Boys for Sale

(Book 1)

By

Marc Finks

Acknowledgements

Even though he doesn't even know me, David Batstone has had a huge impact on my life. I had no idea about the issue of modern day slavery – and especially child sex slaves – until I heard him speak in Seoul, South Korea in the winter of 2011. The stories that he shared were tragic, but even more so because they were real, and these kinds of things are happening to more children than you could imagine.

Victims of Violence, a non-profit organization, estimates that about 2 MILLION children are forced into the commercial sex market every year, and that the children are most often between 11 and 18 years of age, but some may be as young as 18 months.

2,000,000 children

That's more people than are living in Manhattan right now. Imagine if every single person in Houston, Texas were a child sex slave…That's how many children are being raped each year.

If you're interested in learning more, Not For Sale –

http://www.notforsalecampaign.org/ -

- is a good place to start. They seem to be doing a good job of raising awareness about this problem, and yet there is so much that still needs to be done that I'm sure that they would appreciate anything that you could do to help.

To my family,
Who always had their own reasons for believing in
me.

Prologue

"Do you mind if we stop by my office for a few minutes?"

Rachel looked up from the papers she was reading and waited for her son to respond.

"I don't care," Alex said, shrugging his shoulders. "I didn't even want to come to this stupid dinner tonight."

"You know it's helpful when people see my family – you – at these things." She sighed and shook her head in defeat. "Fine. You're old enough to decide if what I'm doing is important to you. If it's not, then I won't make you come anymore."

"Good."

Rachel tapped on the shoulder of the taxi driver. "Could you please stop by 2121 W. 32nd street? It's the KTF building."

As the driver put on his blinker to slide into the left-turn lane, Rachel fought down the urge to share with her son why she wanted to stop by her office so late at night. She glanced at him, and for a second she saw him as a stranger – a sullen, slightly overweight sixteen year old, arms crossed as he stared out of the window, lips petulant, and realized that the twelve year old boy who had been so excited about helping her change the world was nowhere to be seen.

She turned and stared out of the window, watching the city flash by. Her city. Growing up in a nearby suburb, this city was a constant background for most of her memories. Being allowed to come to her father's office on a Saturday, playing on the computer while he finished up his work, and then strolling to a nearby deli for lunch. Shopping with her friends in high school, free from their parents and their boring mundane lives for a few hours. Finding new bars and clubs during college, meeting Alex's dad, working here, and now living here.

But as her eyes slipped past the shiny buildings, the ones lit by neon signs advertising the newest clubs, with lines of people dressed in expensive clothing waiting to get in, the dark shadows in between the bright lights held her attention. Alleyways she had never known existed. Small, dark buildings barely visible from the street with their windows boarded up. Two small shadows disappearing into the darkness as a man paused beneath a street lamp, hands on his knees, exhausted from the chase.

She had first seen this while on vacation in another country. Looking out from her hotel window, she could see the shanties and the poverty and the people struggling to stay alive with the little that they had. She had shaken her head in sadness and wondered why no one tried to help them, why they were allowed to suffer so much when there was a first-class hotel towering over them, but still – she didn't see. She did not see that their problem was her problem, and that those people were also her people, and that she…she was one of those people whom she had shaken her head at, despising for not seeing the darkness that was right in front of her.

Until she had met Tavi.

And that was why she wanted to stop by her office, regardless of the time, to make sure that things were okay. It had taken a long time for Rachel to understand how bad things were, but now that she had seen the darkness that her own culture had hidden from her, she was willing to take the time to help out Tavi and a couple of his friends. She was shining a light through the shadows, and now she would become a beacon that would change the world.

As the taxi stopped in front of her office building, Alex opened the door and hopped out.

"We'll be back down in a few minutes," Rachel told the driver.

"Sure. No rush, ma'am. The meter will keep running."

Rachel slid out and shut the door behind her. "Let's go," she said to Alex.

"What? Why?"

Rachel looked up at the fourth floor and frowned when she saw that the lights were off. "I was hoping that you could meet Tavi," Rachel said, giving her son a hard stare. "I know you don't really care, but I think it would do you some good to meet him. God knows he could use a friend."

Alex stared at his mother for a couple of seconds before rolling his eyes as he walked towards the door. "Fine, but can we hurry it up?" he asked.

Rachel hurried toward the front door. When the security guard, Joe, opened it for her, she began interrogating him before he had a chance to speak.

"What did I say when I called earlier? I said if a kid or two stopped by and mentioned my name, then you should show them to my office and let them in. Why is the light off in my office? Did he not come? Did you turn him away? God help me, if you called the police..."

"Councilwoman Walsh!" Joe interrupted, his eyes wide with a look Rachel couldn't define. "I swear I didn't call the police. I did what you asked."

"And what did I ask?"

Joe took a deep breath and recited, "If any teenager stops by tonight and mentions your name or the name Tavi, then I should let them in and show them to your office. They need a safe place to sleep, and you have promised that your office will be a sanctuary for tonight...ma'am."

"And did they show up?"

Joe hesitated before nodding his head. "I did what you asked."

Rachel studied his face for a second, wanting to question him further. However, Alex walked through the door that

Joe was holding open, and with a curt nod to the security guard, Rachel hurried after her son.

"What's that smell?" Alex wrinkled his nose as they stepped into the elevator.

Rachel pushed the button for the fourth floor and gave her son a disparaging look. "Not everyone is as well off as we are, Alex." Alex looked up at her, exhaled harshly through his nose, and made an effort to hold his breath until the doors opened.

Rachel turned left out of the elevator and immediately stumbled to a stop. Curled up on the floor in front of her office was a small shape. She whispered to Alex to be quiet as they slowly walked towards her office.

From this angle, Rachel could see how worn the shoes wore. They seemed to be so full of holes that half of the toes were protruding at one place or another. The long olive green pants were frayed at the edges and covered with dirt, and she could see a couple of small rips along both legs.

"Tavi?" Rachel said gently.

Tavi jumped up instantly, grabbing the bag that he'd been using for a pillow before his eyes were even open. His eyes focused on Alex and he flinched like a startled deer. When he saw Rachel, though, he relaxed and let out a long sigh, exhaustedly dropping his bag to the floor beside him.

"Tavi, what are you doing out here? I told you that you could use my office if you needed a safe place to sleep." She paused and then said angrily, "Did the security guard not let you in?"

"No, Ms. Walsh," Tavi answered vehemently. He gave a small smile and said, "He was really nice to us."

"But then why are you out here? Wait..us? So you brought some friends too?"

Tavi hesitated and bit the corner of his bottom lip. He stared at her with his wide, emerald green eyes, and Rachel felt herself getting frustrated. "What is it? I told you, you don't have to keep watch out here. You can all sleep safely in my office for tonight. There's plenty of room."

"I know, Ms. Walsh." Tavi swallowed before continuing. "You know how you said I could tell a couple of my friends about this? If they haven't been able to sleep either because they were worried about danger that…" Tavi paused and struggled to find the words. "You told me we could have a safe place. A sanctuary, you said." He shrugged and opened up his hands. "Well, the ones who needed it the most came."

Rachel studied his face as she reached for the door handle.

Tavi grabbed it first and whispered, "Quietly."

He turned the handle and tried to push the door open. It stopped after only a couple of inches. He leaned his shoulder into the door and continued to gently push it open.

"Let me do it!" Alex demanded, roughly knocking Tavi aside and shoving at the door.

There was a shout of pain and some murmurs of dissent as Alex opened the door wide enough for them to slide through.

"Hey!" Tavi shouted, raising his voice for the first time since Rachel had met him. He grabbed Alex's arm and pulled him away from the door. "Be careful!"

"Let go of me!" Alex pushed Tavi away and looked towards his mother for support. "What are his friends doing in there? Selling drugs?"

Rachel looked at Tavi, who was staring at her angrily. "Tavi – I have to see."

Tavi shook his head and dropped his eyes to his feet. "Fine."

Rachel leaned her weight against the door and opened it enough for her to squeeze through. She stepped on something and heard someone near her knee cry out in the dark. "Sorry," she whispered as she rubbed her hand along the wall, feeling for the light switch.

She flipped it on and froze, too stunned to move a muscle. Her eyes flicked around the foyer to her office as her mind tried to tally what she was seeing. The floor – completely filled. The secretary's desk – two. The cabinets…The cabinets had been emptied and she could see a child on each shelf. She could barely see into her office beyond the light, but from what she could tell, it was more of the same.

Rachel looked down at Tavi, who was silently standing next to her. "What is this?!?"

Tavi looked up at her, his eyes brimming with tears. "You told me that I could bring my friends who couldn't sleep safely at night. They also had a couple of friends. I guess word got around." He shrugged as tears rolled down his face. "I'm sorry."

Rachel put her arms around him and pulled him tight. "Oh, Tavi. Don't be sorry. I…I didn't understand."

As Alex silently pushed his way between them, they stared at the room full of children, all of them sleeping in organized rows, on the desk, in the cabinets, on the floor, in her closet. The smallest and youngest ones – maybe seven or eight years old – had the tightest places. The oldest children slept on the edges. And as Rachel, Alex, and Tavi stared at them, the two hundred and fifty children continued to sleep, blanketed by the knowledge that for the first time in a long time, they could sleep safely for at least one night.

Disclaimer

This is a story about life. It won't be one of those stories where the hero is goodness personified, or a character appears and you think, "Ah, he's the bad guy." In real life, the high school principal who fights tooth and nail for his students could be a drug addict who likes underage porn. The drug dealer who sells to children could be doing it because it's the only way that he can keep his own family safe and provide them with food and a home. Bad things are going to happen in this story to good people, but bad things happen in life to everyone. It's what shapes us as humans and makes us real and able to understand one another. No one is all good with just a few quirky traits. I also don't (want to) believe that anyone is all evil, and that they do what they do simply because they enjoy destroying beauty.

While this is a work of fiction, certain aspects have been taken from true stories that actually happened. The prologue is one example. And so, come on a journey and let's read about a life, and how the positive and negative events in a person's life can shape who they become. And at the end, maybe we will have a better notion of how we can be a positive force and make a difference in an unfortunate child's life.

Boys
For
Sale

Chapter 1

The cry of a healthy baby rang out from the dwelling, and the men sitting around outside on the ground gave a cheer.

"To a healthy baby boy!" Emok shouted, as the others raised their glasses and drank down the clear alcohol that he had made the week before.

"May he be a strong worker who will bring great pride to your family!" said Tintin seriously, holding his glass out to the father.

"I pray that your wise words come true as they often do," murmured Raphael, touching his own glass to Tintin's, before gulping his drink down in one swallow.

Emok raised his glass again, grinning at Raphael. "Or may she be a beautiful young girl, with a light touch, and a..." Groans of laughter drowned him out as the others reached for whatever was near and tossed it at his head.

Suddenly, the midwife stepped out into the sunlight, holding a bundle wrapped up in a blanket.

Raphael leaped to his feet and held out his arms. "Is he a..?"

Hyori grinned, as she handed the baby to his father. "Yes. He is a boy."

Emok and Tintin whooped with joy and jumped up, raising their glasses as they did another shot. They crowded around Raphael and stared at the little wrinkled face.

"Look at him," Emok said in a hushed tone. "He's so tiny." He reached for one of the baby's fists and gently squeezed it. "Hello, little man. Welcome to the family."

Raphael beamed with joy and stared at his newborn son. "I shall protect you with my life. You are my firstborn son, and I will cherish you above anything else in this world." He glanced at his friends and swore, "And so will Emok and Tintin."

Tintin and Emok nodded their heads in agreement as Emok asked, "What will you name him?"

Raphael thought for a moment before replying. "I shall name him Tavi, after my grandfather." He gently handed Tavi back to Hyori and bent down and picked up his glass. He held it out for Emok to fill and then raised his glass. "To Tavi! May his life be full of good fortune and joy!"

"And surrounded by loved ones!" Emok shouted.

Tintin closed his eyes and thought deeply for a second. "And may he be someone whom men will look towards for leadership, and his soul will shine as bright as the noonday sun."

The three men gently clinked their glasses together and solemnly said, "Cheers." They each gulped down their drink and turned and threw their glasses as hard as they could against the tin walls of Raphael's house. As the glass shattered and flew through the air, they whooped with delight and drunken laughter and followed Hyori back into the house.

Chapter 2

Tavi's earliest memory was of his younger brother being born. Try as he might, he couldn't remember a time before he had a baby brother. But he clearly remembered the night his brother joined their family because it was one of the most traumatic experiences of his young life.

He remembers his mother screaming in pain for a long time. When it first began, his father's hands – his giant, rough hands – gently picked Tavi up and set him on his shoulders.

He remembers his father saying, "Walk?" as they stepped out of the dark, one-room shack. Tavi squinted in the sunlight as his father slipped on his shoes, and they began walking down the dirt path that ran between the houses. His mother's screams dissipated in the warm afternoon sun, and before they had reached the trail that would take them into the fields, Tavi had already forgotten about her.

He still remembers the golden dog that followed them. He doesn't remember if it had a name, or who it belonged to, or whatever happened to it, but he wasn't surprised to see it, and he laughed as it ran before them and then ran back again, barking excitedly before disappearing into the fields. Tavi loved riding through the fields upon his father's shoulders. He was almost as tall as the plants and he felt like he could see the whole world. He reached out and grabbed one of the tall plants as they brushed past it.

He remembers sitting in the dirt, playing with his small red car, as his father and his uncles sat around him drinking. His mother's screams echoed through the air, but his father kept laughing, and so that meant everything was okay. He remembers Uncle Emok giving him a small sip of something that was so bitter that he spit it out and started crying, until Uncle Tintin laughingly pried his mouth open and put a little bit of dirt on his tongue.

He remembers his father's hands – his hard, gentle hands – setting him down on the ground as Miss Hyori came out of the house and handed his baby brother to his father. Tavi couldn't see his brother yet, but he saw his father's smile; a smile which had only been shared with Tavi before. And then Uncle Tintin and Uncle Emok crowded around his father, blocking his view, and he remembers crying and no one hearing him.

It was the first time he could remember feeling unloved and alone.

Chapter 3

"Tavi! Wait up!" John cried to his eight year old brother as they crashed through the field.

Without slowing, Tavi turned his head and shouted back, "Hurry up! There's a tiger in the jungle! We have to catch it!"

John panted while he ran, dodging in and out around the stalks until he caught up with Tavi at the edge of the forest. Tavi didn't even glance at him as John bent over coughing, his lungs hurting from the sprint from their house.

"Shhh!" Tavi whispered, pointing at the ground in front of him. There was a vague animal trail disappearing into the bushes. "This is where it was seen." He punched John lightly on the shoulder. "Are you ready to catch the tiger?" he asked.

John smiled at his older brother, and they both knew without saying that he would follow Tavi anywhere. He nodded his head and stepped onto the trail.

For the next fifteen minutes, they walked carefully down the familiar path, pointing at indentations in the dirt that may have been tiger tracks, and broken branches that showed where it had passed by. Suddenly, they heard a noise in front of them and they both dived under a bush to their right, wriggling their way deeper into the undergrowth.

The sound of something walking slowly through the leaves got closer and closer. When it was only a few feet away, Tavi looked at John with a grin, and mouthed, "Ready?"

John grinned in response and nodded his head. Tavi held up three fingers as the footsteps stopped next to them on the path. Three, two, one…Both boys leaped out from the bush and tackled the feet that were right in front of them. Tavi's friend, Marco, fell to the ground, and John and Tavi quickly climbed on top of him, pinning him to the ground.

"Got you!" Tavi yelled triumphantly. John giggled as Marco struggled to move his legs that he was sitting on.

"Tavi! I didn't even know you were playing," Marco complained, continuing to struggle.

"Stop it," Tavi replied, lightly patting Marco's cheeks with his hands. "I thought up Tiger Hunt. Why wouldn't we be playing?"

Marco lay still, obviously hoping that the two brothers would get off of him soon. "You didn't meet us. Bryan, Jochi, and Andrew said you weren't coming."

A frown darkened Tavi's face as he stood up. He knocked John to the ground with his knee and watched Marco hop up. "My parents were fighting. We had to wait." He looked around the forest as John tried to tackle Marco's leg again. "Where are they? Stop it, John," Tavi commanded.

"Maybe by the river. That's where we were going to meet if no one found me."

Tavi began walking into the forest and the other two followed him. "Okay. Let's go swimming and wait for them there."

An hour later, the other three boys showed up, yipping with excitement when they saw Tavi and his brother. They ran and jumped into the river without hesitating, trying to land on top of the boys swimming. After wrestling and splashing for a few minutes, they all climbed out of the river and stretched out on the nearest bank. The sunlight flickered on their faces as a gust of wind gently stirred the leaves high above. They lay there unmoving, listening to the breeze brush the leaves above their heads, feeling the water dry on their skin. They had found a rare moment of perfect contentment in their young lives, and they instinctively held onto it for as long as they could.

All too soon, a cloud slid across the sun, and the cheerful, sunny glade changed to something a bit darker. Andrew, the largest of the boys, sat up and asked Tavi, "Where did you guys come from?"

Tavi turned his head and grinned, his light eyes flashing as a sunbeam broke free from the cloud and lit up his face. "We killed the tiger. What were you doing?"

The other boys laughed and sat up. "Let's play again!" Bryan said. He was as lithe as Tavi, but without the same natural grace. "I want to be the hunter!"

"Me too!" everyone else cried instantly. Tavi and John were the only ones who didn't talk. Tavi, because it was assumed that he would lead them in the hunt, and John, because he was too young and had never played before.

"How about…" Tavi began, looking thoughtfully at each boy. He knew that they wouldn't argue with what he decided, but he wanted to be fair. "…we let John be the tiger?"

His friends all shouted in agreement and jumped up, as John looked at Tavi with confusion in his dark eyes. "What do I do?" he asked quietly.

Tavi helped his brother stand up and pointed in the forest around him. "Go hide somewhere. But you can't leave the forest, you can't cross the river, you can only go up to the top of the hill, and don't go into the big flat rocks," Tavi finished seriously. He'd had a bad experience there once, and he still felt fear when he thought of the place. "Understand?"

"Yep!" John shouted. He turned to the other boys and roared. Giggling, he turned around and disappeared into the forest.

"This will be too easy," Andrew complained, as they heard John laughing and crashing through the bushes.

"Good! Then we have more time to swim!" Tavi shouted, jumping at Bryan and throwing him into the river. The rest of the boys jumped in, and they lost track of time as they tried to see who could make the biggest splash.

At the beginning of the eighth round, when Tavi had a slight lead over Jochi in the overall standings, he looked around before jumping and suddenly exclaimed, "John!"

The others looked at him and then squinted back at the forest. "Uh-oh," Jochi said. "We need to find him."

"He's stupid," Andrew said. "Why didn't he come back?"

"I don't know," Tavi said, as he turned and scanned the forest. "But he's been gone too long." He pointed in the direction where they had last seen his brother. "He was going this way. I don't think he's smart enough to change direction. He usually just keeps running until he gets tired and falls down." He looked back as his friends. "Let's go," he said, running into the forest.

They ran in a line, spread out over a hundred meters. Jochi found a small footprint in the mud and they all shifted slightly as a trained unit and continued searching for signs of Tavi's brother.

After twenty minutes, they paused to get their breath back. Bryan looked around and somberly said what they were all thinking, "I think he's heading for the rocks."

Tavi's stomach clenched in fear. They had all had trouble at the rocks, and the only reason they included it in Tiger Hunt was so that everyone would know not to go there. Tavi shook his head and made a sound of frustration.

Everyone looked at Tavi, nervousness, unhappiness, or fear written upon all of their faces. "Maybe they won't be there today," he said quietly. "But we still have to find John."

They nodded their heads and followed him as he sprinted towards the rocks.

Chapter 4

The rocks were a large area of rocky outcroppings which their village had used as a source for stone since it was first founded. No one really went there anymore, and it was a place that a few of the older boys had claimed as their own.

Tavi had first come across them when he was six years old. He had been chasing a lizard that he'd seen from the forest, and as he raced around one of the outcroppings, he stumbled across two boys, who were ten or eleven years old. They had been smoking cigarettes and taking sips from a stolen bottle of alcohol, and they had looked up in fear when he had stumbled over the rocks.

Tavi skidded to a halt and tried turning around and running away before they could get up, but the older one – San – was too quick and grabbed Tavi's arm before he could go more than two steps.

San pulled Tavi towards him and threw him down against the rock wall, as the larger boy, Borthe, stood up with an ugly grin upon his face.

Both of these boys were well-known throughout the village. They were always running from a screaming adult for some reason or another, pushing down smaller children, and they'd even gotten caught – and beaten – for stealing small things from people's homes.

All of this flashed through Tavi's mind in an instant, and tears began streaming down his face as he stood there, too petrified to move.

"Stop crying!" San demanded, slapping Tavi across the face. This only made Tavi cry harder, and so San slapped him again. "Stop it!" he said, as Borthe grinned and reached down for the bottle.

"Maybe he needs a drink?" Borthe held out the bottle towards San.

San slapped his hand away and looked down at Tavi. "You're in a lot of trouble," he said softly, as Tavi tried to control his sniffling. "You can't tell anyone you saw us."

Tavi wiped his face and looked up at San. "I won't. I promise!"

San grabbed the bottle from Borthe, took a drink, and gazed at Tavi. "Pull your pants down."

"Wha…what?" Tavi stuttered.

San slapped him again and said, "Take your pants down now." He pulled out a cigarette from his pocket and lit it with a lighter that Borthe handed him. Meanwhile, Tavi softly cried and slowly pulled down his pants.

San looked at Borthe and grinned. He reached down, grabbed Tavi's shorts from the ground, and handed them to Borthe. As Tavi tried to cover his nakedness with his hands, San slapped his hands away, and then slapped him in the face again.

Tavi cried out, and raised his hands to his face. He began crying again, but San didn't seem to mind anymore.

"Okay, listen," San said. "You can't tell anyone we were here."

"I..I..I won't," Tavi cried.

"If you do tell anyone, then we'll kill you," San said, flashing a grin at Borthe.

"I won't tell," Tavi said.

"And to make sure you won't tell," San continued, "I will give you a stamp to show that we are friends."

"A stamp?" Tavi sniffled. It didn't sound so bad. "Okay."

Borthe suddenly grabbed Tavi and held him from behind, arms locked at his sides. San took a drag from his cigarette, blew the smoke into Tavi's face, and said, "Here is the stamp."

Tavi's eyes widened with horror. "No!!!" he screamed, struggling to get free. San calmly ignored him and pressed his cigarette against the Tavi's left ribcage.

Tavi's shrill scream echoed through the forest for a few seconds before his lungs were empty, and then he just hung in Borthe's arms, sobbing helplessly.

"And one more," San said cheerfully, aiming the point of the cigarette at Tavi's face. Tavi shrieked again and shook his head back and forth. San roughly grabbed his hair and held his head tight.

Tavi closed his eyes as the cigarette got closer and closer. When it was two inches from his left eye, San casually let go of Tavi's hair and stepped back as Borthe released him. Tavi collapsed to the ground, crying and whimpering for help.

"What's your name?" San asked.

Deep sobs wracked Tavi's chest before he managed to whisper his name.

"Go home, Tavi," San said. "If you tell anyone about this, or if I see you here again, then you're dead."

Tavi stood up, his legs trembling. He lightly touched the burn, looked at Borthe, and asked tremulously, "My pants?"

"Do you mean my pants?" Borthe laughed and put Tavi's pants on his head like a hat. Tears streamed down Tavi's face as he looked from Borthe to San.

"GO!" San said, pushing Tavi towards the forest. Tavi slowly started walking until he heard San shout, "You're too slow. I'm coming to get you."

Tavi jumped and ran as fast as his six year old legs could carry him into the forest.

Chapter 5

Tavi was leading them as they approached the rocks when they first heard John yell. They all froze and looked at each other with wide eyes. Tavi's mind was blank and he saw his uncertainty reflected in his friends' faces.

John yelled again, and this time Tavi could hear him calling for help. He looked around and picked up a branch which was as thick as his arm. He swung it against a nearby tree and nodded at the solid sound it made. Without looking at his friends, he ran as quietly as possible towards the rocks.

After he got to the edge of the outcropping where he had seen San and Borthe long ago, he glanced back and gave a ferocious grin when he saw his friends walking behind him. Andrew, Bryan, and Marco each carried a stick the same size as Tavi's. Jochi carried a rock that was the size of his fist in each hand.

"Tigers!" Tavi whispered and smiled.

The fear left their faces as they all replied, "Tigers!"

"Now!" Tavi said and sprinted around the corner. He swung his stick at the first thing he saw, which was Borthe's head. Borthe had been squatting on the ground in front of John, but fell flat with a scream of pain as Tavi hit him across the temple.

By the time San turned around, Marco was swinging his stick at his left knee, while Andrew was hitting him across the back. As he fell, Jochi ran up and hit him in the face with the rock that was clenched in his right hand. He threw it at San's head as San collapsed to the ground, pivoted around, and hit Borthe in the face with the other one.

"Tavi!" John screamed.

Bryan ran past all of them and raised his stick to hit the third boy who was still standing. Tavi looked up and observed how he seemed to be standing in front of John, his arms spread wide as if protecting him. Seeing that John still had his clothes on, Tavi jumped forward and stuck his stick in front of Bryan. "Wait!" he said.

Bryan glared at Tavi in frustration, looked towards where Borthe was struggling to stand up, ran back and hit him across the face with his stick. As Borthe fell back unconscious, Bryan turned and jumped on San's chest. They had all been hurt by San and Borthe at one time or another, but they knew that Bryan had probably gotten the worst treatment out of all of them.

Tavi stared up at the boy who was standing in front of John. His name was Yuri, and he was three years older than Tavi. If they had been similar ages, they probably would've been the best of friends. They were each the brightest student in their age group, and they looked strikingly similar. Yuri was tall for his age, a bit too thin, and had the same sparkling, wide green eyes that Tavi had.

Tavi stared hard at Yuri, unsure of what to do next. "What are you doing here?" he finally asked. Andrew and Marco walked over and stood next to him. John threw himself at his older brother and clung to him.

Yuri watched John hug Tavi and his eyes twinkled a bit as Tavi stroked John's hair and murmured reassurances to him. "I came to say good-bye," Yuri replied. "I'm going to school in the city tomorrow."

Tavi nodded. The whole village had heard about how a special school was paying Yuri's family a huge amount of money just so Yuri could study there. It was a school for future leaders, and Yuri had somehow drawn the attention of the school's owners. All of the mothers in the village were jealous of his family and hoped that their own sons would be chosen for a similar honor someday.

However, that wouldn't protect him now if he'd hurt John. "They're your friends?" Tavi asked, nodding his head towards San and Borthe.

Yuri shook his head and smiled. "Not really. I know them. I've been here a couple of times with them. But…" he paused and shook his head. "This is the first time I've ever seen this kind of thing happen."

Tavi gazed at him suspiciously. He heard San moan behind him and then a thwack as Bryan hit him again. Tavi squatted down and spoke to John. "Hey, tiger. Are you okay?"

John sniffled and smiled. "I roared, Tavi. But they didn't care."

"Did they hurt you? Did he touch you?" Tavi asked, pointing at Yuri.

John glanced back at Yuri and shook his head. "Nope. He stood in front of me and told them to leave little tigers alone." Yuri gave a small smile, and John ran to him and hugged him around the waist.

Tavi stood up and nodded his head. "Thank you." He dropped his stick, looked around at his friends, and held his hand out to John. "Let's go home. I'm hungry."

The other boys nodded and dropped their sticks as well. Andrew patted John on the back and said, "You were the best tiger ever!"

John grinned at his words and roared.

As they walked around the rock cropping towards the forest, Tavi glanced back one last time. Yuri stood there, watching them leave with a smile on his face, as San and Borthe lay unconscious on the ground in front of him.

Tavi held up his hand, and Yuri grinned and waved goodbye. As Tavi turned back and headed home, Yuri walked away from the rocks, following a different path back to his house.

Chapter 6

The two men sat alone in one of the two classrooms in the tiny schoolhouse, crammed into two desks in the front row. They were both wearing expensive silk shirts and trousers, dressed with the sophistication of the big city. One of them was in his early forties and was clearly the leader of the two. The other one was much younger, barely approaching manhood. The schoolmaster – with fresh money in his back pocket – had just left them alone to decide who would be the lucky student this time.

"The schoolmaster recommended these five," the older man said, flicking through the photos on the digital screen of his camera. "However…" He paused as he deleted three of them. "I don't like these. They don't have the look we need."

The younger man nodded his head in silent agreement and looked at the two remaining candidates.

"They're both smart. They're already handsome. The schoolmaster recommended this one," the older man said, tapping at one of the photos, "but only because he's a year younger. What do you think?"

The younger man hesitated and bit the inside of his cheek as he stared at both photos. He took a deep breath and lightly shook his head, remembering why he was there. "This one," he said, choosing the other photo.

"Why?"

"His family is poorer. It'll be cheaper to convince them. Also, I met him before. He has the right personality and a smile that the customers will love."

The older man considered both photos for a moment before grinning and clapping the other on the back. "You see, Yuri," he said, "this is why I brought you with me." He stood up and brushed off his pants, and then picked up the camera. "Go see your mom. It's been…what…four years?"

Yuri nodded his head as he rose to his feet and walked towards the door.

Unexpectedly, the older man reached out and grabbed Yuri's upper arm, squeezing hard enough to leave bruises later. "Remember," he warned quietly, "don't say a word."

Yuri clenched his jaw, and only his eyes showed how frightened he was. "I know," he said, fighting the urge to shake loose of the man's grip.

He had learned long ago what the consequences were for fighting back.

Chapter 7

Tavi irritably squinted his eyes in the encroaching dimness, hoping to finish his homework before the evening light completely disappeared. He sat against the metal wall of his house, feeling the warmth from the day's sunshine through the thin school uniform he wore. Writing as fast as he could, he tuned out the noises around him – his two younger brothers running and giggling around the outside of the house, his mother singing to his crying baby sister inside their dark home, and his father silently drinking as he watched the world around him, the only sound being the clink of the bottle as he refilled his glass like clockwork.

The silence radiating from his father was perhaps the most distracting noise for Tavi. He had learned long ago to judge his mood based on how much he talked while he drank, and this was one of those times where his father hadn't spoken for the last two hours. He had just gazed at the world around him, his eyes growing meaner and meaner.

As his brothers came around the corner, John caught up to their younger brother, Raswon, and gave him a slight push. He stumbled into their father, who reacted with the speed of striking snake and cuffed Raswon to the ground without saying a word.

Tavi jumped up and lifted Raswon from the dirt before he could cry out. He eyed his father with a dangerous glint in his eye, as John stopped and stood next to Tavi.

Raphael struggled to stand up and stood weaving slightly as he stared at his sons. "What?" he said harshly to Tavi. "You got something you want to say?"

Tavi just stared at his father with hard eyes as he gently set Raswon to the ground, still holding his hand. Exhaling slowly, Tavi stepped back, unwilling to confront his father. But before he could take another step, John started talking.

"Hey, Dad," John said, blissfully unable to read his father's moods, "guess what today is?"

Raphael's eyes flicked from Tavi to John and back again, noticing how Tavi put his hand on his brother's shoulder in an attempt to quiet him. He looked back at John and said, "Tell me."

John grinned at Tavi and said, "It's Tavi's birthday today! He's thirteen years old." Tavi grimaced as John continued. "What are you going to give him?"

The anger which had been simmering inside of Raphael all day exploded. "Give him?!?" he shouted, as John cringed behind Tavi. "Why should I give the bratty prince anything? He thinks he's better than all of us, studying, reading his books!" Raphael took a cautious step forward and fought to retain his balance. "Your brother is nothing but a ..."

Tavi stepped forward, struggling to keep his hands down and off of his father. Even in his anger, he knew that touching him would be crossing a line that could never be recrossed. "Nothing but a what, Dad?" Tavi shouted. "Maybe if you worked, we wouldn't be hungry all day, with only rice to eat and whatever we catch in the forest! What else can I do besides study? I don't want to drink my life away like you and Uncle Emok!"

"Don't you talk about Emok!" Raphael spat. He poked his finger into Tavi's chest. "You don't know..."

"Everyone knows he was drunk when he was on the motorbike!" Tavi took a deep breath and tried to keep the words from tumbling out of his mouth, but it was like trying to dam a river with just his fingers. "Even when he was drunk, he was still a better father than you. At least his family had food. And clothes. At least his children didn't cry every night because they're so hungry like Raswon and John do!"

Tavi heard a noise behind him. He turned and saw his mother, Tomoko, standing in the doorway, holding his baby sister, Yasmine, in her arms. Her lips were pressed together in anger and Tavi regretted everything he had just said.

"Mom, I'm…" he began before she interrupted him.

"Tavi, shut up," she said harshly. She turned back and went into the house. When she reemerged, both of her hands were full. She thrust the contents into Tavi's hands. "Here is a chicken that we were going to have for your dinner. And here are the colored pencils that you mentioned you wished you had last summer. Your father is the one who remembered you wanted them."

Tavi stared helplessly at his mother and then glanced shamefacedly at his father. His father once again sat on the ground, his bottle held tightly between his hands. He refused to look up. Tavi turned back to his mother. "Mom, I…" he tried again.

"Just go, Tavi," his mother replied tiredly. "Take your brothers and go enjoy your birthday dinner somewhere else. Don't bring any of it back." She turned and disappeared into the house as Yasmine started crying again.

Tavi gazed into darkened house in silence, hoping she'd come back. When she didn't reappear, he looked at his father, and then down at his two brothers, who were looking up at him in confusion. Tavi sighed, carefully handed the chicken dinner to John, and quickly wiped away the tears that were forming. Grabbing Raswon's hand, he said, "Come on, guys. Let's go eat dinner somewhere."

As they passed his father, Tavi said softly, "I'm sorry, Dad. And thank you."

There was no response as they trudged down the dirt road.

Chapter 8

As Tavi and his brothers slowly made their way home after dinner, he felt the pressure from his argument with his parents weighing on his soul. He knew it wasn't his father's fault that he couldn't find work. Most of the men in the village had only been able to find seasonal work for the last three or four years, and that was sporadic at best. He felt tears forming again as he squeezed the pack of colored pencils tightly in his left hand, and he quickly brushed them away before his brothers could see. He couldn't imagine how his parents had been able to buy his gifts without him knowing, or why they had chosen to use their money in that way. He wished he were older and wiser so that he could understand better.

When they were still about a hundred yards from home, Tavi looked at their house closely and saw that there were two men squatting on the ground with his father. Not wanting to risk his father's anger again that night, Tavi pulled Raswon to the edge of the fields that ran behind the houses and whispered to John, "Follow me!"

They crept down the narrow path between the houses and the fields until they were at the corner of the house nearest to theirs. Motioning for John and Raswon to stay still, Tavi silently tiptoed to the front corner of his own house.

"Enough talk," his father demanded. "Just tell me what you want."

"Sir," said a deep voice that Tavi didn't recognize, "as I said, we are from a school that finds children in villages like yours, and we give them the tools they need to be future leaders."

"Hah!" laughed Raphael dismissively. "And how do you do that?"

The deep voice replied, "I assume you know Yuri here?" Tavi cocked his head. Yuri? He peeked around the corner and recognized the younger man as the same boy he had last seen four years ago.

From somewhere Tavi couldn't see, his mother responded, "I do. Yuri, how have you been?"

Yuri gave a charming smile. "I've been great. I've seen so many things and have learned so much that I wouldn't have been able to learn here." He motioned to his clothing. "They even give us nice clothing to wear and feed us good food."

Raphael looked at them suspiciously. "Why?" he asked. "Why do this?"

The older man nodded his head, acknowledging that it was a good question. "I work for a company. You probably haven't heard of it, since it deals with exporting goods to foreign countries, but the owner of the company grew up in a village like this." He turned and motioned to the village. "One day, a rich foreigner came through and offered scholarships to the brightest boys in the village. My boss was one of them. Because of this man's offer, my boss and several of his boyhood friends became educated and successful. And he has never forgotten how much that help changed his life." He tapped himself on the chest and motioned towards Yuri. "Same with me. And the same will be true for Yuri. And maybe Tavi." He gave a warm smile before continuing. "But what we're doing isn't free, you know."

"I knew it," Tavi's father growled. "Well, we can't pay anything."

"And we don't expect you to," the man continued smoothly. "After Tavi finishes school and university..." He paused when Tavi's mom gasped and he gave her a quick smile and a nod. "When he finishes university, my boss will expect Tavi to work for him for at least five years. He gets a bright, educated, hard worker who feels indebted to him, and Tavi gets a better life."

"And after five years?" Tomoko asked.

"After five years – and during this time, we do encourage our students to send most of their money home to their families – but after five years, Tavi can continue working for us, or he can look for another job, or do practically anything he wants to do."

Tavi's parents were silent as they considered what the man had said. Gesturing towards his wife, Raphael said to the two men, "Could you please step across the street while my wife and I discuss this?"

The older man nodded his head as he and Yuri stood up. "Just call us over when you're done talking," he said, as they crossed the road.

Tavi's mom came into view as she knelt near his father. His mind was swirling with thoughts, and he couldn't focus on anything. Did he want to go? Could he leave his family and his village and his friends? A real school, though, in the city, and maybe university. It was a dream that he'd never dared to dream.

"What do you think?" Tomoko asked Raphael quietly.

Raphael shook his head, and took a sip from a nearby water bottle. "I don't understand it. I still don't see why they would do this."

Tomoko gestured towards Yuri. "But look at Yuri. After four years, he's so tall and handsome, and he looks rich. Imagine Tavi like that!"

"He's been gone for four years!" Raphael retorted. "Do you want to not see Tavi for that long?" He sighed and shrugged. "He's my firstborn son. As hotheaded as he is, he's still the best of all of them. The other fathers talk about it while drinking sometimes."

Tavi felt a rush of pride burn through him as his mother replied, "But what if this is his chance?" She paused, carefully weighing her next words. "I also know that Yuri's mother was paid a thousand talents by the school."

"What?!?" Tavi's father almost shouted. "Why didn't I know this?"

Tomoko shrugged. "She didn't want any trouble. Since her husband died, it's only been her and her children. If people had known that she had extra money…"

Raphael nodded his head in understanding. "Someone would've caused trouble for her." He paused as he did the calculations. "That's as much as money as I would make in a year if I worked every day." Raphael exhaled slowly and softly admitted, "I don't know how to take care of our family. We have no money. There are no jobs. If Tavi left, it would be easier to take care of the other three children."

Tomoko reached out and held his father's hand. Tavi bit his lip while they both watched his father make a decision.

"Okay. Come back," Raphael shouted across the street, waving his hand.

As Yuri and the older man squatted back down with Tavi's father, Raphael said, "Education is a good thing. But Tavi does a lot of work around here. I don't know if we could manage without him."

Tavi saw the older man's eyes flick towards Yuri and the corner of his mouth turned up at the corner. He couldn't explain why, but that one look made Tavi feel uneasy.

"I know that when I left, the school gave my mother one thousand talents," Yuri said to his father. "I'm sure they could probably give you the same. Right?" he asked hesitantly to the man beside him.

The man shrugged. "I'm sure they would. You should be compensated for the work that Tavi probably would have done."

Raphael shook his finger at the man. "Not so fast. You're not taking him for just one year. You want to take him for school, and then university, and then five more years of work. That's a lot of work that Tavi is missing out on."

"Fine." The man sighed and held up his hands in a gesture of surrender. "How much do you think would be fair?"

Raphael looked at Tomoko, counted on his fingers, and said, "One thousand five hundred talents."

Both Yuri and the older man lost their composures for the first time that night. Their mouths dropped in shock, but the older man recovered first. He gazed at Raphael appraisingly, turned and studied Tomoko's face, and then laughed and held out his hand to Raphael. "It's a deal," he exclaimed. "I hope your boy's worth it."

Raphael hesitated for just one second before firmly shaking the man's hand. Tomoko wiped at her eyes and said, "Now we just need to find Tavi and let him know."

Yuri eyes flashed to the corner where Tavi was hiding. "He's over there," he nodded. "He's been there for most of the conversation."

Tomoko and Raphael jumped up as Tavi stepped out into the light, embarrassed to have been caught eavesdropping. His mother ran over to him and squeezed him tight. "Is this okay with you?"

Tavi nodded and clutched at his mother in a way he hadn't done since he was four years old. "It is," he said softly. "I'm going to miss you guys so much." Tomoko squeezed him tighter.

Raphael came over and wrapped his arms around both of them. "Are you sure you're okay with this, Tavi?" he asked. Tavi nodded his head, his father's smell enveloping him. He took a deep breath, not knowing when he would ever smell it again.

"I'm sorry, Dad," he whispered. "I didn't mean the things I said."

"It's okay, Tavi," Raphael responded. "You were right about a lot of it. I'll try to be a better father for your brothers and sister."

"No…Dad," Tavi protested.

Squeezing him and his mother tightly one last time, Raphael murmured, "Happy birthday, Tavi."

Chapter 9

They left the village early the next morning, riding on the backs of scooters of neighbors who had offered to drive them to the nearest bus stop. After a forty-five minute bone-jarring ride over rutted dirt roads half covered with puddles, they arrived at a slightly wider road, paved with two lanes.

This was farther than Tavi had ever been from his village, and he felt a twinge of loneliness as the scooters disappeared down the road, headed back to the village. He looked at Yuri and the older man – Vikram, he had announced earlier when they first got on the bikes - and wondered what they were supposed to do next.

Vikram looked in both directions down the dusty, paved road, heaved a great sigh, and retreated away from the road to seek shade under the nearest tree. Resting his back and head against the trunk, he closed his eyes and called out, "You boys keep watch. Let me know if you see anything coming."

Yuri squatted on his heels without saying a word and stared into the forest across from them. When Tavi kept standing, Yuri looked up at him out of the corner of his eye, shook his head, and muttered, "Sit down. Relax. Last time we had to wait seven hours." He turned his gaze back to the forest, ignoring Tavi as if he weren't even there.

Tavi squatted down next to Yuri, carefully holding the small bag that held all of his worldly possessions in it. Vikram had told his parents that the school would provide clothing, which was fortunate since Tavi only had two pairs of shirts and pants that fit him. Besides the extra pair of clothing, Tavi had brought the colored pencils his parents had just given him, a rolled-up piece of bark on which John had drawn a picture of their family, and – his most prized possessions – three books, which his schoolmaster had given him each of the last three years for being the top student in his class.

After a few minutes, Tavi became bored and then restless with just sitting and waiting. He glanced over at Yuri, only to find that he was still staring at the forest with a look of longing and determination. He opened his mouth to ask a question, but a brief look from Yuri made him change his mind.

He seems so different here, Tavi thought.

The sound of an approaching vehicle made Tavi jump up in excitement. Buses and trucks rarely came to the village, and Tavi was eager to start his journey and ride in one. As he saw it approaching in the distance, he shaded his eyes from the sun, unable to see it clearly. It was too small to be a bus, he thought, and buses were never bright red.

The roar of the engine grew louder as the car neared and even Yuri stood up to look. He put his hand on Tavi's arm and took a step back from the road. Tavi looked at him quickly before turning his attention back to the automobile. "Is that ours?" he asked.

Yuri snorted. "No. That's not a bus. That's a car."

"I know. I just…" Tavi trailed off, feeling embarrassed for asking something so stupid.

Without warning, the car sped up and before Tavi knew it, a red sports car with the convertible top down zoomed past them. The person nearest to them – a beautiful woman with long dark hair – laughed and waved as they flew by, and the dusty wind that followed settled gently upon Yuri and Tavi.

Tavi's enthusiasm for what he had just seen couldn't break through Yuri's stoicism. "Did you see that?" Tavi asked excitedly. "That was…what was that?!? Will we have one of those if we go to university?" He grabbed Yuri's arm without knowing it and tugged on his sleeve.

"Tavi," Yuri said, as he gently pried Tavi's fingers from his shirt, "don't get your hopes up."

"What do you mean?" Tavi felt all of the excitement drain out of him.

Yuri gave a tired sigh and squatted back down. "Nothing," he said quietly. "Let's just wait for our bus."

Tavi squatted down next to Yuri again, feeling lost. He had lain awake all night, imagining everything that was going to happen to him. He could envision the other students who were as excited as he was to be there. And the teachers who would gently guide them and help them get ready for university. And he pictured having long talks with Yuri about everything that had happened in the village since Yuri had left, and hearing about everything that Yuri had seen in the city.

But this…this was something he didn't know how to deal with. He looked behind him and saw that Vikram was apparently sleeping against the tree. Keeping his voice down so as not to disturb him, Tavi told Yuri, "I don't understand, Yuri. Why aren't you excited? We're going to school in the city!"

Yuri opened his mouth to respond, but then clenched his jaw tight. He shook his head slightly and turned his attention back to the forest across from him.

Tavi sighed and tried to think of something to do. Shrugging his shoulders to himself, he opened his bag and pulled out his favorite book. It was a story about a boy who could do magic, and even though he had a terribly difficult life, he was still able to save his friends and defeat the evil king. The cover and pages of the book wore worn thin from constant use, and Tavi flicked through the book with affection. It was his favorite story, and he often imagined that he could be that boy and be the hero who saves his friends. Tavi flipped it open, excited to lose himself in the story once again.

Yuri looked down when he heard Tavi flip open the book and his eyes widened with interest when he saw what Tavi was holding. Tavi looked up as Yuri's shadow moved over the page, and he gave a quick smile. "This is my favorite book," he confided. "I got it last year for being first in my class."

Yuri reached out gently and took it away from Tavi. "I remember winning these," he mused, turning the book over and gazing at the cover. "I haven't seen mine since…" he paused and his eyes went out of focus for a second, "…a long time." He looked at Tavi and held the book up. "Can I read this?" he asked.

"Sure," Tavi answered cheerfully. He dug into his bag and pulled out another book. "I have two others, so I can just read this one." Squatting side by side, there was a comfortable silence which was only punctuated by the sound of turning pages, as the boys waited beside the dirt road for their bus to arrive.

Six hours later, Tavi excitedly climbed onto his first bus. He looked around in amazement at the fan that was blowing by the driver's head and the long aisle that ran between the rows of seats and windows. Rushing to the back, Tavi slid into an empty seat and pressed his forehead against the dirty window. He felt Yuri sit down next to him, and he watched the dirt road that led back to his village slowly pull away behind them.

He turned towards Yuri with a huge grin upon his face. Yuri, who was almost finished with his third book, gave Tavi a sad smile. He nodded his head towards the front of the bus where Vikram was sitting. "Tavi," he whispered solemnly.

"Yeah?" Tavi replied, his cheerfulness fading away as the bus crawled farther and farther away from his home.

"Don't trust Vikram." Yuri's face was an emotionless mask as he turned back to his book. "Don't trust anyone."

Chapter 10

When they were boarding their third bus, Vikram stepped in front of Yuri and followed Tavi to a seat in the back. He sat down beside Tavi and indicated that Yuri should sit across from them. Besides themselves, there were only a couple of other people on the bus, and they were sitting up front near the driver. As the bus pulled away from the station's lights, the interior of the bus darkened until it matched the night outside, and Tavi once again pressed his forehead against the cool glass of the window, watching the never-ending headlights of cars rush by in the opposite direction.

"Tavi," Vikram said softly after watching him for ten minutes, "we have to talk."

Tavi turned around, the surprise on his face plain to see as a headlight beamed across him. He had thought that Yuri was sitting next to him, and those were the most words that Vikram had spoken since they had left the village over a day ago.

"Okay, Mr. Vikram," he said. He briefly checked to see what Yuri was doing in the seat across from them, and he felt a little apprehensive when he saw that Yuri appeared to be sleeping.

"Do you know how much I paid your father for you?" Vikram asked.

"One thousand five hundred talents."

"And do you know what that means?"

Tavi shook his head timidly.

"That means that you have to work to pay me back that money, plus whatever we give you for food and clothes and anything else."

"Um…" Tavi stuttered, wishing that Yuri would wake so that he could help him be less confused. "Um…do you mean after university?" he asked.

Vikram gazed at Tavi and smiled, his eyes cold in the dim light. "You'll see what I mean when we get to…the school," he said, pausing slightly at the word "school".

For some unknown reason, Tavi felt tears come to his eyes, and he couldn't remember ever wanting to see his parents more than he did at that second. Blinking quickly to stop them from falling, Tavi said, "I don't understand."

Vikram just stared at Tavi. "Fifteen hundred talents," he muttered. "You better be worth it."

Tavi shook his head, overwhelmed by fear and confusion. "I…I don't understand," he said again.

A look of anger crossed Vikram's face and he grabbed Tavi's upper arm and squeezed. "Stop saying that," he said. Tavi looked at him in disbelief as he cried out in pain. Vikram squeezed harder. "Lesson number one – don't cry when you're hurt." He continued to dig his fingers into Tavi's arms. "Do you understand, boy?"

Tavi was doing everything he could to keep from screaming. Biting the inside of his cheek and clenching his fists, he quickly nodded his head.

"Say it," Vikram whispered. "Say you understand the first lesson."

Tavi took a deep breath and squeezed his eyes shut. "I understand," he managed to gasp. Vikram eyed him appraisingly as he released his arm. Tavi fought the urge to grab where it was hurting and stared straight ahead instead. He caught a glimpse of Yuri watching him before Vikram blocked his view.

Vikram reached into his pocket and pulled out a little envelope. He stuck his finger inside and pulled out some brown paste. "Here," he said, holding his finger at Tavi's face, "open up your mouth."

Tavi looked at Vikram in disgust and horror and slid away from him until his back was pressed against the window. Vikram sighed and said in a sad tone, "I guess it's time for rule number two. Always do what I say." He shook his head. "I thought you were smarter than this."

Tavi stammered, "Wha...what is it?"

"It'll make you feel better," Vikram promised. "Trust me. You'll love it."

Tavi pressed his lips closed and looked wildly around the bus. His eyes focused on the driver and the other passengers up front, and he took a deep breath as he opened his mouth to scream.

"Fine," Vikram said resignedly. "Watch Yuri. You'll see that I'm just trying to help you." He looked back over his shoulder and said Yuri's name. Tavi relaxed slightly when he saw Yuri lean down in front of Vikram.

"Here," Vikram said, holding out his finger with the brown stuff on the tip. "Have some paste for the rest of the trip."

Tavi stared at Yuri's face and was stunned to see a look of hunger and excitement flash across his eyes as he smiled and quickly opened his mouth. Vikram stuck his finger into Yuri's mouth and ran his finger all along his upper and lower gums, and then he stuck his finger deep into Yuri's mouth. Tavi watched in fascination as Yuri closed his eyes and gently sucked on Vikram's finger. After a couple of seconds, Vikram pulled his finger out with a slight pop, and Yuri partially opened his eyes. He gave them a slow smile and then slowly stepped back and sank blissfully into his seat.

Vikram stuck his finger back into the envelope, and scooped out another blob. "You see," he said in a friendly tone of voice, holding his finger out towards Tavi, "that didn't look too bad, did it?"

Tavi's eyes flickered from Vikram's finger to his eyes and back again. Vikram's eyes weren't smiling, and Tavi could still feel the aching pain in his arm where Vikram had squeezed it. Fearfully, he licked his lips, and then relaxed his mouth open. Vikram jammed his finger in and rubbed it around inside of his mouth. Tavi wanted to gag on the bitter taste, and at the end, when Vikram rested his finger on his tongue, all Tavi could do was jerk his head as he tried to get the taste out of his mouth.

Vikram grabbed his chin with one hand, and mashed his lips together with the other hand. However, Tavi could already feel the effects of the brown paste. The pain in his arm was gone, and his body felt like it was falling…falling…falling. His eyes grew heavy and he felt a warm fuzziness smother his body. As he floated away, Vikram bent over and kissed him gently on the lips. "Good boy," he whispered.

Chapter 11

Tavi struggled to wake up as someone roughly shook his arm. He felt as if his mind were swimming through an impenetrable, sticky black river. His left eye flickered open for a millisecond before he gave up and drifted back into unconsciousness.

"Tavi!" he heard someone shout before a hard slap across the face jerked him awake. He blinked his eyes and looked around groggily. Yuri was standing above him, clearly angry, and reached down to lift Tavi up by his arm. "Get up! We have to go now!"

"Ow!" Tavi exclaimed as Yuri squeezed the bruises that Vikram had left. Fearfully he pressed his lips together and looked around to see if Vikram had heard him cry out. When he saw that they were alone on the bus, he sagged in relief. He grabbed his bag and stepped into the aisle. "Yuri…" he began.

Yuri whirled around and the look on his face scared Tavi more than anything else had since he had left his village. It was a mixture of fear and anger and…scorn? Yuri squeezed his arm again and spoke in a low threatening voice. "We are not friends here, Tavi. I can't help you. Don't even ask."

"What?" Tavi said, jerking his arm free. "What do you mean?"

Yuri breathed forcefully through his nose and shook his head warningly at Tavi. "Trust me. It's for your own good." He let go of Tavi's arm and walked toward the front of the bus.

Tavi watched him walk away. He replied quietly, "You said not to trust anyone."

Yuri put his right hand on the seat next to him and stopped. After a couple of seconds, he turned around and grinned at Tavi. "Good," he said. "I'm glad you remember." The grin vanished and Yuri exited the bus. Through the window, Tavi could see Vikram waiting outside.

After opening his bag to make sure it still had everything in it, Tavi trudged down the aisle, his left hand lightly hitting each seat as he passed by, and he wondered what was going to happen next.

Tavi hesitated briefly as his foot touched the concrete parking lot. He couldn't assimilate everything that he was seeing for the first time. So many buses. So many people. And the smells – where were they all coming from? He could see six different people waving sticks of food from various hot carts, and yet that didn't explain the thick dirtiness that made the air hard to breathe. But the most overwhelming were the sounds – sounds of people, sounds of buses and cars roaring past and honking, people screaming, dogs barking. Tavi looked around anxiously as he tried to separate the cacophony of noise that was barraging his ears.

"Boy," Vikram said, interrupting his concentration, "Let's go. We'll walk from here. It's not too far."

"Where are we?" Tavi asked, as he dutifully began following Yuri and Vikram, his feet dragging on the ground.

"This?" Vikram laughed in disgust. "This is just the Central Bus Terminal. It's not important, so don't worry about it."

Tavi nodded his head as they walked past a line of empty cars that had the word TAXI on the side. Above his head, something made a loud rumbling noise, and he stopped and stared as it thundered past.

Tavi hurried to catch up with Yuri. "What was that?" he asked, pointing upwards.

Yuri responded without looking, "Just the sky train. Don't worry. You won't need to ride that for a while."

Excitement buoyed Tavi's emotions, and he felt that if he jumped hard enough then he could fly as high as the sky train. He ran forward and leaped as far as possible, landing next to Vikram. Vikram looked down at him sharply, but when Tavi flinched away, Vikram just smiled and ruffled his hair. "I remember when I first came here," he said to Tavi. "Everything was so new and loud and amazing." He looked around at the dirty, rundown city, the beggars asking for money, the street vendors selling their cheap rancid food, the boarded up windows of the slums to their left, the hookers standing in their little pink-lit rooms behind the glass walls, waiting for their next customer.

He cuffed a dirty, seven year old street urchin who had gotten too close to him and instinctively checked his pocket as the boy fell to the ground with a cry. "Enjoy it while you can, Tavi," he said with a tinge of regret. "You'll see it for what it really is soon enough."

After walking for twenty minutes, they entered a street which was surprisingly empty for that time of the morning. In the daylight, the facades of the buildings were dingy and run down, and Vikram grimaced when he looked upon them.

"They never seem this ugly at nighttime, do they, Yuri?" he asked.

Yuri looked around and shook his head in agreement. "Nope. I sometimes think everything looks pretty at night, with the lights shining and people laughing and talking everywhere."

Tavi looked to see what they were talking about. Granted, the buildings were a bit dirty, and there was a lot of trash in the street, but the buildings in his village weren't nearly as big or as grand as the ones on this street. His mind automatically read off the different names he saw as he excitedly looked at everything around him. *The Poker, The Joy Luck Club, Bangarang, The School House*. The School House?!?!

"Hey!" Tavi tugged on Yuri's shirt. "Is that our school?"

Yuri and Vikram shared a look before Yuri replied with a cynical smile. "Yep. That's it. That's...our school." He bit his lip and strode forward, leaving Vikram and Tavi behind him.

"Is he okay?" Tavi asked worriedly, watching Yuri disappear into an alleyway that was next to The School House.

Vikram sighed. "Yeah, boy. He'll be fine. Let's get you settled in and show you where you'll be living."

They walked past the alleyway that Yuri had turned into and continued past The School House. It was a wide, two-story building, with several windows on both floors. Tavi ran to peer into a window, but it was too dark to see anything.

"Is it closed?" he asked in disappointment.

"It'll be open later," Vikram replied, grabbing Tavi by the scruff of his shirt and dragging him along. "Keep up. I have a lot of work to catch up on."

Tavi stumbled after Vikram as he tried to regain his feet, but soon he was proudly walking beside him. Now that he was actually here, all of his worries from the bus ride and talking with Yuri had vanished. They turned down the next alleyway, and then made a left down a small path, and a right down an even smaller walkway, both lined with low buildings with doors spaced regularly. Several of the doors were open, and Tavi could see people lying on mats on the floor, some with fans blowing on them, as they tried to stay cool in the heat.

Vikram finally stopped at a door that had a large red circle painted on the front of it. "If you ever get lost," Vikram said, unlocking the padlock on the door, "just look for this red circle. Then you'll know you're home."

The door squeaked as Vikram eased it open, and the smell of unwashed bodies wafted through the air. Sunlight lit up part of the room and Tavi could see half-naked boys, his age and younger, sleeping on the floor in various poses. Two of them looked up blearily, but Vikram said quietly, "Not yet. You boys still have a couple more hours to sleep. I'm just dropping off a new one." The two boys dropped their heads back down on their arms and went back to sleep without a word.

Vikram held the door open, and stepped into the windowless room. Noticing a clear space near the middle, he pointed to it as Tavi entered and looked around nervously. "That can be your spot," Vikram said. Tavi quickly counted and realized that there were seven boys sleeping in a room that was the size of his home in the village. There were clothes strewn everywhere and two buckets by the door. Tavi glanced in one and grimaced when he found it to be half-full with urine and feces. Vikram reached down and shook the boy who was nearest to the door.

"What?" the boy mumbled, batting Vikram's hand away.

"Chouji!" Vikram said warningly.

Chouji sat up immediately, his eyes wide awake. "Mr. Vikram," he said.

"Why do you have so many blankets?" Vikram asked. "Give one to Tavi, the new boy."

"Uh...okay!" Chouji hopped off of the bed he had made and pulled off the top blanket. He handed it to Tavi with a smile. "Here you go, Tavi."

"Thank you," Tavi replied, taking the blanket. Chouji sat back down and Tavi looked at Vikram, unsure of what to do.

"Okay," Vikram said. "I'll be back in a few hours. You boys be good." He turned to step out into the fresh air before pausing as if he'd forgotten something. "Oh, Tavi," he said, turning around. He reached down and took Tavi's bag away from him. "Let me keep this for you. You wouldn't want anything to get lost." He stepped outside and put his hand on the door to close it. Noticing that Tavi was still just standing there, he pointed to the center of the room again. "Hurry up! Go put your blanket down. I'll be back in a bit. Try to get as much sleep as you can."

Tavi opened his mouth in confusion. He glanced around and saw Chouji glaring at him, two of the boys looking up at him unhappily, and Vikram beginning to frown. He felt tears coming again as he resolutely stepped over a couple of bodies and put his blanket in the only free space on the floor.

As soon as he squatted down to spread it out, Vikram said, "Good boy, Tavi," and shut the door. Blackness enveloped him. The darkness was so thick and unending that he felt like he was smothering in it. He heard Vikram click the padlock shut, and then without warning, two beams of light shined through the dark, blinding Tavi. Someone punched him in the back of his head, another person kicked him in the ribs, and his blanket was ripped away from him as he fell to the floor.

Chapter 12

The man froze at the doorway to the bedroom. His right foot had stepped on a creaky floorboard, and all of his senses were alert, waiting to see if he'd been heard. He felt like a tiger, stalking its prey, and as the house remained quiet around him, he crept into the bedroom.

He was a big bear of a man, with a full beard, dark curly hair spilling over his forehead, well-built and six inches taller than average. Despite his size, he moved almost gracefully and was beside the bed in three steps. Gazing upon the peaceful face of the young girl sleeping in the bed, he sighed, knowing in his heart that he had to follow through and do what needed to be done.

He stood there for a few seconds before he heard a noise from downstairs. Glancing to see if anyone was coming, he quickly bent down and scooped up the five year old girl and nuzzled her ear while making growling noises.

The girl shrieked awake and hit the man in the neck. Her eyes focused as he leaned back, and she relaxed and put an arm around his shoulders. "Daddy!" she said, "You scared me!"

Javier Lopez laughed and tossed his daughter back onto the bed where she giggled as she bounced a couple of times. "Wake up, Jasmine," he said, turning and walking to her open closet. "It's time to get ready for school."

Jasmine rolled to her side and watched her father pull out some clothes. "I dreamed I had a horse!" She thought for a second. "Can I have a horse for my birthday, Daddy?"

"We'll see," Javier said. He turned around holding a green dress and socks and laid them on the bed. "Here is what you're wearing today. Do you want help?"

"No, Daddy!" Jasmine reached over, grabbed a sock, and tried to pull it onto her foot as she lifted her leg above her head. "I can do it."

Javier smiled and turned towards the sound of running steps getting closer. "Okay, but hurry up. Your mom says breakfast is almost ready." An adolescent boy dashed into the bedroom, wearing a baseball cap and carrying a baseball glove. "And Billy's up too!" Javier said happily. "This is turning out to be a perfect day."

"Daaaaaaaaaaaaaaaaaaaaad!" Billy cried.

Javier reached down and easily picked the boy up by his armpits. He raised him until his head almost touched the ceiling and then gently lowered him back down. "Good morning, Billy. How may Jasmine and I help you on this fine morning?"

Jasmine giggled as Billy held up his glove. "Tomorrow is tryouts for the baseball team. You said you'd play catch with me and hit some balls for me to catch."

"Well," Javier began, putting his arm on Billy's upper back and guiding him out of Jasmine's bedroom. They walked to the top of the stairs and stopped. "Do you have anything going on after school today?" Javier asked.

Billy shook his head. "Nope. I just wanted to play some baseball."

"Okay. How about I meet you at your school at three-thirty and we'll play on the field there? It'll be good for you to practice where the tryouts will be."

Billy grinned. "Cool, Dad," he said excitedly. He jumped down the stairs two at a time before pausing halfway down. "Can I bring some friends? Matt and Assaf said they wanted to play catch."

Javier shrugged his shoulders. "Sure. The more the merrier. Bring whoever you want."

"Awesome. Thanks, Dad!" Billy called out as he ran into the kitchen.

Javier stood at the top of the stairs in contentment, listening to the sounds of his family getting ready to start their day. It doesn't get any better than this, he thought, as he strolled down the stairs to help his wife with breakfast.

Later, as they scrambled to leave the house on time, Javier and his wife, Laura, bumped into each other as they rushed around the island in their kitchen. Javier put his arms around his wife and gave her a long hug, and she squeezed back and gently kissed him on his neck.

"Busy day today?" she murmured.

Javier inhaled the scent of her hair and kissed her temple. "A bit busy. I have to go into the office today for some paperwork. Baseball at three-thirty. Back to work afterwards. I'll try to be home by ten."

Laura sighed. Javier knew that both she and their kids were so much happier when he was home in the evening, but she understood that he had to work late sometimes, and that hard work paid for their expensive house, private schooling for Billy and Jasmine, and two cars in the driveway when most families struggled to have one. "We'll miss you," she whispered. "Try to get home as soon as you can."

"I will," he promised.

Just then, they were interrupted by Billy sliding in between them. "Daaaaaaaaaaaaaad!" he cried.

"What, Billy?" Javier asked, rolling his eyes at Laura with a smile.

"I can't find my homework."

"What homework?'

"My science project. The one we made last night from a Styrofoam ball. I've looked everywhere!"

Javier let go of Laura's hand and walked into the living room. "Did you look here?" he asked Billy, who had followed right behind him.

"Yep!"

Javier pointed to his study. "Did you look in my study...which is where we finished it?"

"Ahhh." Billy smiled at his dad. "Um, no. I forgot." He ran into his father's study and pulled his science project off of Javier's desk. "Found it," he yelled, as he rushed past his father and into the kitchen.

Javier called up the stairs. "Jasmine! Let's go!" When he heard something that sounded like a murmured assent, he turned and walked back into the kitchen.

"Are you going grocery shopping today?" Javier asked his wife, as she handed Billy a sack lunch.

"I don't think so," Laura replied. "I was going to the office to look over a case I'm handling, lunch with Jane, back to work for a bit, and then pick up Jasmine from school. Why?"

"I'm going to need the Lexus today," he said, referring to the SUV which was the larger of their two vehicles. "I've got some bats and bases in the back of it that I want to take with me when I meet Billy today."

"Sure, honey. No problem. Where are the keys to the Mercedes?" she asked.

Javier stuck his hands into his pockets, looked at the wall mount when he couldn't find them, and then shrugged at his wife with a grin. "I probably left them in the cup holder in the car. Let me check the garage."

Javier ran into the garage as Jasmine appeared in the kitchen, her shoes on the wrong feet. Sighing, Laura bent down and fixed them. "Found them," Javier said, dropping them on the counter.

Laura stood up and helped Jasmine put her backpack on. "Goodbye, baby," Laura said, kissing her on the forehead. "Have a fun day at school."

Jasmine wiped her forehead with one hand and reached up for her father's with the other hand, tugging him along through the door to the garage. "Come on, Daddy," she ordered.

Javier smiled back at his wife as he disappeared into the garage and mouthed the words, *"I love you."*

Laura beamed and whispered, "Me too." Turning to look for Billy, she was surprised to see him standing right behind her, baseball glove in one hand, science project in the other.

"Can we go now, Mom?" he asked.

"Yes, Billy," she said. "Let's go." They walked into the garage just in time to see Javier pulling out of the driveway.

As they both waved goodbye to him, Billy opened the door to the backseat and slid in. One minute later, Laura backed out of the garage, closing the automatic door behind her, and another morning in paradise had come and gone.

Chapter 13

Javier spent the day in his office at work, going through paperwork, mumbling over expense accounts, and checking his inventory supply. He had lunch with a number of executives from competing businesses and over an expensive meal, they agreed on the pricing of their stock for the next fortnight. When Javier had first started out and was struggling to make ends meet, another business had kept undercutting him with prices so low that Javier – and a couple of the men whom he had eaten lunch with – would have soon been out of business. After dealing with the problem of price gouging, they realized that the only civil way to prevent the problem from occurring again would be to fix their prices at a previously agreed upon amount. Since then, there had been no problems, and all of the gentlemen at the table were much wealthier because of it.

At three-thirty, Javier showed up at the baseball field wearing shorts and a t-shirt. He shook his head in amusement when he saw the large group of sixth graders who were waiting for him. Some of them were playing catch, but most of them ran over to the parking lot with Billy.

"Dad!" Billy exclaimed. "We've been waiting forever!"

Javier raised his eyebrow at Billy and looked around at the crowd of boys who called out greetings to him. "This is what you meant by Matt and Assaf?" he asked, walking around to the back of the SUV and opening the back.

"Well," Billy began, grabbing the equipment from his father and tossing it to his friends. "I don't know. They were excited, and we were talking about it in gym class, and some friends asked if they could come too, and…" He shrugged his shoulders as if to show he had no idea how so many people had showed up.

Grabbing the bag of balls and his glove from the car, Javier laughed and slammed the hatch shut. "I'm joking. As I said, the more, the merrier. Let's go play!" Javier suddenly sprinted towards the field, leaving most of the boys behind him. "Last one there has to run a lap!" he called, laughing again as he heard the joyful shouts behind him.

Javier spent the next three hours with the players, running drills, giving coaching advice, and finally, organizing and umpiring a game for the last hour. Over the course of the practice, some boys ran off to go eat dinner, while others showed up late and asked if they could play. Javier welcomed each newcomer cheerfully and got to know the boys he had never met before, and called out last second advice to each player who had to leave early.

Halfway through the game, when Javier had called a quick timeout so that he could show the batter how to stand properly in the batter's box, the coach who was in charge of the next day's tryout ambled over and stood behind the backdrop.

"So, you got it?" Javier asked, his hands on the batter's shoulders. "Stay straight like this. Turn your chin and face the pitcher. And then step and turn your body at the same time, and you should be able to hit the ball pretty far. You've got some muscle on you." Javier turned to walk back to his place behind the catcher, but paused when he caught sight of the coach. "Hey, Coach," he said.

"Hi," said the coach, looking around the field appraisingly. "You're Billy's father, right?"

"I am," Javier said proudly. He walked back and stood next to the chain link that was separating them. "I offered to play catch with him today, and then suddenly...this happened," he explained, motioning to the field.

"Dad!" Billy called out. "Let's play!"

Javier waved at Billy, and said to the coach as he squatted down behind the catcher, "Well, back to work. Hope I'm not stepping on your toes here or anything."

"Actually," said the coach hesitantly, "would you mind if I went to the field and helped out there?"

"No. Of course not," Javier said. "Thanks a lot." He cleared his throat and shouted, "Play ball!"

"Thanks," the coach replied, as he jogged around the fence to the field.

After the game was finished, Javier sat on the bleachers with the coach, sipping from a bottle of water. They watched Billy as he practiced pitching with his friend, Assaf.

Breaking the easy silence, the coach said, "It was good what you did today. I don't think most fathers would've done it."

Javier shrugged off the praise. "I think they would, if they had the chance. What about you? You don't have a son on the team, do you?"

The coach shook his head. "Nope. My son died when he was twelve years old, about ten years ago. Baseball was how we spent time together. I guess this is just my way of holding on to a piece of him."

"I'm sorry," Javier said quietly, imagining what he would do if anything happened to Billy. "It's still a wonderful thing, though. You give these boys a chance to play and get better."

"That's the problem," the coach said. "How many kids showed up today? Twenty-five? Thirty? Each team only has twelve or thirteen players. Last year I had to cut half the kids who wanted to play because there was no place for them."

Javier nodded his head and stared thoughtfully at the field.

"And so," the coach continued, "I was wondering if you wanted to coach another team. I can call the league commissioner tonight and get another team added to the schedule."

Javier hesitated. "How much time does it take?"

"One or two practices a week, and then one or two games a week. Maybe an hour and a half for practices and a couple of hours for each game. It's not much," the coached cajoled.

Javier's mind quickly ran through how much time he really needed to spend at work each week, and who could cover for him if he wasn't there. After a couple of seconds, he nodded as he turned and smiled at the coach. "Sure, it's a deal. But no "A" and "B" team. I don't want these kids to feel like they're losers for being on one of the teams. We'll call tomorrow a skills practice, and then tomorrow night, you and I can fairly split up the teams. Sound good?" he asked.

The coach nodded his head in agreement, relief showing in his face. "Thank God," he said. "I hate having to cut kids from the team."

"Good! Now we won't have to," Javier responded cheerfully. "Oh…about Billy. It'd probably be best if he was on your team. I don't want anyone to feel like I'm playing favorites."

The coach said, "I agree. It's usually best that way."

"However," Javier continued, "there's no reason why YOU can't play favorites." He laughed when the coach looked at him in surprise and clapped him on the back. "Just kidding. If he deserves it, then give it to him. If not, then he'll have to work for it." Javier paused as he watched Billy throw a curveball. "I'm sorry. I never introduced myself. I'm Javier Lopez."

"Tom Jackson," the coach said, shaking hands with Javier.

"Well, it's been a pleasure, Tom," Javier said, standing up, "but I have to go the office now. I'll see you here tomorrow at three." He hopped down from the top row of the bleachers and called out to Billy, "Billy. Let's go. Mom's making dinner and I have to get to work."

To the delight of his daughter and wife, Javier spent twenty minutes eating dinner with his family before hurrying off to work. As he drove through the rundown area where his sales team was located, all of the thoughts about work which he had compartmentalized earlier rushed back to the forefront of his mind.

Parking his car in his private spot, he gave one talent each to a couple of heavyset teenagers and said, "Make sure no one steps near my car."

"Yes, Mr. Lopez," they both said, jumping up and looking alert.

Javier took a deep breath, relishing the scent of his city. Looking down the street he had made his own, Javier strolled through the crowds and turned into the third door on the right. As his eyes adjusted to the dim lighting, he saw his employees straighten up imperceptibly, as if they all seemed to sense at the same time that the boss was in the building.

Nodding to himself in satisfaction, Javier walked to the bar, his eyes constantly scrutinizing everything around him. "Hello, Juan," he said, as the bartender gave him a bottle of water. "How are things?"

"Never better, Mr. Lopez," Juan said, smiling nervously and rubbing a nonexistent mark on the spotless bar with his rag.

"Where is he?"

"Upstairs," Juan replied.

Without saying a word, Javier turned around and bounded up the stairs. He opened the door with a bang and slammed it shut behind him. Making his way behind a wide, expensive looking desk, he plopped down in the leather chair and leaned back, taking a swallow of water from the bottle.

"Vikram," Javier said, without looking around, "please enlighten me as to why you paid one and a half thousand talents of my money for a village rat. He better be worth it."

Chapter 14

Later that night, three boys stood in a row in front of the desk, heads down, as they shifted their bodies slightly and tried to get used to their new clothes.

Javier walked around his desk and studied each boy, judging them by the way they stood, their faces, the coloring of their skin, and a number of other little details that Javier looked for each time he met one of his new boys.

He stopped in front of the one on the right, as Vikram stepped behind the boy and said, "His name is Mac. Jonas found him in a village we haven't been to before. First in his class. Tall parents. I spoke to him a bit earlier. Seems like a good find."

Javier reached out and gently lifted the boy's chin until he was looking him in the eye. "Mac, huh?" The boy smiled at Javier nervously. "So, Mac, are you ready to learn and get to work?" Javier studied his face, liking the bright blue eyes which were a rare find, and mentally wondering how much he could charge for it.

Mac nodded his head and grinned. "I am, sir." Without warning, Javier grabbed Mac's jaw and lifted up the corner of his lip roughly with a finger.

"Damnit, Vikram," Javier said angrily, prying Mac's mouth open as wide as it could go. "He's got two brown, rotten teeth right here." He stuck his nose near his mouth and sniffed, turning his head away in revulsion. "Did you guys not smell his breath? Come here, Vikram! His breath smells like death!"

Vikram hurriedly stepped around Mac and sniffed his mouth. He grimaced and stepped back. "I'll take him to the dentist tomorrow morning. I'm sorry. I should've noticed."

Javier shook his head in disappointment, roughly grasping Mac's jaw and turning his face from side to side. He ignored the tears of embarrassment that were trickling down Mac's face before letting go and stepping to the boy in the middle. "Okay. Other than that, he should be fine. Who's this?"

Vikram cleared his throat. "This is Will. Jonas picked him up in a village we used a few years ago. His parents were eager for the cash and the schoolmaster spoke highly of the boy."

"Smile," Javier commanded, and Will grinned and showed all of his teeth. Bending down to sniff his breath, Javier mumbled, "Well, at least that's something." He grabbed Will's face the same as he had grabbed Mac's, and turned it from side to side, studying every aspect of it. "You look familiar, boy," Javier said thoughtfully. "Any reason why?"

Will swallowed hard and stuttered, "My…my…brother, sir. He came to this school four years ago."

"What?" Javier's voice was flat, filled with a cold anger.

"My brother, Tim, sir. He's here somewhere, I think. He came to study and…" Will trailed off when he saw Javier glaring above his head at Vikram.

"Did you know about this, Vikram?" Javier asked quietly.

Vikram shook his head in dismay. "I…no, sir. I know the rules. This is…I don't know what Jonas was thinking."

Javier stared at him for a few seconds, turned towards his desk, grabbed a glass and threw it at the wall with such force that a couple of the fragments flew back and struck Mac on the arm. "Mac," Javier said without looking at him. "Go downstairs, get a broom, and clean this up!"

"Yes, sir," Mac said, running for the door.

Javier stared at Will, who was trembling in fear. "Your brother," Javier began quietly, "ran away two weeks after we brought him here." Will's mouth opened in surprise. Javier reached out and clamped his hand across Will's face. "You won't do the same, will you?"

Will tried to shake his head, but Javier's grip kept him from moving it even a little bit.

"Because you need to work off your debt, as well as your brother's debt, before you can leave. Do you understand?" Javier let go of Will's face and stepped back, as Mac ran back into the room with a broom and dustpan.

Will nodded his head frantically. "I understand, sir," he said.

Javier held out his hand and stopped Mac with his hand. Taking the dustpan and broom from him, he handed them to Will and gently pushed Mac back into line. "Will, you can start working off your debt now. Clean this mess up!"

"Yes, sir!" Will answered, as he ran to where the broken glass was and anxiously swept it into a small pile.

Javier looked at Vikram and shook his head in disappointment at the first two boys. "And now let's see what you've brought." Javier stepped in front of the third boy and tapped his chin, making him raise his face. He smiled when he saw the fire burning in the boy's deep green eyes. Javier stepped back and eyed Tavi closely. His body was tall and straight, maybe a bit leaner than the customers liked, but that could be easily fixed. His hair was slightly longer than fashionable, and Javier reached out and rubbed a lock between his fingers, pleased with the thickness. Proud chin, intelligent eyes.

"What's his name?" Javier asked Vikram.

"Tavi."

"Smile for me, Tavi," Javier said kindly. He grinned when he saw Tavi bare his lips like a wild animal and show all of his teeth. "I like you," he said, reaching out to pat him on the head. As Tavi jerked his head away from his touch, Javier hit him solidly on the side of the head. "But you're going to have to learn some respect," he warned. He inched his face close Tavi's face, ignoring the carefully controlled deep breaths the boy was taking.

"What happened to his eye?" Javier asked Vikram, pointing to Tavi's left eye.

Vikram shrugged and poked Tavi in the back. "You can answer, boy."

Tavi glared straight ahead, refusing to make eye contact with Javier, and said in a loud voice, "I fell in the dark. I hit my face. I shouldn't be so clumsy."

Javier glanced up at Vikram who smiled at the lesson that Tavi had already learned.

"Well, make sure it doesn't happen again," Javier said. "We don't want you scaring away any of our customers."

"It won't," Tavi promised crossly, briefly making eye contact with Javier.

The only sound in the room was Will sweeping up the last of the glass. As he hurried back to the others, carefully carrying the dustpan in front of him, Javier went and sat back behind his desk, sipping from his bottle of water.

"So what's the schedule then for these boys?" Javier asked Vikram, who was still standing straight at attention.

"The dentist for this one," Vikram said, motioning to Mac who had just moved over to make room for Will. He put his hand on Will's head. "I want to have Doc come in tonight and see if we can do anything about this one's rash." Vikram twisted Will around by his head and lifted up his shirt. A pink rash with whiteheads covered most of his back.

Javier felt sick for a second, and mentally cursed Jonas. "Where IS Jonas?" he asked, as Vikram dropped Will's shirt and turned him back around.

"Drunk somewhere," Vikram answered. "I haven't seen him since I've been back, but I heard he started a couple of fights tonight in two different bars."

"Goddamnit!" Javier stared at Vikram furiously. "Next time you see him, tell him I need to talk to him immediately."

Vikram nodded his head, silently pleased that Jonas was losing face, as Javier continued, "Maybe it's time to promote your little protégé. Anyway, we're getting off topic. Finish telling me what the plan is for these guys."

"I was going to have Yuri take Tavi to the hairdresser, cut some of it off, and maybe get the tips of his hair frosted," Vikram said, touching Tavi's hair.

Javier nodded in agreement. "Good. That'll work. And then?"

"We have enough boys now to do a training session. The others have been sitting around for a few days. We'll cover the basics - how to talk, how to make people happy, that kind of stuff. We'll ease them in, just let the customers eye them for the first few nights, jack their prices up…" Javier waved his hand for Vikram to move on since Javier was the one who had created the training schedule. "And," Vikram continued, "we caught Tiki. Little fucker was hiding in the alley next to *The Poker.*"

Javier sat up excited. "Really? That was fast. Who found him?"

"Yuri did," Vikram said proudly, the name jolting Tavi from his reverie. "He's been out looking for him all day. He had to beat up a couple of street rats, but they eventually showed him where he was hiding."

Javier nodded his head happily. "When he has time, tell Yuri to stop by. I want to talk to him about his future." He paused to flip through his planner on his desk. Picking up a pen, he asked, "This was Tiki's first offense, right?"

Vikram nodded his head.

"Okay," Javier said, making a notation on the calendar. "Let the new boys watch tonight. We'll do it at four after we close."

"Sounds good," Vikram said, stepping forward and putting his hands on Mac's and Tavi's shoulders. "Anything else?"

Javier shook his head, "I don't think so. You got anything?"

Vikram froze in the act of shaking his head as Tavi stepped forward. "I have a question," he said loudly.

Javier raised his eyebrow at Vikram curiously before motioning Tavi forward with his finger. "Yes, Tavi? What can I do to make you happy?"

Tavi swallowed and looked back at the other two boys. Will shook his head slightly, eyes glassy with fear, while Mac imperceptibly nodded his head. "I was wondering," Tavi began, swallowing hard again as his throat dried up, "um…when can we have flashlights too?"

Javier looked at Tavi in stunned silence and then leaned back in his chair, roaring with laughter. Vikram smiled along, but grabbed Tavi by the scruff of his shirt and yanked him back. Javier's laughter turned into chuckles, and he said, "Don't be hard on the boy, Vikram. That's an order." He looked at Tavi and smiled. "I like this one. Give him and these other two their own flashlights. No reason they should have to fight over them like dogs."

Vikram nodded his head in acknowledgement.

"Anything else?" Javier asked. "New clothes? A new house? Anything?" He waited a heartbeat and said, "Good. Get the hell out of here. Vikram – I'll see you when it's time to deal with Tiki." Turning his attention to some papers on his desk, he didn't even notice Vikram hurrying the boys out of the room and closing the door softly behind them.

Chapter 15

"No! What is wrong with you?!?" Tavi smiled for the first time that night as Ben, one of the older men who worked security for Javier, slapped Chouji hard across the back of his head. "You do not talk about how you miss home! You don't say that we paid your parents for you! You just talk about how happy you are to be here, and you love what you do, and how handsome I am!" Ben hit Chouji again and grabbed him by the hair. "Do you understand what I'm saying?"

"Yes!" Chouji cried out, making Tavi smile again. Tavi was sure that Chouji was the one who had given him a black eye the previous night, since he had been reclining on six blankets when Vikram finally unlocked the door that afternoon. Looking around quickly, Tavi had seen that two of the larger boys each had a couple of blankets while the rest of the children had none. When Chouji saw Tavi looking at him, he had just smiled at Tavi and mocked him by holding his hand up to his eye and pretending to cry in pain. Tavi had tried to tell Vikram about it and had been rewarded with a cuff on the side of his head as Vikram told him that he had fallen and shouldn't bother anyone with those kinds of problems.

However, Tavi was still confused about what they were learning. He had quickly picked up on the things that he was allowed to talk about with the customers, but he didn't understand why he would be talking to old men in the first place. Eventually, Chouji was able to have a successful conversation with Ben, and the boys were motioned to sit in a circle on the floor with Ben and Vikram.

"Next, your money," Vikram said, holding up a silver talent. "I have seen some boys make over ten talents in tips in one night." He paused and watched the boys look at their friends and whisper excitedly. "Yes," interrupted Vikram, "that's a lot of money. I even know a few boys who made over three thousand talents in one year, and that was just from tips." He looked around the circle and seemed pleased to find them all staring at him, eyes filled with greed. "If you work here for two or three years, then you could have enough money to buy a house in your village."

Excited murmuring from the circle. "Or a car?" someone asked quickly.

Vikram replied, "With that kind of money, you could buy four cars!" This time, there were whoops of joy.

"However," Vikram said. "We have rules. And you'll soon see…" Vikram paused to check his watch. "…what happens to boys who don't follow the rules." He glanced at Tavi who was unintentionally rubbing his arm where Vikram had bruised him. He dropped his hand, embarrassed, when Vikram flashed him a knowing grin. "So are you ready for the rules?" he asked the circled.

Nodded heads and murmurs of assent followed.

"The customer pays all money to the counter. If they do give you money for any reason inside of the bar, then you give it to me or Ben or someone else in charge immediately, understand?"

The children nodded their heads.

"Outside of the bar, whatever money they give you is yours, do you understand?"

The nods accompanied with smiles this time.

"However, we've had problems in the past with boys stealing from one another." Vikram shook his head sadly at the thought of it. "It just boggles my mind. I don't understand how you boys can't get along. But we won't have that kind of problem now, will we?" he asked, noticing how half of the circle glanced uncomfortably at Chouji, who was whispering to his friend with a grin. "WILL WE?" Vikram asked louder.

Most of the boys jerked in surprise and loudly agreed.

"However, as I said, we have had problems. And so when you come back home, give me or someone else your tips, and we will keep the money safe for you. At the end, when you're finished and you want to leave, we'll give you back everything that you have given to us to keep safe for you." He paused and looked around the circle for any suspicion or dissension. When he saw none, he said, "Okay, well now…" Vikram pursed his lips thoughtfully at Tavi's raised arm. "Yes, Tavi? Is this really important?"

Chouji and his friend elbowed each other and snickered at Tavi. "I don't really understand why the customers would pay money," Tavi said hesitantly.

Vikram looked around at the expectant faces. I always forget how innocent they are, he thought. "Who else isn't sure what's happening here?" Slowly, one by one, the entire circle raised their hands. Vikram gave a sad smile and said, "Usually, we would do that tonight, but we have special surprise tonight, and so you will learn the rest of what you need to know tomorrow night." Getting to his feet, he said, "Now, everyone stand up and back up a little."

As the boys hopped up and moved back, Vikram glanced at his watch – four o'clock in the morning on the dot. He heard a knock on the door, and hurried over to open it up. Unlocking the door and pulling it open, he saw Yuri patiently waiting, holding a boy by the scruff of his shirt.

"Tiki," Vikram said pleasantly, stepping back and letting them enter. "It's nice to see you."

The circle of boys edged closer, fascinated by Tiki. He looked to be about twelve years old, tall and strong. He might've been handsome, but his nose and mouth were rimmed with dried and wet blood, and his left eye was swollen shut. Frantically looking around with his good eye, his shoulders slumped with defeat when he saw no one who could help him.

The door banged open, making everyone jump. Javier strolled in, twirling a baseball bat in his right hand like a walking stick. His face was serious as he glanced around the room before resting his eyes on Tiki.

"Tiki," Javier said, shaking his head with displeasure, "you disappoint me."

Tiki stared at Javier's feet with his one good eye as tears started to fall. "I'm sorry," he said, barely louder than a whisper.

"And so am I," Javier said. "You know what I have to do, right?"

Tiki nodded his head, his body shaking as he wept silently. Javier looked over at Yuri and frowned.

"Stop it!" Yuri snarled, grabbing Tiki by the collar and slapping him in the face. Tavi flinched, unwilling to accept what he was seeing. "You stole money AND you ran away!" Yuri punched him in the stomach.

Tiki groaned, bending over as he grabbed his stomach. "It was MY money," he coughed.

"Stop," Javier commanded Yuri. "Let's just get this over with." Javier turned and faced the boys who were watching. "You get two chances here. This is what happens the first time you disobey us." He nodded to Yuri and Ben. Yuri went behind Tiki and put his arm around his throat, forcing him to stand up. Ben grabbed Tiki's right wrist and pulled it onto the empty bar where the boys had been sitting earlier.

"Tiki," Javier declared emotionlessly, "This is your last warning." He lifted the baseball bat over his head and swung it down as hard as he could, cleanly breaking Tiki's lower arm bone.

Tiki's piercing scream filled the room. Javier reached over and gently ruffled Tiki's hair as he clutched his broken arm, sobbing loudly. "Don't forget," Javier said softly. Walking towards the door, he looked at the stunned children who were staring at him with frightened eyes. "I'm glad you guys got to see this," Javier said. "Remember the rules."

He turned and walked out of the room, softly closing the door behind him as Ben and Vikram sat Tiki on a stool and began splinting his arm.

Chapter 16

They sat with their backs against the walls, in three separate groups, as far from each other as possible. Next to the open door and enjoying the night breeze, Chouji and his two friends, Brent and Anouram, reclined against the wall, laughing at a joke Chouji had just told. They had been there the longest – maybe a week or so – and were bigger than the other boys in the room.

Tavi, Mac, and Will watched them in silence from the wall facing the door. They could still feel a bit of the fresh air and were anxiously waiting for their dinner to arrive. Against the far wall to their right were the two other boys. They'd arrived a couple of days after Chouji and his friends and had been tormented endlessly since then. They were both younger than the others and stared at everything around them with frightened eyes.

Tavi sighed, as his eyes flicked back and forth between the other two groups. "So, when did you guys get here?" he asked Mac and Will. It was the first chance they'd had to converse since being grouped together in Javier's office.

Mac looked at Will, who shrugged his shoulders. Mac shook his head and said to Tavi, "Will and I got here two days before you. Those guys have been pretty rough with him." Tavi glanced at Will and saw him staring at Chouji and his friends in obvious hatred.

"What happened?"

"I don't know. It was dark, you know?" Tavi nodded. Mac continued, "Ever since I met Will, all he's talked about is seeing his brother here. How great his brother is. How amazing everything will be once he finally gets to be with his brother again. When we get here, he asks Chouji and them where Tim is. They laughed at him, Will pushed Anouram, and then all three of them jumped on him."

"What'd you do?" Tavi asked.

Mac stared at the floor shamefaced. "What could I do? There's three of them. They're bigger than me. I didn't know Will would start a fight." He shook his head and scuffed his foot on the floor. "I would, though," he said with conviction, raising his eyes and looking at Tavi. "If I could do it all over, I would jump in and help him."

Tavi nodded his head in understanding. "Did they take your blankets?"

"Yep," Mac said. "They're the only ones with flashlights." He grinned at Tavi and touched the flashlight in his pocket. "Or, at least, they WERE the only ones with flashlights." Tavi grinned and touched his own flashlight in response. "They just took my blanket and pushed me," Mac said, "but they kicked Will and blinded him and kept tormenting him both nights...until you arrived." Mac motioned to Tavi's eye. "And then they gave you that."

Tavi grimaced, remembering how embarrassed he had been when Vikram laughed at him for talking about it. He peeked at Will, who was staring at something in his hand. "Is he going to be okay?" Tavi asked.

"I hope so," Mac said. Yuri entered the room and started setting down plates of food. Mac whispered quickly, "I think Chouji made him pull his pants down!"

"What? Why?!?" Tavi asked, remembering his own experience at the rocks.

"I don't know."

Mac went silent as Yuri called over to them, "Tavi. Mac. Tim's brother. Come grab your food before Chouji eats it all." He looked at the two younger ones against the wall. "You too. Hurry up!"

They all ran over and scooped up their bowls of food, starving from their busy night. Yuri held out four extra bowls for Tavi, Mac, and the two youngest boys. "Javier said you guys need to fatten up a little bit, so eat this as well," he said.

"What about me?" Chouji said, almost whining.

"Javier says you're too fat, and you're lucky I'm giving you anything," Yuri retorted. Tavi and Mac snickered and Chouji shot them a look full of promised pain to come.

Chouji finished his bowl quickly and looked up at Yuri, who was standing in the doorway. "You don't have to watch us eat," he said charmingly.

"Shut up, fatty." Yuri yawned and checked his watch. "I'm supposed to make sure everyone eats what they should eat." He looked at Chouji and sneered, "Or what they shouldn't eat."

Chouji flopped back against the wall, eyeing everyone around him angrily. When they were finished eating, they hurried to the door and placed their bowls on the tray that Yuri had brought and then rushed back to their spots. Only Tavi didn't return to his seat.

"Yuri," he beseeched. "Can I please go to the bathroom in the outside toilet really fast? I'll be back in one minute." He wrinkled his nose and pointed at the bucket. "It stinks so bad here when it's full, and these guys don't let…" Tavi hesitated. "Never mind. It just smells really bad. Please."

Yuri nodded his head and asked, "Does anyone else need to go?"

Mac jumped up, as did the two younger boys. They followed Tavi out and ran down the narrow alleyway. Yuri listened to their steps recede and looked at Chouji. "I'd be careful, if I were you," Yuri warned him. "Bullies don't usually last a long time around here."

Chouji looked at his friends and laughed. "Me? A bully? That's just silly," he insisted.

Yuri shrugged and looked outside, waiting for Tavi and the others to return. "I've seen Tavi angry. But since you're not a bully…" Yuri trailed off and they could hear the four boys running back down the alleyway. He picked up the tray and stepped outside, letting Tavi, Mac, and the two young ones pass into the room. He glanced around once to make sure that everyone was where they wanted to be, and then he shut the door, padlocking it closed for the next ten hours.

Chouji and his friends laughed and relaxed next to the door, enjoying the little bit of light and fresh air that came in through the cracks. Silently, Tavi stood up and tiptoed over to where he had last seen the little ones.

"Hey," he whispered, his voice so low that it would've been inaudible from more than two feet away.

"Hey," one of them said.

"Come sit with us," Tavi breathed. "It'll be safer."

The one who was speaking hesitated slightly before whispering, "Okay."

"Take my hand." Tavi held out his hand and felt a small sweaty hand grab it. For a split second, it felt like his brother's hand, and he took a deep breath to keep from crying. Standing up as quietly as possible, Tavi led the boys back to Mac and Will.

As they sat down, Tavi asked Mac, "You know what to do, right?"

"Yeah," Mac replied quietly. "I just told Will. He's ready."

"Yep," Will said in a normal tone of voice.

Chouji's corner was suddenly quiet. Someone rummaged on the ground for something and then CLICK. Tavi and his friends were blinded by a flashlight shining on them.

"Well, what do you know?" Chouji said, a smile in his voice. "All of the little rats are sleeping together." Holding up their hands, they tried to shield their eyes from the light. "Will," Chouji called out in a friendly tone, "you want to come play with us?"

"Go fuck yourself!" Will shouted.

Chouji and his friends laughed and darkness returned with a CLICK. "We'll come play with you guys later," Chouji promised. He and his friends resumed talking as Tavi's group tried to regain their composure and steady their breathing.

"They made us take our clothes off too," one of the small boys whispered to Tavi, making him jump in surprise.

"Wait..What?" he asked.

"Every night before the other Will and Mac came. They touched us and laughed and made us touch them."

Tavi lightly banged the back of his head against the wall, rage filling his body with strength. "Those fuckers." He turned his head in the direction of Mac and whispered, "Ready?"

"Yeah."

"Let's go." He leaned his head towards the two young ones. "You guys stay here," he said, silently rising to his feet. When they had come back from the bathroom, Tavi and Mac had casually kicked aside anything that they might step on, and so the path to Chouji and his friends was clear.

They crept towards the voices with Tavi in the lead and Mac and Will lightly holding on to his shirt. From the door to the wall was twelve steps, and after ten of them, Tavi halted and lightly tapped Mac on the shoulder three times.

On the third tap, Tavi and Mac shined their flashlights at the corner by the door, immediately joined by Will's flashlight. Chouji and his friends yelled and held up their hands to protect their eyes.

Tavi and Mac jumped forward, each carrying a large stone they had picked up on their way to the bathroom and hidden in their pockets. Tavi hit Chouji across the temple with his rock, and he fell to the ground moaning as he held his bleeding head.

Mac punched forward, holding his rock in front of him, and Brent's nose exploded in a shower of blood. He fell back into the corner, screaming and holding his nose as blood poured through his fingers. Anouram jumped up with his eyes squeezed tight and his arms extended, but Tavi hit him in the face with the rock, and he collapsed to the ground as well with a bloody nose.

Suddenly, Tavi heard Will make a sound like a growl and the hairs on the back of his neck stood up. He spun around only to see Will drop his flashlight as he jumped forward and grabbed Chouji by the hair. Lifting his head up, Will reached into his pocket and pulled out a large shard of glass that he had picked up and pocketed earlier without Tavi or

Mac knowing. He held it under Chouji's chin, where the sharp point was already cutting into him.

"Will…" Tavi said, the calmness of his voice belying the fear that was threatening to paralyze him. "Don't do it, man. It's too much."

Will's body shook as he began sobbing. "This fucker. He thinks he can do whatever he wants." He turned and looked at Tavi for a second, tears streaming down his face. "He made me pull down my pants and then he made me touch them, Tavi!"

Tavi shook his head, his gaze never leaving Will. "I know, but…" He took a deep breath and continued. "You saw what they did to Tiki. What will they do to you if you kill him?"

"And where's my brother?" Will cried, as if Tavi had never spoken. "I just wanted to see him. We're supposed to be going to school together. Where's my brother, Tavi?!?"

"I don't know," Tavi said softly. "But…"

"Your brother is dead, you stupid fuck," Chouji interrupted, mumbling his words. "And so are you as soon as I stand up." Chouji raised an arm to Will's wrist, still too stunned to move quickly.

"NO!" Tavi shouted, watching Will's eyes, as Mac jumped and tried to grab Will from behind.

Will thrust his hand forward and the piece of glass slid deep into Chouji's throat. Will sat back, a stunned look upon his face, as Chouji made gagging sounds and fumbled at the piece of glass. Blood dripped down his neck and covered his hands before he finally managed to grip it. His eyes wide with fear, Chouji struggled to pull the glass out of his throat for a few seconds. Suddenly there was a slurping noise, and when the piece of glass slid free, blood gushed out everywhere.

Will's flashlight had landed facing Chouji, and they could all see his eyes rolling around in horror as he clutched at his throat. Within seconds, he was dead, his blood pooling on the floor around his body.

Mac's arms fell to his side, too shocked to move. Will's legs gave out from under him, and he collapsed to the ground. He pulled his knees up to his chest and wrapped his arms around them, silently sobbing as he stared at Chouji's body.

Tavi and Mac stared at each other in horror, two young boys faced with death for the first time in their lives, and they had no idea what they should do.

Chapter 17

After dropping Jasmine off at school in the morning, Javier sped to a nondescript office downtown as fast as the speed limit would allow him. He only had a short amount of time to finish this errand and hoped to get it out of the way with a minimum amount of trouble.

Stepping from the bright sunshine into the dimly lit real estate office, Javier paused for a second to allow his eyes to adjust to the light, and he wrinkled his nose at the stale smell of cigarette smoke.

"Can I help you, sir?" said a man from behind the desk, standing up respectfully.

Javier strode forward and stuck his hand across the desk. "Javier Lopez," he said, gripping the man's hand tight and giving it a brief shake. Easing himself into one of the two uncomfortable wooden chairs facing the desk, Javier got right to the point. "I saw your listing in the paper last night."

"I see, sir," the real estate agent replied. He slid a thin plastic folder across the desk to Javier and flipped on a light switch behind his head. The overhead lights flickered on, barely adding any light to the office. "Here is a list of properties which you may be interested in."

Javier slid the folder back. "The only one I'm interested in is the fifty acres of land, right outside of the city. Is it still available?"

"It is," the man replied, unable to hide the excitement in his voice. "It's a prime piece of land. I've had several callers set up appointments for later today."

Javier laughed. "I have a source that tells me that it's been on the market for over two years, and no one wants to buy it," he said in a friendly tone of voice. "So how about we don't play any games today? I'm either going to buy it in the next five minutes, or I won't. It's entirely up to you."

The real estate agent swallowed. "Okay," he replied quickly, "what do you need to know?"

"Is it isolated?" Javier asked. "Do people cross the land to get to other places, do teenagers go there, is it a private place?"

"Yes, no, no, and yes," the man answered. "It's surrounded by highways on three sides, and it's mainly farmland and a small forest. There's also a fence around the place which you could renovate into an electric fence for a small price."

Javier nodded his head in satisfaction. "Good. I'll consider it. I want a place that's safe from the prying eyes of anyone I don't want to be there."

"Then it's the perfect place," the man answered, opening the folder and showing Javier photos of the land and the structures that were still on there.

Javier quickly studied the photos, his eyes taking in every small detail. Glancing at his watch, he shut the folder again. "Okay. We have two and a half minutes left. Let's talk about the price."

Two minutes later, he stepped out of the office, followed by the real estate agent. Javier walked to his car and opened the door. As he climbed into his car, Javier said, "Call my accountant now. Set up a time and place with him and get this done by noon. I'm going to have men working on that barn to make sure it's secure by twelve-thirty today, so the paperwork had better be done!"

"Yes, sir!" the man called as Javier slammed the door shut. He waved to an uncaring Javier as he drove away and rushed back inside, eager to seal the deal.

Javier drove like a madman to get to Jasmine's school on time. He had volunteered to be one of the parents who would help out on the trip to the zoo. He slowed down just as he got to the school parking lot and was pleased to see that the bus was still in front of the school. Jogging to the front door, he met Jasmine's class as they came out of the school.

"I'm sorry I'm late, Mrs. Turville," he apologized to Jasmine's teacher, who was leading the class towards the bus. "My business meeting ran later than I had planned."

"It's okay," she said, smiling forgivingly. Javier was the only father who ever volunteered for these kinds of things, and she was always happy to see him. "You'll be in charge of group number five, which has Jasmine in it."

"Sounds good," he started to say, but was interrupted by a scream of joy.

"Daddy!!!" As Jasmine ran straight at Javier, he caught her in his hands, whirled her around, and tossed her in the air. The rest of the class stopped for a second to watch, and Mrs. Turville had to call to the other mothers to keep them moving.

Javier looked around, gave an embarrassed smile, and put Jasmine back down, shooing her to her place back in line.

"Hi, Javier," said two young, pretty mothers as they walked by. Wendy, the blonde, and Winnie, the brunette. Javier had been as courteously non-flirtatious as possible since he had met them which only seemed to encourage them more.

"Wendy...Winnie...A good morning to you," Javier said politely.

Wendy smiled and said, "When are you and Jasmine going to come over for a playdate with Mackenzie and me?" She turned and giggled with Winnie as Javier ducked his head shyly.

"Sometime when we're not so busy," he replied, turning away and following Jasmine into the bus. Stupid bitch, he thought viciously. What's wrong with those two women? Why do they act like that around children? Swallowing his anger, Javier sat next to Jasmine on the bus and they began planning which animals they wanted to see first.

After they got back from the zoo, Javier jumped in his car and drove quickly to Billy's school, hoping to get there before the non-tryout started. He sighed with relief when he saw that Tom was the only one there. Checking his watch, he realized that school wasn't going to let out for another five minutes.

He opened his car door and climbed out, calling out a greeting to Tom who was setting up the bases on the field. He walked around to the back of his car and opened the hatch. As he was reaching in to grab the bags with the bats and balls, his cell phone rang. He looked at the caller id before answering, cursing slightly when he saw that it said *Sales Manager2.*

"This better be important," he answered.

"Javier," Vikram began, speaking quickly. "We have a problem. One of…"

"Wait a second, Vikram," Javier interrupted. "Is this a big problem that you're sure you need me to solve, or is this a small problem that you should be able to handle?"

He could hear Vikram's mind ticking. With Jonas fucking up so much lately, Vikram should move into the number two spot, but if he showed that he couldn't do things without guidance, then… "It's a big problem," Vikram decided.

"Fine, what?" Javier pressed the phone to his ear with his shoulder, grabbed the bags, and headed towards the field.

"Um…One of the boys is dead."

"The fuck you say!" Javier exclaimed, dropping both bags as he stopped walking. "What happened?"

"From what I can gather, Chouji's been tormenting the younger kids, and last night Will stabbed him in the throat."

"Will, the pimply one? What'd he stab him with?" Javier asked angrily. "Did you leave anything dangerous lying around?"

"He kept a piece of glass from when he was cleaning up yesterday," Vikram said. Javier closed his eyes and silently cursed as Vikram continued. "The body is just lying in a huge pool of blood. It looks old, so it happened a while ago. What do you want me to do? We've never had this happen before."

"Touch the body," Javier commanded. "Is it stiff yet?'

"Uh," Vikram said, sounding unhappy. "Yeah."

"Alright," Javier said, thinking quickly. "It probably won't fit in a bag right now, and I don't really want you guys chopping it up to make it fit."

"Me neither," Vikram said.

"So, go get the biggest plastic bag you can find, fit as much of the body as you can inside of it head first, and put it in the back of Ben's pickup truck. Cover the body with blankets or something and then tell Ben to go dump the body somewhere outside of the city where no one's around."

"Yeah, sure, Javier."

"And make sure you guys wear gloves when you touch anything or else there's a chance you could get caught and go to jail."

Vikram gulped. "Anything else?" he asked.

"Yeah. Once you put the body in a bag, get the rest of those boys filling up buckets with water and soap and bleach, get them sponges, and have Yuri watch over them and make sure they get all of the blood up."

"Okay." Vikram hesitated a moment before blurting out, "Do you think anyone will notice that he's missing?"

"Nah," Javier replied. "It's just one more dead dirty street rat. No one cares about them anyways."

"Yeah," Vikram agreed, giving a nervous laugh.

"But be fucking careful anyway, got it?"

Javier could hear Vikram nodding his head as he said, "Yep."

The sounds of children screaming made Javier look up in alarm. When he saw a bunch of boys running towards the field, he quickly said, "Vikram. I have to go. You were right to call me, but I'll talk to you next when I get to work. Take care of everything before then." He hung up before Vikram could reply, put his phone in his pocket, and picked up the bags.

Reaching the field at the same time as the boys, Javier smiled and called out, "You boys ready for some baseball?"

The sound of their cheering voices was more than enough to wash away his problems for at least a little while.

Chapter 18

Javier regarded the line of boys in front of him with cold eyes. They all looked exhausted. Not really in a physical sense; it was more of a weariness of the soul. Javier's eyes studied each face, lingering on Will the longest. Shaking his head in disappointment, Javier looked up at Vikram, who was standing behind the boys with Ben and Yuri. "Where's Jonas?"

The three men shook their heads, and Vikram answered, "I don't know, Javier."

Javier sprang up and banged his desk with his fist. "Where the fuck is Jonas?!?" he screamed.

Ben and Vikram dropped their eyes as if they were schoolboys who were getting in trouble with the headmaster. Yuri glanced at them, however, and said quietly, "He might've been arrested last night. Someone who sounded like him killed a man with a knife in a bar on Front Street. I just heard about it downstairs."

Javier sat back down slowly, looking at everyone in the room, daring them to make eye contact with him. "What is happening?" he asked incredulously. "We need to clean house right now." He studied the boys one last time. "Vikram!"

Vikram flinched and looked at Javier. "Go call the police station," Javier said, "and find out if it's Jonas. If it is, see if bail has been set and have someone pay it. If not, come back here immediately because we have a lot of work to do tonight." Vikram nodded and hurried out of the room.

"Yuri," Javier said, after pausing to think for a second. "Take Will downstairs. It's time for him to go see the doctor about his rash."

Will and the other boys looked up, different degrees of hope lighting up their faces for the first time that night. Yuri nodded knowingly at Javier as he put his hand on Will's shoulder to turn him around, and they quickly walked out the door.

After they had left, Javier gazed at the boys quietly until they started to fidget. He slid out a drawer from his desk and pulled out a thin metal container that originally held mints. He stood up and walked around the desk and faced the boys.

"Okay," he said, "stand in order of age. Brent and Anouram, you're both fourteen, right?" They nodded their heads and he motioned for them to stand in front of him. "Next is Tavi, you are thirteen years old, correct?" Tavi nodded. "Next to Tavi should be Mac. Mac, you are twelve years old, right?"

Mac smiled and said, "I am."

"Mac, don't smile until you get your teeth fixed," Javier said. Mac's bottom lip started to quiver as Javier spoke to the last two boys. "Sven and Francois, you are both eight years old, right?" The two smallest boys nodded their heads as they held each other's hand for comfort.

Vikram burst back into the room, receiving a dirty look from Javier for slamming the door open. "Sorry," Vikram said. "Two things – bail is not set, and the VIP customers are ready in the upstairs bar."

Javier scratched his chin and wondered what to do about Jonas. Putting it in the back of his mind, he opened up the tin and pulled out a tablet. "Starting today, you will take vitamins whenever we say," Javier said holding the pill out and dropping it into Sven's open hand. "We want you to be healthy." He took out another one and dropped it into Francois's hand. "Do you understand?" Javier asked.

"Yes," the boys mumbled together, each taking a pill. Ben handed a bottle of water to Brent, who swallowed his pill and passed the water bottle to Anouram, who did the same and passed it on down. After they had each swallowed their vitamin, Ben took the mostly empty bottle back, swallowed the remaining water, and walked towards the back stairs.

"Follow Ben," Javier commanded. The boys turned around, and filed behind Ben in a line, with the oldest children in front. He opened up a door at the rear of the office, and they followed him up the stairs, with Vikram following close behind. Sven tripped on the second step, giggling as Vikram caught him. Helping him stand up, Vikram gently pushed him up the stairs.

"Should we have given the younger ones only half a tablet?" he asked, looking over his shoulder at Javier.

"No," replied Javier, sliding open the drawer and returning the container to where it belonged. "It just hits them the quickest." Vikram nodded and turned to go. "Oh, Vikram," Javier called out, just as the door was shutting.

"Yeah?" Vikram asked.

"Two goals tonight – One, make our VIP's satisfied, and two, make sure those boys learn what they're supposed to do."

"Yes, sir," Vikram replied, gently closing the door behind him.

At the top of the stairs, he looked around the room where the boys had practiced the night before, making sure everything was set up how it should be. Their best barman was working the bar and several of their best customers sat on the barstools, sipping their drinks, and ogling the boys who were swaying slightly on their feet and randomly staring at things with glassy eyes. The rest of the VIP customers were sitting in comfortable chairs and deep sofas that lined the walls, and they too were eyeing the boys with calculating expressions.

Vikram entered the room and announced, "Can I have your attention?" The men all turned to look at him, as did a few of the boys, albeit rather slowly. "A few of you have been here before. As our way of saying thank you to you for being such wonderful customers…"

"Don't you mean for spending so much of our money in your club?" one of the men shouted with a laugh. The others quickly joined in, relieved that someone had broken the ice.

"Exactly," Vikram said with a smile. "And so we offer to you these beautiful, untried, inexperienced boys, who need some experience before our shrewd customers start paying for them." The men turned their attentions back to the boys, who were smiling happily in the center of the room. "We will also be taking photos for the newsletter that you all subscribe to. Your faces will be blacked out if you want, but you all agreed that it wouldn't be a problem, so I don't really think it's an issue."

A man with a cowboy hat raised his hand and asked, "What can we do?" The other men looked at Vikram eagerly.

Vikram gazed at each man with a stern expression upon his face, ignoring the lust in their eyes. "These boys are virgins now, and they will remain virgins until we sell their cherries in the bar. You do not want to cross us on that issue." He shrugged and continued, "Other than that, this is class and you are the teachers. Try to start out gentle, though."

He walked through the room and took a seat at the bar. After ordering a drink, he turned around and watched the men discuss and select who was going to start with each boy, as casually as if they were at a grocery store and deciding on which cut of meat they wanted.

Chapter 19

Tavi swallowed the vitamin and passed the water bottle to Mac. He studied Javier's face, wondering why Will wasn't being punished for killing Chouji.

Suddenly, and unexpectedly, Tavi felt a warm tickle move from his stomach up through his chest and down his legs, until his fingers and toes were tingling. He smiled and felt happier than he had felt in a long time. Blinking his eyes slowly, Tavi suppressed a giggle as he almost fell to the side.

"Follow Ben," Javier commanded, and Tavi smiled at him, liking the man, and really hoping that he was happy with him. Tavi turned and followed Anouram and began humming along with whatever song Anouram was humming. He didn't know what the song was and he had never heard it before, but he knew without a doubt that they were in harmony.

A bit of time passed, and Tavi remembered Vikram talking, and a bunch of men smiling kindly at him. The next thing he knew, a large man was leading him back to a chair. The man sat down and patted his knee for Tavi to sit on. Tavi hopped up, and the man rested his hand on Tavi's back for a second, before sliding his hand under the back of Tavi's shirt and gently rubbing him.

Tavi smiled at the man and said, "That feels really nice."

"What's your name?"

"Tavi. What's yours?" Tavi asked, smiling at the man and thinking he had a really handsome face.

"I'm Scott." He paused and then touched Tavi's cheek with his other hand. "You're a beautiful child," he said.

Things became fuzzy there and the next thing Tavi knew he was squatting in front of Scott and Scott had his pants off.

Scott took Tavi's hand and showed him where to hold him. "Like this?" Tavi said happily, enjoying how it felt against his hand.

Scott gave a deep sigh. "Yeah," he grunted, and placed his hand on the back of Tavi's head. "And bring your mouth here...like an ice cream stick."

Tavi woke up with a start, breathing heavily in the dark, and rubbed his aching head with his hand. He put his face near the crack of the door, letting the light touch him as he smelled the fresh air. "What happened?" he whispered. He pressed his other hand to his temple. "Ow!" he moaned. He gently laid his head back on the ground, feverishly trying to make sense of the disjointed images in his mind.

"Mac," he said, nudging the body next to him.

"Ugh!" said Brent. "What?!?"

"Sorry," Tavi whispered. Ever since they'd been attacked the night before, Brent and Anouram had stopped bullying the other children and were now doing their best to get along with everyone. "MAC!" Tavi whispered more loudly, kicking the person on the other side of him.

"Ow! My head" Mac whined. "Why does my head hurt?"

"Mine too," Brent murmured. "I remember the worst things from last night."

"Like what?" Tavi asked, dreading the truth.

"Those men!" Brent hissed. He was about continue, but Mac's gasp stopped him.

"Those men!" Mac whispered to himself. "And...and...we kissed each other?" he asked.

"What?" Tavi asked, as images of him kissing Mac and Sven with his tongue flashed through his mind. "And we were naked?"

One of the other bodies shifted and Anouram crawled closer. He said in a shaky voice, "Did I let Francois suck me...down there last night?"

Tavi squeezed his eyes shut; the disgust at what he had done filled his mouth with saliva. Turning to the piss bucket, he spat, trying to get the familiar filthy taste out of his mouth. "Last night," he asked quietly, focusing on the only thing that wouldn't make him go crazy, "did they give us brown paste before we slept?"

Mac replied uncertainly, "I think so. I remember Vikram stuck his finger out and you ran to him – naked – and started sucking his finger. So we all did."

Tavi couldn't get the taste out of his mouth. Not just the brown paste, but the bitter sliminess from the men. How many men were in his mouth? he wondered. Tavi hit the door with his fist. "I need some water!" he shouted, immediately moaning from the pain in his head. He buried his face in his arms, overwhelmed and wanting to cry from the shame and revulsion he was feeling.

"Will!" Mac said suddenly.

"What?" Tavi asked warily, not wanting to remember anything else.

"Don't you guys remember? Maybe it's because I was one of the last to eat that brown stuff," Mac said.

"Shit!" Anouram said. "I remember. Vikram said... they're going to kill Will today?"

Mac nodded his head in the dim light as Tavi started weeping helplessly, his sobs the only sounds they could hear.

Chapter 20

For the first time since he had arrived in the city, Tavi was relieved that they were kept in a darkened room all day. Even the thought of looking at one of his friends was too unbearable. The day slowly passed, each boy lost in his own fragmented memories from the night before, the silence only broken by an occasional sob when things became too overwhelming to think about, especially in the dark.

After the boys had been awake for a long time – with no clocks or windows, they were never sure what time it was or how much time had passed – they heard the rattle of a key in the padlock. Sven and Francois, who had slowly squirmed their way forward and were lying with their faces near the crack of light, jumped back and scuttled away from the door like two frightened cockroaches as the door opened and sunlight lit up a small section of the room.

Squinting his eyes against the brightness, Tavi was relieved to hear Yuri's voice, and then instantly he looked down at the floor, ashamed that Yuri might know what he had done the night before.

"Hey, Mac," Yuri said, his voice sounding abnormally loud in the small room.

Mac stood up and faced Yuri, covering his eyes with his hands.

"Come with me," Yuri commanded. "I'm supposed to take you to the dentist." Mac stumbled out the door and stood next to Yuri, still holding his arm over his eyes. "The rest of you can eat and have some water," Yuri continued, as he bent down beside the door and started tossing water bottles into the room.

Two of them rolled near Tavi and he snatched at them, dying of thirst. As he twisted open the first one, he saw Brent and Anouram already gulping down their bottles. He looked around for Sven and Francois and saw that they were still huddled against the far corner. Remembering again that they were only eight years old, he screwed the cap back on, and walked over to them. "Here," he said, holding out the water bottles. "You guys have to drink something." He waited patiently until they each slowly grabbed one. Tavi grimaced as a memory of them from the previous night flashed through his mind. Biting his lip to hold back his anger and shame, he turned and walked back to the door.

Yuri had ordered Brent and Anouram to carry the bowls of food into the room. He stood at the door and watched them, while Mac hurriedly shoveled food into his mouth from the bowl he was holding. Anouram walked over, carrying two bowls, and set them down gently in front of Sven and Francois.

Yuri watched this with a cynical smile, which Tavi was beginning to associate with him. "Okay," Yuri said. "I'm taking Mac to the dentist. We should be back in a couple of hours. I'm going to leave the door open, so you guys clean up this mess, dump out the buckets, and go shower in that room over there." Yuri pointed to a doorway next to the bathrooms. "Any questions?"

No one said anything, their eyes all focused on the floor. Yuri sighed and said, "You guys, it will get easier. You just have to..." he hesitated a second before saying more softly, "...not think about it or feel anything." He gave his cynical smile again and said in his normal tone, "And don't think about running away. Remember what happened to Tiki." Turning around, he tapped Mac on the shoulder and they walked off towards the main street.

Later that evening, after Mac had returned from the dentist, they were all sitting near the open door, relishing the fresh air and dim light from the deserted alleyway. After sitting in silence all day, speaking had suddenly become awkward and no one knew what to say or how to say it.

Tavi and Anouram each cleared their throats a couple of times as if they wanted to speak, but in the end, it was Mac who spoke first. "Fucking dentist," he complained. "He yanked out four of my teeth."

"Let me see," Tavi said, and everyone crowded around to look at the spaces in Mac's mouth.

"They're just going to leave you with holes there?" Brent asked, sitting back against the wall.

"No," Mac said. "I have to go back in tomorrow and they'll give me fake teeth."

"That's not a bad deal," Anouram said, nodding his head knowingly. "My sister needed a fake tooth but it was too expensive for my parents. You get four of them for free."

"Which he probably has to pay back," Tavi added darkly.

"Ah," Anouram said, as Mac frowned and tried to calculate how much it would cost.

"So…about last night," Tavi began.

"No!" Brent said firmly.

"I don't want to talk about it either," Anouram agreed quietly. Mac just stared at the ground, his eyes focused on a line of ants that were walking into the room.

"We have to," Tavi insisted. He jerked his thumb at Sven and Francois. Neither one of them had spoken all day. "Look at these two. We have to…"

"What about us?!?" Brent said, almost hysterically. "Do you know what I did last night?!?" He shuddered and wrapped his arms around his knees, huddled into as small of a ball as possible.

Tavi swallowed, reaching for a bottle of water as the taste from the previous night came back to him. He rinsed out his mouth and swallowed. Setting the bottle down, he said quietly, "We could run away and go back to our homes."

"Run away?" Brent scoffed. "Did you see what they did to Tiki?"

Anouram added, "And I don't even know how to get home from here. And we have no money for buses even if we did." He reached for his own bottle of water and rinsed out his mouth as well, before spitting the water into the alleyway.

Tavi looked at Mac, who was still staring at the ants. "Mac," he pleaded. "What do you say?"

Mac finally looked up, his eyes brimming with tears. Just from looking at him, it was easy to see that Mac was one of those cheerful, laidback children who was always smiling and being mischievous, and he never let bad things get him down. But now, he looked...*broken*, was the only word Tavi could think of. He had the expression of a dog that had been beaten so often by the master it loved that it didn't know what to do, and it lived each minute in fear of being hit again.

"I don't know Tavi," Mac said. He closed his eyes and took a shaky breath. "I can't do it again what we did last night. I can't believe that I did that, and I don't know who I am if I keep doing it because I wouldn't do that...But I did do it," he finished softly.

Tavi stared at Mac speechless. He had just described everything that Tavi had been thinking about all day. Brent and Anouram nodded their heads in agreement.

"Me too," said a soft voice, and Sven, the little blond boy, crawled into their group and leaned against Mac. "Is it me or not me? I can't remember," he said sadly.

Tavi whispered urgently, "And that's why we should try to run away now. It has to be better than this place."

"But what about Tiki?" Anouram asked. "I don't want my arm broken."

"If that's the worst they'll do, then I think it's worth the risk," Tavi insisted. He froze, eyes wide, as footsteps rapidly approached from the alleyway.

A few seconds later, Yuri appeared in the doorway. "Back up," he said. Everyone scooted away from the door. "Keep going," Yuri ordered, and they all crawled and sat against the back wall.

Yuri stepped into the room, followed by Vikram. And then Will stumbled into the room.

"Will!" Tavi shouted, rising to his feet.

"Sit down, Tavi," Vikram said, catching Will before he could fall.

Will looked around the room anxiously, blinking his eyes so that he could see in the dim light. When he saw the boys sitting against the wall, he relaxed and smiled, giving them a quick wave.

Ben stepped in behind Will and nudged him forward. Remembering what Mac had said when they had awoken that day, Tavi felt his hands go cold, and he started breathing quickly, hoping that he was in a nightmare from which he would soon escape.

Finally, Javier filled the doorway, at least a head taller than anyone else. He stretched his hand above his head on the outside of the doorway and FLICK.

Lights around the edges of the room flickered on, and soon the room was awash in bright fluorescent light.

Tavi and the other boys looked at each other in stunned silence before turning their attention back to the doorway. Javier smiled at them, stepped inside, and closed the door behind him.

"You were right, Vikram," Javier said. "They didn't try to escape."

Vikram smiled and replied, "After seeing what happened to Tiki, I didn't think they would." He shrugged and continued, "But we had men watching, so there wasn't ever really a chance."

"Still, it's good to know that you judged them correctly," Javier said. He stepped forward and studied the group of boys who were huddled together against the wall. "I know you don't like me right now," he said, "and you're unhappy and confused. But trust me; you won't mind it after a while." He stared at them, awaiting a response. "Well, somebody say something!"

Tavi glanced at the others, cleared his throat, and said, "You're wrong. None of us will ever be happy."

Javier beamed at Tavi, who shrunk back in confusion. "There…You see? How we present something is a huge part of how effectively we can sell it." Tavi looked at him quizzically as Javier turned to Yuri. "So, Yuri, let's see how your idea worked."

Yuri stepped forward and said, "Did they talk about running away?"

Tavi looked at Mac, who shrugged his shoulders.

"They did," said a voice to their left. They whipped their heads around as Brent stood up and walked over towards Yuri. "Mainly it was Tavi. He didn't think Tiki's broken arm was that scary. I think the others might have agreed to it pretty soon, though."

"Brent?" Anouram said weakly. "Why are you doing this? We came together and…"

"Brent's been here for two years," Javier said. He clapped Yuri on the shoulder, who was staring at Tavi. "Yuri had the idea of putting one of our old boys in with the new ones. I think it's worked pretty well." Javier looked at Brent and smiled. "Good job, Brent. You can have the next two days off. If you need some money, talk to Ben later."

Brent beamed at the praise as the other boys stared at him in disbelief. Tavi remembered Yuri's words of warning on the bus – "Don't trust anyone" – and vowed that he wouldn't ever make the same mistake again. He suddenly looked at Mac and Anouram with uncertainty, and saw that they were doing the same to him.

Inside, he felt like crying and wished for a second that he could just die right then and there.

Javier approached the boys, disappointment written across his face. "Why do you boys want to leave?" he asked. "You can make a lot of money here." He nodded towards Brent and Yuri. "And look at them. They were once like you, and now look how happy they are."

Tavi looked down at his feet, feeling scared and alone.

"Tonight," Javier continued, "you're going to entertain our V.I.P. guests one more time, and then…"

"No!" Anouram covered his mouth in surprise, as if he hadn't intended to speak. Seeing Javier's attention focused on him, he begged, "Please. Don't make me. I can't do it again. I won't…"

"You won't?" Javier interrupted softly. "You will…" He paused and looked at the other four boys. "You all will. And you will smile and enjoy it, and starting tomorrow, you will start working in the bar."

Mac shook his head, the fear in his eyes plain to see.

Javier smiled at his courage. He turned around and walked towards Will. "You said that you didn't think that what happened to Tiki was that big of a deal, right?"

Tavi looked at the others desperately, knowing what was coming. When they wouldn't return his gaze, he stammered out, "Please, sir. I didn't mean it."

"But I agree with you," Javier said, reaching into his pants pocket and pulling out an eighteen-inch long rod of steel. "And so now you should see what happens if you really disobey me and make me angry."

Javier stood in front of a quivering Will, as Yuri, Ben, and Vikram each pulled out their own batons. "Chouji cost me one thousand talents, and you killed him." Will shook his head and tried to run, but Ben and Vikram quickly grabbed him. Javier continued, "I debated if I should let you live, but once you've killed one person, you're a killer. You'll never change and I could never trust you." He reached out and ruffled Will's hair.

"I'm sorry," Javier said seriously.

Suddenly, the four men began swinging their batons forcefully at Will, on his arms, his legs, his torso, and his head. After the first couple of swings, Javier stepped back, watched for a second, and then turned and gazed at the boys against the wall, who were watching in horror as their friend was beaten to a pulp.

Will cried out at first and tried to cover his body, but after a few seconds, he collapsed on the ground, making the most terrible noises Tavi had ever heard. After what seemed like an eternity, Javier called out, "That's enough."

Yuri, Ben, and Vikram stepped back, breathing heavily. In front of them on the floor, Will was crumpled in a bloody pile, still making high-pitched keening sounds, as blood dripped down his face, his arms and legs broken, and a large flap of scalp was hanging off of his forehead.

Tavi tried looking away, but couldn't. He reached out and found Mac's hand, squeezing it as hard as he could. Mac squeezed back and Tavi prayed that it was finished.

"This is what happens if you disobey us," Javier said again. Vikram knelt next to Will, but Javier shook his head and said, "Let Yuri do it."

Vikram stood up slowly, looking like he wanted to argue. But Yuri stepped forward, and Vikram pulled a switch blade from his pocket, flicking it open.

"Do it fast and deep, boy," he murmured softly to Yuri as he handed him the knife. "No reason to make him suffer anymore."

Yuri took the knife and knelt down next the body. He looked up at Javier, his eyes glittering oddly in the dim light, and then they roamed unseeingly across the boys against the wall. Taking a deep breath, he grabbed Will's hair with his left hand, pulled his head back, and slit his throat.

Tavi squeezed his eyes shut and sobbed silently before fear for his own life made him take control of himself again.

When he opened his eyes again, the body was gone, and only Javier and Yuri were left standing in the doorway. "The cleaning supplies are here," Javier said. "Use the water in the bathroom and clean up this blood. We'll be back in two hours to give you your vitamins."

He turned and disappeared down the alleyway. Yuri made as if to follow, but hesitated and looked at the pool of blood on the floor. A look of regret seemed to cross his face, and for a second, he looked to Tavi like a sad little boy. But as he turned to go, his face once again wore that same cold, cynical smile. Tavi closed his eyes and leaned his head against the wall, knowing in his heart that it had only been a trick of the light.

After scrubbing and cleaning for an hour and a half, they finally got the floor spotlessly clean again. Vikram popped his head in, glanced at the floor, and said, "Good job. Hurry up and go shower. You have thirty minutes." He disappeared and the boys slowly stood up from where they were sitting against the far wall. Even though the door was open, none of them wanted to sit near the spot where Will had died.

Tavi was the last one to shower. When he got back to the room, Vikram was already standing there, with the boys lined up inside the room behind him. "You took your own sweet time," Vikram said, as Tavi squeezed by him to stand with the other boys. "Who do you think you are – a prince?" Vikram laughed and Tavi felt anger stirring inside of him.

"I'm sorry, sir," he said in a controlled voice. "I just felt extremely…" He paused and swallowed before he could finish. "…dirty."

Vikram studied Tavi and then his eyes flicked to the other boys. He smiled understandingly, the joking expression gone from his face. "You boys probably won't believe it," he said gently, "but I was just like you. Only they just threw me into the bar my first night, no vitamins, no warning, nothing, and some fat, rich bastard took me home, and…" Vikram shook his head and gazed at the floor. "Some boys end up enjoying it. I'm not going to say it gets better, but it gets easier," he said, still staring down with a faraway look in his eyes.

Tavi felt a shimmer of hope. "So you understand," Tavi said excitedly. "You can help us and…"

Vikram interrupted him with a hard look. "Stop. Don't say anything else, Tavi. No one will help you, especially not me. Don't ever mention it again."

"But…" Tavi tried to argue.

Vikram stepped forward and slapped Tavi hard across the face. "Stop," he ordered Tavi.

The crack of his hand hitting Tavi's face echoed through the room, and everyone froze. The rest of the boys looked at Tavi, who was staring angrily at Vikram, tears of frustration in his eyes. Vikram calmly returned his gaze, and after a few seconds, he dropped his hand and cleared his throat.

"Let's not have any more trouble tonight, okay, boys?" Vikram said, walking out of the room. He looked over his shoulder at them. "I want to show you something before we go upstairs." He turned to his right and started heading for the bathrooms with the boys trailing behind him. After passing the bathrooms, he turned right into a larger alleyway. The boys glanced around, none of them ever having gone this far from their room. Vikram stopped after about twenty yards and opened up a door in a building on his left. Holding it open, he motioned the boys to enter.

Inside was a room about twice as large as the one they were staying in, with sofas, chairs, and a television. Vikram took them through a door to the next room, which was filled mostly with beds, as was the adjoining room.

"What is this?" Mac asked.

"This is where the boys sleep who leave with customers each night. Since we don't know what time they'll be returning, this is where those boys come back to after leaving the customer's house or hotel."

"What about the boys who don't go home with customers?" Tavi asked.

Vikram shrugged. "They go back to the locked room until the next day. You guys have the circle room. Other boys have the diamond or triangle rooms."

"So no one is living in here now?" Tavi pressed.

"The boys who slept in here last night are back in the bar, trying to find their next customer. No one wants to go back to the locked room after staying here. This door is always open, you can watch television; you have a lot more freedom," Vikram explained.

He reached into his pocket as the boys looked around. Anouram sat down and bounced on the edge of a bed, testing it to see how it felt. None of the boys had ever slept in a bed before. "Okay," Vikram announced, grabbing one of the bottles of water that was sitting on a nearby table. "Come take your vitamin." He held out his hand, and one by one, each boy took a pill, put it in their mouth, and swallowed it with a gulp of water. With the memory of Will's death fresh in their minds, none of them wanted to argue.

Tavi tried to fight off the effects of the pill, and for the first few minutes, he thought he was winning and that he could stay in control of himself. But then he felt the warm tingling feeling spreading through his body, and he relaxed as his worries were washed away.

"Come," he heard Vikram say, and they all trooped happily after him.

As they passed by an open side door of the bar, Tavi later remembered hearing someone announcing to a cheering crowd, "And starting tomorrow, we are going to be auctioning off our new, fresh, young…" a significant pause. "…VIRGIN boys!" Cheers and applause drowned out the next couple of words. "…over the next four nights, so if you don't win tomorrow, come back the next day for another chance of winning!"

The cheers followed them up the back stairs, and Tavi smiled, feeling as if they were cheering for him. The boys followed Vikram through a door and Tavi saw all of the men stand up and smile at him. He smiled back, feeling loved and happy, as two of them came over and started talking to him and touching him.

Chapter 21

Javier took a sip of coffee, relishing the peacefulness around him. Sitting at the kitchen table with the early morning sunlight shining through the windows, the sounds of birds chirping in the backyard, his wife sitting across from him, and his children sleeping soundly upstairs, Javier gave a deep sigh of contentment as he thanked God for giving him such a perfect morning.

"I love you," he said, looking across the table at his wife. "I would do anything to make you happy."

Laura's smile was so beautiful that he felt his heart aching with love. "I love you," she replied. She reached across the table and grabbed his hand. "Are you sure we're not making a mistake?"

He smiled and squeezed her hand reassuringly. "I don't think so," he said. "I found this woman; her name is Jenny something or other. She comes highly recommended, and she'll meet us out there today. If we like her, then most of it will be on her."

"Okay," Laura said with a smile. "I trust you." She looked at the clock on the kitchen wall. "I can't believe you already have your first baseball game today," she said. "What time is it at?"

"Two-thirty," Javier said. "Since they had to add us to the schedule, the only way to make it work was to add games to the beginning of the season. At least we get to see Billy play today."

Laura grinned and asked, "Will you be rooting for our son or for your team?"

"I hope that our son is the best player on the field, and yet my team still wins at the end." Javier laughed and stood up, pulling Laura up so that he could he put his arms around her. "However, if you want everyone to think that you're cheering for your own son's team, then it's okay. I understand." He bent forward and kissed her softly, feeling her fingers on the back of his head.

Pulling away with a sigh, Laura said, "Should we go wake up the birthday girl?"

Javier yanked her towards him and gave her one last kiss. "I suppose," he said with a smile. He reached down and grabbed his wife's hand. Turning around, they walked out of the kitchen and up the stairs towards their daughter's room, holding hands the entire way.

"Happy birthday to you, happy birthday dear Jasmine, happy birthday to you!" Jasmine's grin was so wide that it seemed to reach her eyes, which were squeezed tight during the entire song as she pretended to be asleep.

Javier winked at Laura and quickly scooped Jasmine up, nuzzling her neck. "Jasmine," he growled while Jasmine giggled and screamed. He handed her to his wife and gave them a bear hug, squeezing them tight. "Happy Birthday, baby," he said.

Jasmine tried squirming free as her mother said happy birthday as well. Javier stepped back and Jasmine relaxed and sat comfortably in Laura's arms. Just then, Javier saw Billy peeking in the doorway. "Billy!" Javier pounced on Billy and picked him up. "Family hug!" Javier announce, turning towards his wife.

"NO!" Jasmine and Billy both screamed, struggling to get free. But Javier just laughed, held Billy against his body with one arm while wrapping the other one around his wife.

After a quick squeeze Javier dropped Billy on the bed. "And done," he said. "Who wants breakfast? I'm making eggs and bacon because we have a super busy day today! Everyone be in the kitchen in fifteen minutes." Javier jogged out of the bedroom and they could hear him running down the stairs. "And if you don't come to breakfast," he called out, "then no baseball OR presents today!" His deep laugh rolled up the stairs when he heard their squeals of protest.

When breakfast was finished, Javier had Billy bring his baseball gear with him to the car, and they all climbed into the SUV to celebrate Jasmine's birthday.

After driving for twenty minutes, they had almost reached the outskirts of the city. Taking a break from the word game they had been playing, Javier asked, "Who knows where we're going?"

"To the beach?" Jasmine asked hopefully.

"Nope!" Javier replied cheerfully.

"Stupid!" Billy said, lightly hitting Jasmine on the arm. "We have a baseball game today. We can't go to the beach."

"Daaaaaaaaaaaaaddy!" Jasmine whined. "Billy hit me and called me stupid."

Javier looked at his son in the mirror. "Sorry, Jasmine," Billy said contritely. He relaxed when he saw his father smile and then exclaimed, "Oh! Hey, Mom. Can I give Jasmine her present now? I think Coach is going to have the team over for swimming and barbecue after the game."

"Sure, honey," Laura said. "Where is it?"

Billy undid his seatbelt and knelt on the seat so that he could dig through the stuff in the back. "It's in my bag," he mumbled, hanging over the back seat and moving everything around. "Got it," he said after a few seconds. He slid back down and sat in his seat, handing the wrapped package to Jasmine. "Here, Jasmine," Billy said. "Happy birthday!"

"What is it?" Jasmine cried out, shaking it.

"Maybe you should open it, silly," her mother said, smiling at her only daughter.

Jasmine grinned at everyone around her, making sure that she was the center of attention, and then she ripped off the wrapping paper, throwing it everywhere. "Ohhh! A Barbie horse!" Jasmine squealed with delight. She tried to rip open the box so that she could take it out to play with.

"What do you say to your brother?" her mother asked sternly.

Jasmine paused for a half a second to smile sweetly at her brother. "Thank you, Billy!" she said, and then tried ripping a hole in the plastic again.

"You're welcome," Billy said. He reached out and took it away from Jasmine. "Let me open it. Dad, do you have your knife on you?"

Javier cautiously reached into his pocket and pulled out his switchblade. He flicked it open, and gently handed it back to Billy. "Be very careful," he said. "It's really sharp."

"Javier!" Laura said, the displeasure in her voice obvious to everyone.

"He's fine," Javier said. "He's a careful boy. I had one of those when I was his age." He glanced at her with a smile. "And look how I turned out."

Laura returned his smile as Billy said, "Got it. Here, Jasmine." Billy clicked the knife shut and handed it back to his father.

"Someday, Billy, you can have this knife," Javier said. And then with a quick glance at Laura, he said quickly, "Not today! But someday when you're older, okay?"

"Awesome! Thanks, Dad!" Billy replied enthusiastically.

"What? It's my birthday," Jasmine said, with a hint of whine in voice. "What do I get?"

"What do you want?" Javier asked.

"A horse!"

Javier laughed. "You can't have a horse. You're not old enough yet. And anyway, Billy already gave you a horse."

Jasmine stroked the horse that Billy had given her, clutching it tight in her hand. "But I want a reeeeeeeeeeeeeeeeeeeeal horse, Daddy!"

"Ask your mother," he said, smiling at Laura as he turned off of the highway and drove down a dirt road.

"Maybe when you're older," Laura said. "You're too small to ride a real horse right now, Jasmine."

"Poot!" Jasmine said, crossing her arms and looking out the window. They were approaching what used to be a farm, with a flat grassy area on their right, and a sparsely wooded area on their left, where they could see a number of trails and paths running through it.

As they pulled into the driveway in front of the barn, Javier stopped the car and said, "Okay. Everyone out. It's time for a pee break."

"Where are we going?" Billy asked, as he climbed out and stood next to his father.

"Here," Javier whispered. He grinned conspiratorially at Billy and walked behind the car. A woman in her mid-twenties came out of the barn to meet them.

"Is everything ready?" Javier asked her.

She smiled and nodded her head as she looked over his family.

"Jasmine! Come here!" Javier called. Laura walked over holding Jasmine's hand. "I want you all to meet Ms. Jenny."

"Hi!" Jenny said.

"Miss Jenny will be teaching Jasmine her classes here," Javier continued.

"Teaching me what, Daddy?" Jasmine asked as she squatted down, cautiously eyeing the strange woman who was smiling at her.

Just then, a man walked out of the barn, leading a small pony. When Jasmine heard the clip-clop of its hooves, she jumped up, her mouth open in shock. "Daddy!" she whispered, tugging on Javier's shorts. "Look at that horse!"

"It's a pony," Javier said, grinning at his wife. "You're too small to ride horses."

Her eyes got really big and she looked from her father to her mother. "Is it mine?"

Javier nodded at Laura, who said, "Happy birthday, baby! This is your very own pony!" Jasmine screamed in joy and ran up to the pony, stopping when she was just a few feet away. Her family watched as the man murmured something to her, and Jasmine slowly held out her hand. The man reached down and gave her a sugar cube, and then he led the pony forward a couple of steps. Jasmine squealed and looked proudly at her parents as the pony snuffled her hand and ate the sugar cube.

Billy and Jasmine each got to ride the pony once before they had to hurry to the baseball game. Driving as fast as he dared, Javier constantly checked the time, mentally cursing himself for cutting it so close. He listened to his children arguing in the back seat as he pulled into the parking lot of the sports complex with a sigh of relief.

"You can't name a horse 'Puppy'," Billy argued.

"I can," Jasmine insisted. "He's a baby horse like a puppy!"

"But he's not a dog," Billy replied, and Javier smiled at the frustration in his voice. "He's a…" Billy hesitated as he tried to think of the word.

"Foal," Javier whispered.

"He's a FOAL!" Billy said triumphantly. "Not a puppy!"

Laura leaned over and kissed him on the cheek. She whispered, "I think it's best if we let them settle this one on their own." He smiled and mouthed 'okay' at her and climbed out of the car as soon as he turned it off.

"Billy," he said, pulling open Billy's door, "we have to go! The game starts in twenty minutes!" Billy hopped out as his father hurried to the back of the car and pulled open the hatch. "Here," Javier said, handing him the bag of balls, "you carry this."

"What?" Billy exclaimed. "You're not on my team. I'm not going to help you carry…"

"Billy!" Laura reprimanded loudly. "Don't argue! Do what your father says!"

"Aw, fine!" Billy grabbed the bag of balls, picked up his own bag, and started walking towards the field.

"Thanks, honey," Javier said, blowing her a kiss. "Field eleven. We'll see you there?"

"I wouldn't miss it for the world," she said with smile. "However, you do know that we have to sit behind Billy's team's bench, and we have to cheer for him?"

Heaving a huge sigh, Javier said, "I know. My family is deserting me today. I shall see you afterwards." He hefted the bags onto his shoulders and turned to walk away. After one step, though, he paused and turned around. "Can I have just one kiss for good luck?" he asked.

Laura laughed and ran around the car, wrapping her arms around him and giving him a long kiss on the mouth. "Bad luck!" she whispered, giggling as she went to help Jasmine get out of the car.

Billy's team won by two runs, mainly because of Billy's outstanding pitching. When the game was finished, Javier shook hands with Tom and the rest of his team.

"Good game," Javier said to Tom. "That's a hell of a pitcher you've got there."

Tom smiled, nodding his head as he searched for Billy. Seeing him in the midst of his friends, he said, "Yep. That boy's got something special."

Javier beamed, feeling so proud. "So," he said, "Billy said you're having a barbecue at your house."

"Yep," Tom said. "It's something I try to do after games. It's good for team unity. Also, my pool doesn't really get used that much anymore, and so it's nice to hear children enjoying it again."

Javier nodded his head, remembering how Tom had lost his son. "Sounds like fun. We're just going to get pizza with the parents and kids from my team." He held out his hand and shook Tom's hand goodbye. "Maybe you can have a pool party for the families as well sometime," Javier said, turning to walk away.

"Maybe," Tom said. He watched Javier walk away and then turned and ran to where his team was celebrating. "You guys ready for some fun?"

The sound of Billy's team's cheering carried over to where Javier was trying to give his own team a pep talk. "Don't worry, guys," he said confidently. "We'll beat them next time. Let's go get some pizza!"

His own team cheered just as loudly, and he strolled off to find Laura and Jasmine as his players ran off to find their own families.

Chapter 22

The next three days passed by in a blur as Tavi constantly tried to cope with all of the changes happening in his life. The day after Will's death, he and the other boys didn't say a single word to one another as they sat in the dark room and waited for someone to unlock the door. The shame and confusion from the memories of what they had done the second night kept flashing into Tavi's consciousness as he tried to keep his mind blank. Uncertainty about who he was or why he seemed to enjoy doing those kinds of things kept rattling around in his mind, only to be interrupted by images of Will getting beaten, and Will dying, and the puddle of Will's blood that they had to scrub clean. And just when he couldn't take it any longer, and he knew he had to talk about it or go crazy, he remembered Brent's pleased expression at betraying them, and he would bite his lip to keep from talking, wondering who else he couldn't trust.

Yuri came and picked up Mac for his dentist appointment early in the morning, and then returned him a couple of hours later. He didn't come back until eight o'clock that night, and the boys were so thirsty by the time he arrived that both Mac and Anouram had each tried to force themselves to drink a bit of urine from the piss bucket before giving up in disgust.

Opening the door with his normal grin, Yuri said, "Aren't you guys ready to move out of here yet?" He set a pile of clothes on the floor. "The water is out here, along with your food. Here are the clothes you should wear tonight. Sven's and Francois's are on top, then Mac's, then Tavi's, and Anouram's are on the bottom." He looked at the new watch he was wearing and said, "You have forty-five minutes. Make sure you shower!"

Forty-five minutes later, freshly scrubbed and full from dinner, the boys followed Yuri into the bar. This was the first time they had been in there when other people were there, and it was a revelation. It was softly lit, with recessed alcoves spread throughout the room. Each one had its own muted lighting that could be adjusted by the customers with a twist of dial. The customers sat at a horseshoe shaped bar at the far end of the room where bottles of various liquors lined the walls, and men and boys filled the stools around it. There were more tables in the center of the room, an even mix between two-person tables and four-person tables. There was a small stage next to the bar with a microphone stand, but what surprised Tavi was that a majority of the men were playing children's games with the boys, such as Connect Four, dominos, and several kinds of card games.

And the boys! Tavi hadn't realized that there were so many. Looking around quickly, he guessed that there were maybe thirty or so spread throughout the bar. They were all busy talking to different men, and as Tavi watched, several of them got up for different reasons. A couple of them stood up with the men they had been playing games with, and when the men left, the boys went and sat with other men who were boy-less. Another boy walked up to the bar with the man he had been playing games with, watched the man pay the bartender some money, and then the boy and the man left the bar together, holding hands.

Tavi poked Mac to see if he had been watching, forgetting his own suspicions of Mac for a second. Mac nodded his head and then discretely pointed to a darkened nook where they could barely see a man and a boy of their age kissing passionately in the dark.

He felt Anouram, Sven, and Francois pressing tightly against him and Mac, and he realized that they were as scared as he was. "Be brave," he whispered without thinking. "Like tigers!"

"What did you say?" Anouram whispered back.

"Nothing," Tavi said, as Yuri led them to the stage. He had them face the crowd and stand in order of age. After they were in place, Yuri stepped down, disappearing into the dimness of the room. Suddenly, a row of lights was turned on and aimed directly into their faces. Tavi tried to squint his eyes to see, but someone jumped in front of him, temporarily blocking the lights.

"Good evening, friends and valued customers!" Javier said, speaking into the microphone. "Tonight, and for the next three nights, we have a special treat for you." Cheering and clapping interrupted him, and he waited for it to die down. "As some of you already know, we have five brand new boys who have chosen to become a part of our family." He stepped to the side, and the light once again blinded Tavi. "Who should we auction off first tonight – this strong, young buck? He'd be fun for someone who likes wrestling!" Javier said, pointing at Anouram. A few of the men whooped with joy and applauded.

"Or," Javier said, pointing to Tavi, "this tall, pretty boy. Look at these green eyes, gentleman. And his smile…" Javier poked Tavi, who responded with his brightest smile. A large number of the men cheered and started hollering.

"But wait!" Javier shouted, putting his hand on Mac's shoulder. "There's more. Eleven years old, happy-go-lucky, cutest smile you've ever seen." Mac smiled obediently. "And if you thought you liked green eyes, well look at these baby blues." The crowd was on its feet, cheering and stomping as Javier got them pumped up.

"And finally," Javier said, his voice not much louder than a hush, "two eight-year old boys, Sven and Francois. I don't think I've ever seen such sweet innocence before in my life." The crowd was silent while they ogled the two boys, who were holding hands as they trembled in fear upon the stage. "And you know what?" Javier whispered. Suddenly he shouted with excitement, "They have volunteered to be first prize in this auction, and that kind of enthusiasm will not be denied!!!" The crowd roared its approval and edged closer to the stage.

"Hold your horses," Javier commanded. "First you need to hear the rules of the house. One, this auction has three rounds. You can bid on one of these boys or both of them together. It is a silent auction, and if you would like to participate, you simply place your bid in this box with your name on it, and write down if you want to bid on both of them, or Sven –the cute little blond one, or Francois – the handsome brunette. The bottom half of the bidders who bid the lowest will be eliminated from the next round's bidding, and we will tell the remaining bidders what the highest bid was for the previous round, which will then be the minimum bid for the next round."

Javier paused to make sure everyone understood. "And if you want both of them, then you have to bid at least twice as much as the highest bid for just one of them. That makes sense, right? Two for double the price of one?"

The crowd, thinking that Javier was done, erupted into conversation, as everyone tried to make themselves heard, while continually looking at the stage to check out the new boys.

"Wait!" Javier said, pretending to laugh but getting frustrated. Greedy perverts, he thought. "Finally, you cannot take home these other three boys until they have been auctioned off first, which won't be tonight. You should talk to them and get to know them, maybe buy them a drink, but no hanky-panky until their auctions. Got it?" he asked, the warning in his voice cutting through the exuberance of the crowd.

Murmurs of assent reached his ears, and Javier announced, "The first round of bidding for Sven and Francois will close in thirty minutes." He put the microphone back and motioned to the boys to follow him as he headed up the stairs. They found Vikram waiting for them in his office.

Javier sat down in his chair with a groan of relief, and looked at the boys thoughtfully. "You're not enjoying this, are you?" Seeing their unhappy expressions, he continued, "Well, I don't really enjoy it either, but this is work, and you

work for me now. You do what I say, and things will get
better. You've seen what happens if you don't."

He snapped his fingers at Vikram, who hurried around
and took the tin that Javier had taken from the drawer. "It's
up to you if you want the vitamin while working in the bar. I
will insist that you take one before you leave with a
customer and so Sven and Francois, you guys must take one
later. Not now because I don't want you giggling and falling
down on stage. Understand?"

Sven and Francois both nodded their heads solemnly.

"So, you three," Javier continued, looking at Mac, Tavi,
and Anouram. "Any of you want to take one tonight?"

Tavi couldn't imagine why Javier would think that they
would want to take it. He couldn't even think about the
things he had done the two times he had taken the pill, and
so there was no way that he was going to…

"I'll take one," Anouram said. Tavi looked at him in
shock which was quickly replaced by despair when Mac
raised his hand.

"Me too," he said, eyes staring at the ground.

Tavi looked back and forth from Mac to Anouram,
wanting to ask them why, and wanting to tell them not to do
it, and wishing he could just shake some sense into them, but
they wouldn't look at him. They wouldn't look anywhere
except at their own feet. Javier was looking at him, however.

"Tavi? It's just you. Do you want one?" Javier asked.

Tavi bit his lip in indecision, remembering the happy
feeling that had warmed his body after taking the pill. He
closed his eyes and quietly said, "No, thank you."

He opened them to find Javier still looking at him. With a
tilt of his head and a small smile, he seemed to show Tavi a
little bit of respect. Tavi didn't care, though. He lowered his
eyes and stared at Javier's desk as he listened to Mac and
Anouram swallow their pills.

"Okay," said Vikram. "Here is your job for tonight. Go
downstairs, sit at the bar, and if a man comes up to you, start
talking to him like he was the most interesting, most
handsome man you've ever met. Okay?"

Everyone nodded their heads.

"Not you two," Vikram said, lightly tapping Sven and Francois on the back of their heads. "You two will just sit on the stage until the bidding is finished. I don't want anyone feeling jealous or hurt that they don't get a chance to talk to you, and so no one gets to talk to you."

Vikram looked at Javier to see if he had anything to add. Javier just waved his hand and said, "Have fun, boys."

"Thank you, Mr. Javier!" Mac said with a smile.

"Yeah. Me too," Anouram chimed in.

Tavi grimaced, nodded his head, and followed Vikram down the stairs.

It wasn't as bad as Tavi had been expecting. A short, thin man with a tiny mustache sidled up to him and asked if he'd like something to drink.

"Um...cola?" Tavi asked hesitantly.

"One cola for...what's your name?" the man asked.

"Tavi."

"One cola for Tavi, and one tequila sunrise for me. Just put it on my tab," the man told the bartender. He looked at Tavi and held out his hand. "My name is Terry."

Tavi shook it, and tried to remember what to say next. "Um...it's nice to meet you. Are you having fun tonight?" he asked, dredging the question from his memory from the night of training that seemed so long ago.

Terry smiled at Tavi. "I am now." He handed Tavi the glass of cola that appeared on the bar, and sipped his own drink. "Do you want to play a game?" he asked.

"Um...sure," Tavi said. "But I don't know how to play any of them," he admitted.

"Really?" Terry said excitedly. "This is going to be so much fun." He reached for a game behind Tavi. "This is called Connect Four. We take turns dropping in our pieces, and you try to get four in a row, either up and down, sideways, or diagonal."

"Ah. I see," said Tavi, reaching for a red piece and dropping it in. Terry followed with a black one. After only nine moves, Terry laughed and said, "I win." He pointed to a place on the board and explained, "You see, you should never let anyone put their pieces like this because then they'll always win." He opened the bottom and all of the pieces fell out. "Do you want to play again?"

"Sure," said Tavi, strangely enjoying himself. They kept playing the same game through the next round of the auction, and with Terry's advice, Tavi quickly got better and better until he won a couple of games in a row.

Terry continuously bought Tavi drinks and seemed happy to just play with him and to take care of his needs. After Tavi started winning at Connect Four, Terry suggested dominos, and again, Tavi had fun learning how to play. After he'd almost beaten Terry for the third consecutive game, he said, "You're a good teacher, Terry."

Terry giggled, and played a domino. "I should be," he said. "I've been teaching kids who are about your age for six years."

"Really?" Tavi asked. "At a school in the city?"

"Sure," Terry replied. "It's close by. To be honest," he confided, "it's one of the best schools in the city."

"Wow," Tavi breathed, thinking about how close he was to achieving his dream. "Do you think I could go there?"

Terry looked at him in astonishment, and then slapped his knee and roared with laughter. "Oh, Tavi…You're so cute." He covered his mouth when he saw Tavi's hurt expression, but he couldn't stop giggling. He said, "But I think it's probably too expensive for you. And, in case you forgot, this is a schoolhouse. It's THE School House."

Tavi swallowed hard and nodded his head as he played a domino. I hate you, Tavi thought. You and your stupid mustache and your stupid school. He looked around for Mac and Anouram, and thought he saw Mac in one of the darkened nooks, kissing a man. He felt tears spring to his eyes and stood up quickly. "Bathroom," he muttered, walking towards the side door.

As soon as he stepped outside, Yuri appeared in front of him. "Where are you going?" he asked.

Tavi wiped his eyes and said, "I'm just going to pee. I'm not running away. I've seen what happens to people who do that," he said bitterly.

"Okay," Yuri said. "I'll walk with you."

They walked in silence to the bathroom, and Tavi stayed in there for as long as he dared. With Mac kissing a man on top of this school teacher laughing at him, Tavi felt things were just getting worse and worse. He stared at himself in the mirror, surprised that he couldn't see the pain of the last few days written on his face. He splashed some water upon his face and went outside.

As they approached the bar, Yuri said, "I have your stuff."

"What?" Tavi asked.

"Your stuff. Usually they give the new boys' stuff to whoever wants it, and I grabbed it all first."

"Oh," Tavi said, thinking that that was just one more thing that had gone wrong...and he hadn't even wondered about it.

"I'll keep it safe for you and give it back to you after you've been here for a couple of months," Yuri said surprising him. "You should be able to take care of it by then."

"Why?" Tavi asked. "I mean, thank you, but I don't understand why you would do that."

Yuri opened the door to the bar for Tavi. "They took my books and I never saw them again," Yuri answered, shrugging his shoulders. "I never thought that was right."

"Well, thanks," Tavi said, flabbergasted, as he walked back into the bar.

Yuri shut the door behind him without saying a word.

That night, Sven and Francois were sold together, and they didn't return to sleep in the circle room with Mac, Anouram, and Tavi. Tavi was the only one not to take the brown paste, and he laid awake for most of the day, while Mac and Anouram snored beside him.

The following night, Anouram was sold, and Sven and Francois went home with a different man. Mac chose to take the vitamin again, and even though Mac was there when they went to sleep, Tavi had never felt so alone.

The third night, Mac was auctioned off to Terry, and Tavi was surrounded by different men, all touching him and offering to buy him drinks and play games with them. He had seen Anouram and the two younger boys leave with men that night, and he shared a look of hopelessness with Mac, who was silently waiting on the stage to find out which lucky winner he would have to go home with that night. That night, Tavi was the only one left in the locked room. Even though he had the whole room to himself, he curled up next to the door, his face pressed against the crack, and cried himself softly to sleep.

He knew that his life would be changed forever the next time the door was opened.

Chapter 23

"Good afternoon!" Yuri said cheerfully, awakening Tavi as he opened the door. Early afternoon sunlight filled part of the room, and Tavi sat up in an exhausted daze, his eyes still closed.

"You're early today," Tavi mumbled.

"It's a big day for you, so get up. Here's your food and water," Yuri announced, setting them on the floor in front of Tavi. "I'll be back in twenty minutes."

"Okay."

Yuri looked around the room, his eyes lingering on the spot where Will died. "Isn't it lonely in here? And it stinks too. At least you won't have to sleep here tonight."

Tavi grabbed the water bottle and took a big swallow. "I'm not sure if my other options are any better," he said bitterly.

Yuri gave Tavi his cynical smile and said, "You'll get used to it. We all do." He turned and walked away before Tavi could say anything else.

After Tavi had finished eating, Yuri hurried him out of the room, locking the door behind him. He took the lead and headed towards the nearest busy street.

"Where are we going?" Tavi asked, looking around with less awe than when he had first arrived.

"We're taking the sky train to Vetinari Station which is where you'll get your haircut."

"Really?" Tavi said with a trace of eagerness in his voice.

"Yep. Javier thinks you'll need to learn how to get around on the train because not all of our customers stay in the ratty old places that are around here."

Tavi nodded his head and felt a spring in his step for the first time in a while. "What kind of a haircut?" he asked, touching his hair and checking to see how long it was.

Yuri gave a genuine chuckle and smiled. "Ah, right. I'd forgotten. Before I came here, only my mother had cut my hair. Same for you, right?"

"Yep," Tavi said, as he focused his attention on the sky above him, trying to find the nearest train tracks.

"Well, Javier wants you to look good, so he's paying five talents for you to get your hair done today."

"Really? Five talents?" Tavi asked in surprise. He frowned a second later in understanding. "That means I'll have to pay him an extra five talents, huh?"

Yuri laughed and patted Tavi on the back. "You see, I knew you were smart. You're already figuring out how everything works around here."

Tavi ignored him and pointed above their heads to their right. "There it is," he shouted proudly to Yuri.

Yuri looked down at him and smiled, and then started sprinting to the stairs that led to the station. "Well, then let's go!" he called back over his shoulder. Tavi yelled in surprise and raced after Yuri, almost beating him to the top of the stairs. They both took a second to bend over to catch their breath, hands on their knees, as they grinned at each other.

Tavi followed Yuri to the ticket counter where Yuri bought him a refillable pass. He put enough money on it for thirty trips, which Tavi mumbled again about having to pay back. His bad mood vanished, however, as the train pulled up and the doors opened. Tavi ran in and sat down in one of the few empty seats. Yuri came and stood in front of him, and after a couple of seconds, he kicked Tavi in the shin.

"Ow!" Tavi exclaimed. "What was that for?"

Yuri leaned over and whispered, "It's polite to let the old people sit on the train when there aren't any seats available." He nodded his head at old woman who was standing next to him.

"Oh," Tavi said, feeling chagrined. He stood up and held out his hand to the old woman. "Here you go, ma'am. You can have my seat."

The old woman smiled gratefully at Tavi, and he followed Yuri to stand by the door. Looking out through the window, he watched the city fly by. The train slowed down, and Tavi asked, "Are we there?"

"No," Yuri said, pointing to the map above the door. "Okay, look. This is the map for the green line of the train."

"There's more than one line?" Tavi interrupted.

Yuri pointed at the other door behind them. "That one has the map for all of the lines," he said. "But look at this one. The light tells you where you are. We got on at Metcalf Station, so if you ever need to find your way home, just look for the green line, find Metcalf Station, and work your way to it."

"Okay," Tavi said with enthusiasm. "So we are at Primrose Station," he stepped aside to let the people who were entering and exiting to pass him. "And the next stop is Vetinari Station, right?" he said proudly.

"Right," Yuri answered, giving Tavi a friendly smile.

Tavi decided that it was a good time to try and take advantage of Yuri's good mood. "Will it be horrible tonight, Yuri?" he asked, ready to flinch away if Yuri became angry with him.

Yuri sighed and gazed out of the window at the buildings going by. "If you don't take the vitamin," he said softly, "then it's really hard at first. It's terrible. But if you do take it, then it becomes simple. However, if you take it too often, then you can't sleep. And then you need to start taking the brown stuff just to sleep at night. But if you don't take the pill before you go home with the men, then it's…" he paused as if he couldn't find the right words. "If you don't take the pill, then it's really difficult," he finished weakly.

Tavi nodded his head, not surprised. He took a deep breath and accepted the fact that he would have to take a vitamin and go home with a man that night, and probably every night for the foreseeable future, but he swore to himself that he would do everything possible to escape as soon as he knew how to survive in the city. "Thank you," he said simply.

The doors opened and they stepped off the train. Yuri told Tavi what exit they needed to go out of, and he let Tavi lead them out, discovering for himself how to find his way. After they exited the station, Yuri turned down a street, and entered a large shop near the corner.

Tavi looked around as he entered, sniffing the air appreciatively. It smelled clean, he thought, and he was amazed at the number of hairdressers he saw. "Fourteen people work here?" he asked Yuri in surprise.

The woman at the front desk smiled at him and answered for Yuri. "More like twenty," she said, "but today's a slow day."

Yuri cleared his throat, and said shyly, "Um…We have an appointment with Liz…um…at two-thirty."

The receptionist checked the book in front of her. "Okay," she said and pressed a button, "just one second."

A few seconds later, a beautiful woman with long, flowing brown hair came around the corner. "Yuri!" she said with a smile. "It's been awhile. Are you here for another haircut?"

Tavi was interested to see Yuri blush as he smiled and motioned towards Tavi. "Um…no…My brother needs one and I…um…said you were good," he stammered.

Liz smiled and touched Tavi's hair, pulling it out and looking at the sides. "Sure…what's your name?" she asked.

"Tavi," he answered, enjoying the sensation of her fingers playing with his hair.

"Hmmm," she said thoughtfully, "what were you guys thinking of?"

"Um," Yuri quickly answered, "just something stylish. He has to get his school photo taken tomorrow. And maybe have the tips frosted?"

Liz nodded and let Tavi's hair drop. "I like it. I can work with this. Let's go wash your hair, Tavi."

Tavi awkwardly followed after her, but looked back when he saw that Yuri wasn't coming. Yuri motioned him forward with his hand and whispered, "Don't say anything."

Tavi nodded and turned to follow Liz.

An hour later, they burst out of the hair salon. Tavi couldn't stop touching his hair and Yuri was smiling because he had made a hair appointment with Liz for later that week.

"That was awesome!" Tavi said cheerfully, as he led the way to the train station. "She washed my hair twice and massaged my head the second time." He ran up the stairs taking them two at a time. "And one woman just stood there so that she could brush off my face whenever a hair fell on it." He laughed and reached into his pocket for his transit card. "This must be what it's like to be rich, huh, Yuri?"

"Probably," Yuri said agreeably. Javier was going to be really pleased. The highlighted tips combined with the cut that Liz had given Tavi made him as cute as most of the child actors and models he had seen on TELEVISION and in magazines. He let Tavi chatter about everything he had seen the entire way back to The School House. Yuri led the way to the circle door, and unlocked the padlock. Tavi walked in, his happiness fading away as he remembered why he had gotten a haircut. He stopped short when he saw two boys sitting in the dark.

"Who are you?" he asked.

"Boris," one of them said.

"Danny," the other replied.

Tavi looked back at Yuri in surprise. "They probably just came today," he explained. "I think Michel is the one who just got back. He probably found them."

"Oh," Tavi said, seeing himself four days ago when he looked at the boys, his heart filling with pity when he thought about everything that was going to happen to them over the next few days. He turned away, ignoring them, and asked Yuri, "So what do I do now?"

Yuri thought for a second, and then said, "Stay here for a while. I'll leave the door open. And then I'll bring you guys dinner, bring your clothes for tonight, and then we'll go see Javier and get ready for tonight."

"Okay," Tavi replied, settling down against the wall by the door.

Yuri turned to leave. He paused for a second to murmur, "You shouldn't say too much to the new boys. I can't stop you, but it probably wouldn't be best." He walked away without waiting for a response.

Tavi brought his knees up to his chest, and rested his head on them so that he could look out the door. He closed his eyes when one of the boys asked, "Is this the school? Where is everyone?"

He sat there like that for a couple of minutes, discarding possible answers that he could say to that question. Realizing there was only one thing he could say, he raised his head and looked at the boys with a blank expression on his face. "You guys," he said, "all I can say is don't trust anybody. And don't ask me any more questions." He put his head back on his knees and continued staring into the alleyway.

Chapter 24

"Let me see," Javier said, walking around his desk to get a better look at Tavi. He lightly touched Tavi's hair and then held Tavi's head straight, appraising his look with the eye of an expert. He turned to Yuri with an approving nod. "Good job, Yuri," Javier said. "Let me know where you found the hair stylist and we can send some of our other boys there as well."

"Okay," replied Yuri, after a moment's hesitation. Tavi wondered if Yuri paused because he wanted to try to keep Liz separate from his work life.

Javier turned back to Tavi. "Take your pants down. Let me see which underwear Yuri picked out for you."

Tavi grimaced. He undid the snap on his pants and pulled them down to his knees. He had tried arguing with Yuri when he had first seen what Yuri had given him, but it was to no avail. Yuri had lost his patience and slapped Tavi across the back of the head, effectively ending the conversation.

"Superman underwear," Javier noted, "and tight like a little boy's underwear." He turned to Yuri with a smile. "I'm impressed. Tell me what you were thinking."

Yuri flushed a little at the compliment as he explained, "I think that most of our customers probably want younger boys than what we offer, but they take what they can get."

"Yeah," Javier said seriously. "They're a bunch of sickos."

"And so," Yuri continued, "Tavi will be playing into their fantasy a little bit when they see the tight Superman underwear, which means they could be extra happy, which is better for everyone." He stopped for a second to chew the inside of his cheek. He wasn't sure if Javier wanted to hear a new idea from him, but he had seemed pleased so far, so he barged ahead. "I was thinking – and it's just an idea – that right before the bidding for the last round tonight, we should give the final bidders a peek at Tavi's underwear. Maybe it'll excite them and they'll bid more."

Javier studied Yuri for a second before breaking into a huge grin. "Yuri," he said proudly, clapping him on the shoulder, "the highest bid we've had so far for one boy has been eight hundred talents. I think we'll try your idea, and if the highest bid for Tavi is higher than eight hundred, I'll give you ten percent of the difference. So, if Tavi's price is nine hundred, then you just made ten talents. How's that sound?" Javier asked, holding out his hand.

Yuri grinned and shook Javier's hand with enthusiasm. "Thank you, sir! Thank you, really!"

"No. Thank you, Yuri," Javier said honestly. "You have good ideas and you do good work. I like you." He looked at Tavi and said, "I like you too, Tavi. And I have a feeling that the customers are going to love you. Let's go have an auction, and just make sure that you smile a lot."

He turned and walked through the door near his desk and down the stairs. Tavi took a deep breath and followed slowly. Yuri trailed behind Tavi, closing the door behind them.

"Ladies and Gentleman!" Javier announced. "And yes, if you look around, there are a couple of ladies here tonight." He grinned at one of the women as the crowd looked around curiously. Javier was pleased with the size of the audience. It had been growing with the passing of each night, and he had a feeling that tonight would be the best night. "Tonight, I hate to say, is the last night of our Cherry Auction – at least for a while." Good-natured boos filled the air. Javier held up his hand for silence. "But luckily for you," he continued, "we have saved the best for last. Some of you may have spoken with him over the last couple of nights, but no one has truly…" he paused for a split second and then stressed the next word. "…*known* Tavi. That will all change tonight." Javier beckoned to the stairs. "Tavi, come on down!"

Tavi stepped onto the stage, the bright lights blinding him, but he felt a rush of pleasure when he heard the roar of the crowd and he gave them a huge smile. Blinking his eyes, he was soon able to see the edge of the stage, and his grin grew even larger when he saw Mac and Anouram standing there with smiles, waving at him.

Javier said to the crowd, "I don't really think there's anything I could say that would do him justice right now, so just look and stare, folks. He's pretty enough to be in the movies, isn't he?" He ran his eye over the audience with a measured eye and made a quick decision. "For the first round of bidding, the minimum bid will be two hundred talents. After all," he explained, "when's the next time you'll get a chance to be a young boy's first?"

Javier waited for a few seconds, letting the crowd ogle Tavi. He spoke into the microphone and said, "Bidding closes in twenty minutes. We'll leave Tavi here for a bit, but don't bother him. I don't want everyone getting jealous because he's only talking to one person." He put the microphone back in its stand and walked over to Tavi. "Just stand here for another minute or so, and then sit down on this chair in back. Yuri will bring you juice or a cola or something, and then I'll be back in twenty minutes to announce the results of the bidding."

The next twenty minutes stretched for an eternity for Tavi. Yuri brought him some orange juice and as Tavi sat there, sipping on a straw, men kept waving to him and saying hello. Tavi, not knowing what else he was supposed to do, waved back and said hi, which made a number of the men giggle and they rushed to drop in bids in the ballot box. He caught sight of Sven for a second as a man picked him up and swung him like a doll, but he soon vanished into the crowd. Tavi wondered where Francois was, and whether they always did everything together. His mind immediately shied away from thinking about what they might do together, and he tried to make his mind blank, automatically waving to people as he waited for Javier to return.

When he did return, Javier was brimming with happiness. "Your bids have been tallied," Javier announced to the crowd. "You guys must really like Tavi," he said confidentially. The audience cheered and hollered at that remark, and Javier waited for it to die down. He read off a list of fourteen names who would be eligible for the next round. "And the lowest minimum bid for the second round is…" Javier paused, letting the tension rise. "…seven hundred and fifty talents!" The crowd oohed and aahed and roared their approval. "And for those of you who make it to the third round," Javier said over the noise of the audience, "we'll have something special to show you!"

Javier approached Tavi with a huge grin on his face. "Tavi, they love you. You've already beaten Mac. Let's see if you can get the highest bid ever."

Tavi just smiled at Javier, not knowing what else to do.

"Oh," Javier said, as if just remembering, "Yuri will bring you upstairs before I announce the winner at the end of the auction." He looked Tavi in the eye and said clearly, "So you can take your vitamin."

Tavi nodded. "I know. I understand."

Surprise showed in Javier's eyes for the briefest moment. However, he quickly masked it and said, "Good. Now just keep on doing what you've been doing. It seems to be making them happy." He turned and went up the stairs to his office, and Tavi returned to smiling and waving at the crowd, as he tried to make them happy.

Javier returned to announce the results of the second round. After he read off the names of the last seven bidders, he said, "Ladies and gentleman, we are approaching a record tonight. The minimum bid going into the final round is one thousand talents."

Tavi gasped when he heard the amount. That was more money than his father was paid in one year. Tavi started daydreaming about what he would do with that kind of money, but was rudely interrupted with a poke from Yuri. "Go up to the front of the stage," he hissed.

Tavi stumbled in his haste to move forward, but Javier casually reached out a hand and caught him. "You see," he told the crowd, "Tavi's so excited to meet you that he's tripping over his own feet." He paused to let them laugh, and then squatted down and spoke to the seven men who were gathered at the front of the stage. "Well, I promised you a little surprise," Javier told them. "And the surprise is that we think it's only right for you to see what you're bidding on, and so we're going to let you have a little peek of Tavi in his underwear."

The men grinned, staring at Tavi either flirtatiously or with hungry eyes. Tavi smiled nervously and tried to look at all of the men. This just seemed to make them want him even more.

"It's up to you," Javier said. "We can show you in private upstairs, or we can just do it here, in front of the whole crowd. What do you say?"

"I don't care," one of the men said. "Just do it down here." The others nodded their heads agreeably.

"Okay," Javier said, standing back up. He turned and spoke quietly to Tavi. "I know this will be hard for you since it's your first time. I would give you a vitamin to make this part easier, but I think they'll like seeing you nervous." Tavi looked at the crowd, biting his bottom lip in trepidation. "When I tell you to," Javier continued, "just turn around so your back is to the crowd, pull your pants down to your knees, and bend over and touch your toes. After a couple of seconds, you can slowly pull your pants back up, okay?"

Tavi nodded his head.

"Good," Javier said. "You won't even have to look at the crowd while you do that. And then turn around, smile and wave, and come up to my office with me."

Javier stepped up to the microphone. "And now, what you've all been waiting for – a little peek at heaven." He paused for a second before saying, "Tavi, show them what you've got."

Tavi turned around, watched his hands undo his pants, and then closed his eyes. He pushed his pants down, but had to wiggle back and forth to get them to his knees. The crowd roared louder than it had all night, and when he bent down and touched his toes, showing them the red "Superman" written across his blue underpants, they were so loud that it felt like the stage was shaking. He slowly counted to five in his head, pulled his pants up, and opened his eyes so that he could snap his pants tight. He turned to the crowd and waved. Javier walked up to Tavi as the audience cheered and clapped their hands.

"Tavi, that was nice," Javier said, putting his hand on his shoulder. "Those men were literally drooling." He saw Yuri on the stairs in front of them and said, "Yuri, you're a genius! That little ten percent I'm giving you is going to add up tonight."

Yuri grinned in response and the three of them walked up the stairs.

Javier went around his desk and reclined in his chair, while Tavi and Yuri sat down in two chairs across from him. Javier rested his head against the back his chair, not saying a word. Tavi's heart started racing faster as he thought about what was going to happen.

After a few minutes, Javier blinked his eyes and shook his head, bringing his mind back to the present. He reached into his drawer and pulled out the tin with the pills in it. He stood, grabbed an unopened bottle of water from his desk and walked around to where Yuri and Tavi were sitting. He leaned against the desk and studied Tavi, noting how much he was trembling.

"Tavi," Javier said gently. "Do you want a pill for tomorrow morning as well?"

Tavi looked up at Javier questioningly. "Why?"

Javier shrugged and replied, "Because he'll probably want you to stay for part of tomorrow as well."

Tavi shook his head, not wanting to take the pill in the first place. "No, that's okay."

"Are you sure?" Yuri asked, speaking for the first time.

Tavi looked from Yuri to Javier and back again. "Yes," he said with more certainty than he felt. "Just give me one for tonight."

"Okay," Javier said, holding out the open tin and handing the water bottle to Tavi. "Here you go."

Tavi picked out one pill with his fingers, and quickly swallowed it down in a gulp of water. I can't believe what I'm going to do tonight, he thought hysterically. I don't want to. God, please, I really, really don't want to do this. After a minute or so, he felt the tingling spread through his body, and his frantic thoughts slowly faded away as the stress eased from his body.

Javier watched his body relax and took the bottle from his hand. "Feeling better, Tavi?" he asked.

Tavi breathed out slowly. He had to think about the question before replying, "Yes."

"Good. Let's go downstairs and meet the winner."

Tavi followed Javier downstairs, smiling because he felt so happy. He barely heard Javier announce, "And the winning bid is a new record of one thousand five hundred talents!"

When he met the winner, he could only focus on his eyes and his hands. He remembered those hands from the previous night. They were thick, fat hands that were always moving and playing with things. When they had been playing games, the man kept fondling the games pieces, twisting his napkin, and touching Tavi's knee. Tavi looked into his pale blue eyes and smiled, feeling ecstatic that this man looked so pleased to see him.

They went upstairs with Javier, and Tavi heard Javier saying, "If you don't use protection every single time, we will find out, and we will come and kill you," but he didn't understand what it meant.

Javier mentioned a hotel and the sky train, but by then, Tavi was feeling so fuzzy and happy that he didn't really care.

When Tavi awoke the next morning, he felt as if he were sleeping on a cloud. He had never experienced anything so soft and comfortable. A huge arm was wrapped around his body, and he could feel a fat, hairy belly pressing into his back. He lay there, trying to remember the previous night, hoping nothing had happened. Bits and pieces of memories came back to him, and Tavi suddenly had to go to the bathroom and wash himself. He tried to slip out from under the arm, but as he moved, he felt the sheets caress his body, and he realized that he was naked.

He had a vision of himself bent over the bed with the man…Squeezing his eyes tight, Tavi tried to block out the memory. He wiggled more vigorously and managed to slip out from under the arm. He tried to sit up, but the man suddenly wrapped his arm around his chest, and covered Tavi with one of his legs. Tavi could feel the man's penis pressing against him, and to his horror, he felt it growing harder.

"Where are you going?" the man whispered, kissing Tavi on his temple.

Tavi tried to move away from the whiskers and felt a wet spot remaining where the man had kissed him. "I…um…need to go to the bathroom," Tavi managed.

The man sighed. "Okay," he said, rolling off of Tavi. "But hurry back."

As soon as the man released him, Tavi jumped out of the bed and looked around the room. It was huge. There was a giant flat screen TELEVISION on the wall, another room with a sofa, desk and chairs, and the biggest window that Tavi had ever seen was overlooking the city from way up high. Tavi could even see a sky train going by in the city beneath him.

Tavi glanced down at his own nakedness, feeling embarrassed. He looked around for his underpants and saw them on the floor. He ran to pick them up, only to find that they had been ripped in half. Staring at them in dismay, Tavi dropped them and ran into the bathroom. He flicked on the lights and gasped at what he saw. A glass shower and a giant bath tub. A long marble countertop with two sinks that looked like they were made from gold. Towels everywhere. A huge mirror.

Tavi turned on one of the sinks and splashed water on his face. He looked at himself in the mirror and noticed red marks on his neck. As he rubbed them, he became aware of a burning pain in his butt that he had ignored up until then. Grimacing, he hobbled over to the toilet. He sat down to go to the bathroom and yelped in pain. It felt as if someone were ripping him open. He peed quickly and pulled off a piece of toilet paper. Hesitantly reaching back, he dabbed at the spot where the pain was the worse. Whimpering at his own touch, he pulled the tissue out to look at it, and began hyperventilating when he saw that it was covered in fresh, bright red blood.

He dropped it in the toilet and stood up, looking for a way to escape.

"Tavi," the man called from the bed.

Tavi closed his eyes, remembering what had happened to Tiki and Will. Swallowing his fear, he went out to the bedroom. "Hi," he said timidly.

"Tavi!" the man rolled over to face him, and Tavi saw his huge belly slide over and land on the bed. His penis flopped around and the man seemed disinclined to cover it up. "Come here," he said, patting the bed next to him.

Tavi walked to the bed, each step sending a burning pain through his bottom. He gently climbed onto the bed, and the man put his arm around him and started kissing him on the mouth. Tavi closed his eyes and did the best he could, feeling more and more disgusted. The man then reached down and grabbed Tavi's penis and gently started stroking him.

Tavi wanted to cry…and die in shame and revulsion.

But he knew he had no other choice, so he laid there motionless until the man grabbed his head and forced it down. Tavi knew what he wanted. He had vague memories from when he had taken the vitamin and so he opened his mouth, gagging at the taste and texture of the man's penis.

"Use your hand like you did last night," the man said, and Tavi did, unconsciously doing what the man wanted.

Tavi felt as if he were going to throw up, but he knew that he couldn't. He had no choice. There was nothing he could do except do what the man told him to do.

Finally, when Tavi thought he couldn't go on any longer, the man pulled Tavi away and rolled over to the other side of the bed. He fiddled around with something while Tavi leaned over and furtively spat out the saliva in his mouth onto the floor.

The man reached around Tavi and put his hand on his shoulder. Tavi could feel his leg sliding between his own, and thought that the man just wanted to cuddle again. Suddenly, he knelt behind Tavi and pulled him up and backwards, and Tavi had to put his hands out to catch himself.

"You ready to do it again, baby?" the man whispered. "You were amazing last night."

On his hands and knees, Tavi heard the man take the cap off of something, and then a finger was rammed into his butthole. Tavi yelped out in pain and glanced backwards. There was something plastic covering the man's penis and he was slathering something onto it. Tossing the tube aside, the man grabbed Tavi's hips and thrust.

Tavi bit his lip so hard to keep from screaming that he quickly tasted blood. Tears streamed down his face and silent sobs wracked his body as the man ~~made love to~~ ~~had sex with~~ raped Tavi for the first of three times that day.

Chapter 25

Tavi left the hotel and hobbled around the city in shock for most of the afternoon. The memories of what he had done, along with the burning, crippling pain in his bottom, were so overwhelming that Tavi's only way of coping was to try and block everything out and to make himself as numb as possible. From time to time, his skin would crawl as he remembered the feeling of the man's touch on his body seep through to his consciousness, and he would shudder in disgust and tightly squeeze the two talent silver piece that the man had given him for a tip, rubbing it until his mind was blank again.

He walked aimlessly through the streets, not noticing or caring where he was going. At one point, he bought a small snack from a street vendor and stuffed the change into his pocket without counting it. He continued limping down the street, nibbling absently on the piece of chicken he had bought.

As the shadows grew longer, Tavi became a bit more aware of his surroundings, and he began searching the skyline for the sky train tracks. When he passed two buildings on his right, he looked between them and saw it off in the distance. Turning into the alleyway, he walked in the right direction, keeping his eyes focused on the tracks.

Without warning, two boys who looked to be about his age jumped from between a pair of dumpsters. Tavi stepped back in alarm. They were both thin and dirty with long scraggly hair. Tavi looked at where they had come from and saw a piece of sheet metal lying on the space in between the dumpsters, with a blanket hanging down behind it. He tried to look around the boys to see more, but the taller one pushed him, making Tavi stumble backwards.

"Hello," he said, as his friend circled around to stand between Tavi and the entrance of the alley. "What are you doing in our alley?"

"I didn't know it was yours," Tavi said quickly. He pointed to the tracks in the distance. "I'm just trying to get to the sky train."

"You have money for the sky train?" the shorter one asked. The taller one stepped closer to Tavi with a mean smile on his face.

"My...brother gave me a card," Tavi said, turning to look at the smaller boy, while trying to keep an eye on his friend. "It's all I have."

Suddenly, the taller boy leaped forward and grabbed Tavi's arms from behind. "I don't believe you," he said menacingly in Tavi's ear. "Kurt, check his pockets."

Tavi thought about the money that he had in his pocket and what he'd had to do to earn it. All of the frustration and anger that he'd been feeling over the last few days suddenly exploded, and he howled in fury as he kicked Kurt in the crotch when he tried to get close to Tavi. Before the taller one even realized what was happening, Tavi was spinning around with him hanging onto his back. He let go as Tavi crashed backwards into the dumpster, and then Tavi accidentally smashed the back of his head into the boy's face. The boy dropped to the ground with a cry, holding his face in his hands.

The smaller boy, Kurt, tried to stand up so that he could charge Tavi, but Tavi was already on top of him, punching and screaming and hitting him as hard as he could. It was over within seconds, as both of the strange boys lay on the ground moaning and bleeding.

Breathing heavily, Tavi stood over them with his hands on his hips. Determining that they wouldn't be a danger to him anymore, Tavi turned and started walking towards the tracks. He glanced into their little home and saw two bags, just like the one he had brought with him to the city. Glancing at the boys to make sure they were still on the ground, Tavi knelt down under the sheet metal and rummaged through the bags. They were both stuffed with miscellaneous items – a couple of shirts, a little bit of food, one of them contained a book and a photo of a family, the other had a letter and some money hidden at the bottom. As he sifted through the contents, he realized that everything contained within these bags meant something special to the two boys. Carefully packing the items back into the bags, Tavi made a decision and sat down on the ground, waiting for the two boys to come to him.

They approached him warily. They had seen him digging through their stuff and obviously didn't understand why he hadn't taken everything. For that matter, why was he just sitting there, looking at them?

"Hey," Tavi said, holding up his hands in a conciliatory gesture. "I just want to talk."

The two boys glanced at each other and the taller one nodded at Tavi as they both squatted down in front of him.

"My name's Tavi," Tavi said, holding out his hand to the taller one.

He looked at it suspiciously before reaching out and giving it a brief shake. "I'm Kyle. That's Kurt," Kyle said, as Tavi reached out and shook the hand of the shorter boy.

Tavi looked around at the meager dwelling and said, "You guys live here?"

Kyle shrugged and cautiously reached for his and Kurt's bags. "Nah," he said, tossing Kurt's bag to him, as he opened up his own and looked through it carefully. "It's just a place we use to rest sometimes during the day."

"I didn't take anything," Tavi protested. "If I had wanted to steal your stuff, I wouldn't have waited around to talk to you."

"Well, what do you want?" Kurt asked, closing his bag and slinging it over one shoulder.

Tavi hesitated. "I don't know," he said. "I just...your bags...they reminded me of..." He studied their faces and said, "Why do you live here?"

Kyle scoffed, "Where should we live? In a house with a loving mother and father like you do?"

The anger bubbled up inside of Tavi again and he shouted, "I had a fucking fat man have sex with me four times in the last day because he paid my…" Tavi laughed bitterly. "…my school money for me. So don't fucking talk to me about living in a nice house with my parents!"

He stared at Kurt and Kyle, daring them to say anything, but was taken aback when he saw a knowing look cross their faces as they looked at him with pity. "We had to do that," Kurt said quietly.

"That's why we're here," Kyle added. "We ran away after two years of being sold to different men every night."

"You ran away?" Tavi asked in surprise. "No one runs away. They get killed for doing that."

Kurt and Kyle smiled grimly. "Some owners are worse than others. Ours is a lazy sod, but we still see his men sometimes, roaming through the alleyways." He motioned to the dumpsters. "This is one of the places we come to stay when it gets too dangerous to walk around on the streets."

"But what do you do for food and everything else?" Tavi asked.

Kurt shrugged. "We beg sometimes, and sometimes steal things. There are a couple of men we know who will buy stuff from the street kids." He glanced at both ends of the alleyway guardedly, and he and Kyle crawled in to sit with Tavi between the dumpsters. "There are also places that will give us free food. And sometimes the other street kids will help each other out."

"Are there a lot of you?" Tavi asked.

"Tons," Kyle said, while Kurt answered, "Hundreds and hundreds."

Tavi was tempted to ask if he could stay with them. It was on the tip of his tongue, but his fears stopped him. Fear of Javier's retribution, fear of hearing them tell him no, fear of dying homeless on the streets. He also felt like he owed something to Anouram and Mac, and Sven and Francois, and he thought about his own bag of memories, which Yuri had stashed somewhere. "Can I come back and talk to you guys again?" he asked hesitantly.

Kyle studied his face. "You're going back?"

Tavi just nodded, not sure if he would be able to explain his reasons. Not even sure if he understood them himself.

"Okay," Kyle said, not pressing him any further. "We aren't often here, though. You can usually find us near the playground at Polston Station, or maybe down by the night markets on Saturday and Sunday. If you ever really need a place to stay and hide, go to the back door of the church at 5th and Grand, and ask for Pastor Mike. He'll at least give you a piece of bread or whatever he can spare, and he can maybe tell you how to find us. Just remember," he said with a grin, "Kurt and Kyle."

Tavi shook his head and said, "I don't know where any of those places are."

Kurt said impatiently, "Can you remember what we just told you? Polston Station, night market, 5th and Grand?"

"Yeah," Tavi said.

"Then start exploring the city whenever you can get out, or when you're going home in the mornings. You have to know the city if you want to survive here."

"Okay," Tavi answered. He stepped into the alleyway and turned to leave. "Thanks for the advice."

"No problem," Kyle said, as Tavi started walking away. "Oh," he called out, "one more thing."

"What?" Tavi said, turning around.

"Wherever it is that you work..." he began.

"The School House," Tavi said helpfully.

Kyle and Kurt shared a look. "Ouch," Kyle said, as Kurt shook his head. "That's one of the more dangerous places. I've heard stories...and I've seen them run down a couple of kids who tried to escape."

"Great," Tavi said sarcastically.

"Anyways," Kyle continued, "they're not going to give you your money back. I mean, maybe if you stay there for a long time and become one of the enforcers." Tavi thought briefly of Yuri. "But try to save and hide what you can without getting caught. You're going to need it if you're ever going to get away."

Tavi stuck his hand in his pocket and played with the change. "Thanks," he said, turning away and walking towards the sky train. He pulled the change out of his pocket, put one talent back in his pocket, and then stopped for a second as he took off his right shoe and hid the rest of the coins under the sole.

Putting his shoe back on, he slowly started walking towards the sky train, his head constantly moving as he tried to absorb and learn everything that he could about the city he was walking through.

Kurt and Kyle popped their heads out to watch him leave and then shrank back into their hideout. "You think he'll make it?" Kurt asked.

Kyle rubbed his still tender nose and said, "He beat the crap out of both of us. And he seems smart. I think he has a chance."

"Yeah," Kurt agreed. "But he's working at The School House. No one gets away from there."

Kyle nodded his head in agreement and crawled behind the blanket to the hidden alcove behind one of the dumpsters where they usually slept most nights. He had liked Tavi, but there was no sense in trusting him with that kind of information.

Chapter 26

Tavi managed to find his way back to the door with the circle painted on it. However, he had forgotten that it was padlocked during the day, and he spent the next five minutes wandering around until he found the room that Vikram had showed them earlier.

As he approached the door, he glanced through the window and saw some boys sitting around watching television. Only two of the houses in his village had televisions, and Tavi had never really been allowed to watch it. He wondered what the attraction was as he cautiously opened up the door.

He peeked in, and when no one said anything, he stepped into the room, relishing the air blowing on him from one of the fans that was turned on. When he shut the door behind him, a couple of the boys turned around to see who it was.

"Tavi!" Mac shouted, leaping over the back of his sofa and giving Tavi a hug. "You're finally here!" Tavi squeezed back, feeling happier than he would've expected at seeing Mac again. "Come!" Mac said, pulling Tavi by the arm to the room beyond the living room. Mac threw himself onto one of the beds, and since no one else was in there, Tavi jumped onto the bed next to Mac's, wincing a bit at the pain that he still felt.

"How was it?" Mac asked sympathetically, noticing Tavi's grimace.

Tavi gave a short laugh. "It was terrible, to be honest. I didn't have a pill for this morning, and he wanted to do it again and again."

"I'm sorry," Mac said. "My first one was like that. The one from last night let me leave this morning. From what other people say, I think that's more normal."

They rolled over on their sides so that they could look at each other while talking. "What's it like living here?" Tavi asked.

"So much better," Mac said enthusiastically, before adding in a more somber voice, "But we have to pay the price to stay here."

"Are you getting used to…it?" Tavi asked, still feeling filthy from that morning.

Mac sighed and started tracing a line on the bed. "I don't know. I've never done it without a pill. It still makes me feel sick to think about what I'm doing, but the pills make it okay for a while, and other times I just don't think about it."

"But the men…" Tavi began.

"I know," Mac said, raising his voice. "But we have no choice."

Tavi rolled over onto his back and stared at the ceiling. "I'm sorry," he said.

"For what?"

"I stopped trusting you after what happened with Brent. And I am really sorry. I shouldn't have not trusted you."

"It's okay," Mac said. "I thought the same about you. You came in with Vikram and Yuri, and you seem to talk to Yuri more than we do."

"He's from my village," Tavi explained. "I thought we could be friends."

"Ha." Mac gave a bitter laugh. "I don't think you want to be friends with him."

"I know," Tavi said, but for a brief second, he remembered the Yuri he had seen when they had gone to get his haircut, and he wondered if that was the real Yuri.

"Where is Brent?" Tavi asked. "I didn't see him when I came him. I want to talk to him."

Mac smiled and said, "Anouram and I had the same thought. But I guess there's another place like this for the other boys who have been here for a long time."

"Ah," Tavi said. "Well, I hope we can talk to him in private someday." He rolled back over on his side and faced

Mac again. "What about Anouram and Sven and Francois? Where are they?"

"Anouram is working the early shift, which starts at four in the afternoon. Sven and Francois were bought for a week by a couple of men."

"How are they doing?" Tavi asked with concern.

"Strange," Mac answered with a frown. "They sleep together now, and have started kissing each other even when they're not at work, and they seem happy to go home with the men now. They have no problem talking with each other about everything they do. It's disturbing."

"Well, there's nothing we can do about it right now, I guess," Tavi said. He felt the silver in his shoe pressing against his heel. "Have you gotten any tips?"

"The first night I got one talent, and this morning I got about half a talent, which I guess is typical. What about you?"

"Oh...about the same as you," Tavi said, pleased with himself for guessing the right amount to keep in his pocket.

"Don't forget to turn it in when you go to the bar," Mac warned him. "Things get ugly if you don't." He looked at the clock that was on the wall above the door. "We have to shower soon," he said. "We're supposed to be in the bar by seven-thirty."

"What about food and stuff like that?" Tavi asked.

"Yesterday it came around this time," Mac said. "Or a lot of the boys will use some of their tip money to buy food on their way home from the hotel."

"Okay, good," Tavi said. "Because I did that."

"But don't tell anyone," Mac cautioned. "I know I can trust you and Anouram, but I don't know about anybody else here."

"Yeah," Tavi agreed. Debating how much he should tell Mac, he said, "I met a couple of kids today on the way home."

"Really?" Mac said. "What were they doing?"

"Trying to rob me," Tavi said as Mac's eyes widened in surprise. "So we had a little fight, and then we talked for a while afterwards. They used to be like us," Tavi said in quiet voice, "until they ran away. They say there are lots of boys like them."

Mac shook his head at Tavi and flicked his eyes to the main room. "Stop joking," he said loudly, his face pale with fright. "That's not even funny to talk about. We have a good life here, we make good money, we get fed. Who would want to live on the street?"

Tavi gave a weak laugh. "I don't. They were miserable and dirty and living in a box." He heard a noise outside of the bedroom window, and when he turned to look, he saw one of the barmen walking past.

He whipped his head back around and faced Mac. Mac shook his head and whispered, "He didn't hear anything, but you need to be more careful, or we'll be dead like Will."

Tavi nodded his head and was about to answer when shouts of "Dinner" rang through the house. Mac hopped up and ran to the living room, leaving Tavi alone to dwell upon his thoughts and hopes and fears and sadness.

Chapter 27

"Where's Billy?" Javier asked Laura as he carried in the bags of groceries for the picnic later.

Laura looked up from the table where she had been doing a crossword puzzle. "Tom stopped by to pick him up about ten minutes ago."

"Again?" Javier asked. "He's been spending a lot of time at Tom's house lately."

Laura stood up and gave Javier a hug. "Don't be jealous, Javi. Billy just likes his swimming pool, and his friends are always over there as well."

Javier kissed Laura on the forehead. "If you say it's okay, then I believe you," he said, turning around and pulling the hamburger meat out of a bag. "Is he going to ride with us to the game?"

"No," Laura replied. "I guess his team is helping Tom paint his house today, and so Billy will just meet us there. He took all of his stuff with him."

"What?" Javier demanded. "Now they're painting his house for him?"

"I don't know," Laura said, sounding annoyed that Javier was still on the subject. "I guess he needed help. Do you want Billy to help you paint our house?"

Javier looked quickly at the wall-papered room, the spotless ceiling, and thought about how much money he'd paid to have the exterior of their house painted the summer before. "Well, no," he admitted grudgingly. "I'm just saying it sounds weird."

"I'm not going to argue about it anymore," Laura said, folding up the newspaper on the table and stacking it into a pile. "Talk to Billy about it later if you want."

"Maybe I will," Javier grumbled to Laura's back as she walked out of the kitchen.

Later, as they walked to the field, Laura carried the ball bag in one hand and held Jasmine's hand in the other. "Are you nervous about today's games?" she teased Javier.

He smiled at her and said, "I don't know how I'm supposed to feel. The championship game, and my own son is pitching against me."

"I want Billy to win," Jasmine said, surprising her parents.

"But it's my team," Javier tried to explain. "Those boys have grown on me. Do you know how hard they have worked and practiced to get better?" He shook his head in exasperation as they reached the field. "I hope we tie."

Laura and Jasmine made their way over to the bleachers on the other side of the field. She smiled when she heard her husband roar with enthusiasm as he met his team. She looked across the field to where Billy was playing catch with one of his teammates, with Tom standing next to him. She suddenly had an ominous feeling and prayed to God that everything would work out for the best that day.

Two hours and six and a half innings later, Javier glared at the scoreboard, his desire to win wrestling with familial loyalty. He turned to the dugout and shouted, "Assaf, you're up next." Assaf jumped up, grabbed a batting helmet, and hurried to the on-deck circle. He picked up a bat and did a few practice swings as he watched the batter in front of him face Billy.

"Strike three!" the umpire shouted. Javier cursed silently in his mind while he clapped his hands and shouted, "We've got this one! Everyone put on your rally caps. Assaf is going to bring it home!" Matt, the batter who had just struck out, walked by with his head down, dragging his bat behind him. "Hey," Javier said, grabbing him by the shoulders. "Look at me! You've played a hell of a season. Don't let this one at-bat get you down, you hear me?"

"Yes, Coach!" Matt said, perking up a bit.

Javier watched Billy throw his first pitch. It was way outside of the strike zone. "Ball one!" shouted the umpire.

"Time out!" Tom yelled from across the field. He hurried out to the pitcher's mound where Billy was standing with his hand on his hip, obviously tired.

Take him out of the game, Javier thought, calling Assaf over. Keeping an eye on the pitcher's mound, Javier squatted down to talk to Assaf. He frowned, however, when Tom rubbed Billy's back in a disconcerting manner, and he felt a twinge of worry in the back of his mind.

Ignoring it, Javier spoke quietly to Assaf. "Listen, Billy's exhausted but he's going to stay in. So here's what you do – ignore the next two pitches he throws."

"But, Coach, what if I can hit it?" Assaf asked.

"We don't need you to just hit it," Javier argued, speaking quickly. "I need you to hit that ball so far that they never find it. There's two outs, and runners on second and third. We need both of them to score." He leaned closer and whispered confidingly, "Junior's up next and he hasn't had a hit all season. So I need you to finish this right now."

"But, Coach…" Assaf protested.

"I know Billy," Javier said, as Tom walked back to his dugout and the umpire motioned for Assaf to come back. "He's going to throw that killer curve to get you swinging, but he's exhausted. You wait two pitches and the only thing he'll be thinking about is getting the ball over the plate. And then you kill that third pitch, understand?"

"Yes, Coach," Assaf said, as he turned and took his position at the plate.

Billy went into his windup and threw his first pitch. Curveball, thought Javier, recognizing the pitch by how Billy threw it. Assaf tensed up and Javier thought for a second that he was going to swing, but his body relaxed as the ball curved out of the strike zone. "Ball two!" the umpire shouted.

He loves that pitch, Javier thought. I know he has to do it one more time.

Billy wound up and threw what looked to be a perfect strike. Assaf shifted his weight to swing, but checked himself at the last moment. The ball curved mightily away from him. "Ball three!"

Javier watched Billy lick his lips as he took off his hat and wiped his forehead with his arm. He glanced at Tom, who smiled and shouted encouraging words. Billy suddenly looked back at his father, and before Javier could mask his look of distrust, Billy had wrinkled his brow at what he had seen.

Javier turned away from Billy and shouted to Assaf, "Come on, Assaf! Just one hit!" Javier sensed, rather than saw, Billy's frown as he pulled his hat on tight. Javier watched him go into his windup, and smiled when he saw that it was going to be a fastball.

CRACK!

Assaf connected solidly with the pitch, and the ball flew out of the infield towards the fence. Javier thought at first that it was actually going to be a home run, but it ricocheted off of the fence about two feet from the top. The runners on second and third base easily crossed home plate before the center fielder even picked up the ball.

Game over. Javier's team eight, Tom's team seven.

Javier whooped with joy as he threw his clipboard in the air and ran onto the field, past the other players, and scooped up Assaf with a big hug. His team crowded around him, cheering and jumping with joy as their parents cheered in the stands.

Too late Javier remembered Billy. He put Assaf down and tried to find him, only to find him sitting with his head down disconsolately on his bench, with Tom's arm wrapped around him. Squeezing his way through his own ecstatic players, Javier jogged towards the dugout, getting there at the same time as Laura.

She pulled Billy up by his arms and gave him a hug while Javier stood uncomfortably behind her. He cleared his throat and everyone turned to look at him. "Hey, Billy. Great game!" he said, struggling to find the right words.

"Thanks, Dad," Billy replied, wiping his eyes with his hand. He stepped back from his mother and stood next to his coach, leaning his body in slightly for support. Suddenly, Assaf ran past Javier and gave Billy a quick hug. "Good game, Billy!" he said. "Sorry about that last hit."

Billy smiled his first real smile since the game had ended. "That was a nice hit," he replied. "I was hoping you'd swing at my curveball."

"Yeah," Assaf said, his eyes lit with joy. "Your dad told me to ignore those pitches and to wait for your fastball on the third pitch."

The smile disappeared from Billy's face and he looked at Javier with hurt eyes. Laura glanced at Javier with pity, knowing that he was in a no-win situation. "Well..." Javier tried to explain. "It was a lucky guess."

Billy's lower lip quivered as he stared at his father, until Tom put his arm around Billy's shoulders, cleared his throat, and said, "Well, we have to get going for the team barbecue at my house. I'll give Billy a ride."

Javier looked at Tom, not liking him anymore. "How was the painting?" he asked flatly.

Tom smiled at Javier, but the smile didn't reach his pale blue eyes. "Good. We got a lot done. Thanks for letting Billy come over and help."

As Tom bent down to pick up the bag with the bats in it, Javier had a thought. "Wait – did you have your entire team painting your house? Do you have that many paintbrushes and stuff?" Laura put her hand on his arm to calm him down.

"Um, no," Tom said. Billy came and stood next to Tom with his gear and the bag of balls for his team. "It was just a few of the boys who came over this morning."

Javier studied Tom's face, wishing he could read his thoughts. He wanted to say something else, but Laura quickly said, "Well, you guys have fun at the barbecue. Billy, call me when you need a ride home."

"Sure, Mom," Billy said, exiting the dugout without looking back.

"Good game, Javier. Good-bye, Laura," Tom said, following Billy.

"Bye, Tom," Laura said, while Javier silently watched him leave. When Tom was gone, she turned to her husband and said, "What is wrong with you today?"

Javier watched Billy and Tom until they disappeared around a corner. "That doesn't seem strange to you?" he asked.

"No," she exclaimed. "The only one who is being strange right now is you."

Javier shook his head in disagreement, but knew not to press it any further. Giving Laura a brief smile, he leaned over and kissed her on the cheek. "You're right. I'm sorry. Will you still help me organize the barbecue picnic?"

She smiled and put her hand in his as they strolled towards his team and their waiting parents. "Of course," she said. "Oh, and honey, great game today!"

Javier grinned with pride as he let go of Laura's hand and ran towards his team.

Chapter 28

"That was Jane, Paul's mother," Laura called to Javier, hanging up the phone in the kitchen. "She said that she'll pick up Billy as well."

Javier's yawn cut off his reply. He closed his eyes and relaxed in the chaise lounge on the deck, enjoying the early evening sunshine as it fell upon his face. Laura walked out to the deck and smiled lovingly at her husband who was stretched out like a cat basking in the sun. She sat in the chair with him, and as he shifted over, she curled up against him, resting her head on his shoulder.

"So," she said invitingly, "Jasmine's at a friend's house, Billy won't be home for forty-five minutes. We've already eaten…" She ran her hand lightly over his chest. "Is there anything special you'd like to do?"

Javier grinned knowingly and stretched. "Sleep," he murmured, wrapping his arm around Laura and pulling her close. Laura gave a sigh of contentment and quickly fell asleep, with the scent of her husband enveloping her like a blanket.

They were jolted out of their catnap when the kitchen phone rang jarringly. "I would say don't answer it," Javier said in annoyance as it rang again, "but that's a horrible sound. Do you want me to get it?" He stretched and tried to get up.

"No," Laura answered sleepily. She pushed Javier back down and kissed him on the lips. "I'll get it." She stood up and stretched, and calmly walked into the kitchen to answer the phone.

Just then, Javier's cell phone vibrated against his leg. He was tempted to ignore it, but when he glanced at it, he saw the number for the downstairs bar. "What?" he answered angrily, pressing the TALK button on his phone.

At the same time, he heard Laura say, "What? That's not possible. Okay, well then how long until you're here?" He knew by the tone of her voice that something was really wrong. Wondering what it was, he tried to concentrate on his own phone call.

"Can you repeat that?" he asked. He heard Laura slam the phone the phone into its holder and stomp towards him.

"This is Juan, Mr. Lopez. We have a big problem."

"Fuck!" Javier whispered. In a normal tone of voice, he said, "Where's Vikram? I'm not coming in today."

"I don't know," Juan said. "Him and Ben aren't here. And someone just took the boys!"

Javier sat up in alarm as Laura came and stood in front of him, hands are her hips. "I need to talk to you," she said angrily.

"Wait a second," he whispered to her. He spoke into the phone, "Say that one more time."

"I need to talk to you now!" Laura insisted. He held up his hand as Juan explained that two women had just marched into his bar with a police officer, ordered all of the boys who were working to follow them, and then marched out with the boys in tow.

"I'll be right there," he said and hung up the phone.

"No, you won't," Laura said. "I need you here."

"Why?" He asked, unable to show her any concern as he tried to consider the ramifications of what Juan had just told him.

"Jane's dropping off Billy in one minute. She claims that he and Paul are drunk."

"What?" Javier said. "That's…I don't think that's true."

Laura sat down next to him and gazed steadily into his eyes. "Jane says they're acting drunk and that her car smells like beer." Javier clenched his jaw as she continued, "I don't care if you have a problem at work right now. Your family needs to come first and we need you now."

Javier took a deep breath and shoved aside his impatience to get to work. He put his hand on Laura's back and gently rubbed it. "Okay," he said. "You're right – as always. Family comes first." She sighed with relief and rested her head on his shoulder for a moment. "Let's go meet Billy at the door," Javier said, standing up and helping Laura to her feet.

A few minutes later, they stood on the stairs and watched Billy stumble in, dropping his bag haphazardly on the floor. He tried to take off his right shoe, but swayed dangerously and had to quickly put his hand on the wall to keep from falling over. After he managed to take them both off, he turned towards the stairs and gasped in surprise when he saw his parents waiting for him.

"Billy," Javier said. "We need to talk. Let's go to the living room."

Billy looked at his parents for a couple of seconds, slightly swaying back and forth, and said, "I'm okay. We can talk tomorrow."

Javier raised his voice. "Billy! Now!" he said so sternly that Laura put her hand on his arm.

Billy heaved a sigh and said, "Fine!" and stomped off to the living room. Javier and Laura followed slowly behind, not looking forward to what had to be done.

They sat on either side of him on the sofa. He looked at his parents suspiciously as they leaned in, and when he saw them sniffing, he knew that they knew. "What do you want?" he asked.

Laura looked at her husband and spoke first. "Billy, we know that you've been drinking. You smell like beer."

Billy looked like he wanted to deny it, but then said, "So? It was just one or two."

"Where did you get it?" Javier asked quietly.

Billy shrugged. "I don't remember. One of the boys brought it."

"Who?" Javier demanded.

"I don't remember!" Billy said angrily, raising his voice.

Javier and Laura looked at each with concern. "Does Coach Tom know about this?"

"No," Billy quickly answered. "He didn't see us."

"I think I'm going to call him," Javier said, thinking that Billy had been too quick to deny it.

"No!" Billy shouted, leaping to his feet. "Why do you always have to ruin everything? You don't understand me anymore like Tom does."

Javier felt like someone had stuck a knife in his stomach. "What?" he asked, the pain in his voice obvious to Laura. "What do you mean?"

"Nothing," Billy said. "Can I PLEASE go to my room now?"

Laura answered before Javier could reply. "Yes, but we're going to talk about this more tomorrow. You're too young to be drinking."

"Fine," Billy retorted, marching off to the stairs. "Whatever."

As they listened to him clomp up the stairs, Javier said quietly, "I'm going to call Tom." Laura opened her mouth to say something, but then closed it quickly when she saw the angry look in Javier's eye.

He pulled out his cell phone and called Tom.

"Hello?"

"Tom, this is Javier."

"Oh, hey, Javier. How was your picnic?"

"It was fine," Javier said, looking darkly at his wife. "The reason I'm calling, though, is about Billy."

"Is everything okay?" Tom asked, concern in his voice.

"Actually, no, he's not. He just walked through the door and he's drunk. He smells like he's had a few beers. Jane said the same thing is true about Paul."

A brief pause. "Really?" Tom asked in surprise. "That's…I had no idea."

"So you had no idea that they were drinking at your house?"

"Honestly, today was a huge mess," Tom explained. "One of the boys fell and cut his leg near the pool, and I spent about thirty minutes taking care of that and talking to his mother."

"You left the rest of the kids unsupervised for thirty minutes?" Javier asked angrily. Laura frowned and asked for the phone. Javier shook his head at her and waved her away.

"Javier, I promise you, this is the only time something like this has happened."

"Wait a minute," Javier said. He covered the mouth piece and explained to Laura what Tom had said.

"Let me talk to him," she said, reaching for his phone. He opened his hand and let her take it and leaned back against the sofa. "Hey, Tom, this is Laura. If what you say is true, then why did one of your players come to your house with multiple cans of beer? Do you normally let them drink there?"

"Uh-huh," she said, listening to his reply. "It just seems a bit of a coincidence that you have an emergency at the same time someone brings a case of beer for the first time. Do you keep beer in your house?" A pause. "Can you go check and see if any cans are missing?" A longer pause. "No, it's no problem. I can wait."

She covered the mouthpiece and shook her head unhappily at Javier. He gave her a quick smile and said, "Now I remember why you're the lawyer in the family."

Laura uncovered the mouthpiece. "Yes, Tom, I'm still here." A beat. "Okay, I see. Well, that changes things slightly." She took a deep breath while she listened to him talk. "Listen, Tom. The baseball season is finished, and so there's no need for Billy or any of the other boys to go over to your house anymore this summer, right?" Javier heard Tom protest before Laura cut him off. "Well, I think it's our decision, and until you hear differently, that decision is final." She paused and then interrupted him again. "Okay, Tom. I understand. Have a good night." She hung up the phone and tossed it onto Javier's lap.

"What'd he say?" Javier asked.

"He says he checked and maybe twelve or thirteen beers are missing from his refrigerator."

"Do you believe him?"

Laura thought for a second. "No, not really, to be honest. I think he gave them the beers and he lied to us and he told Billy to lie to us."

"That…fucker," Javier said angrily.

"Well, that's that." Laura shrugged her shoulders. "We can't prove it, but I'll tell Billy tomorrow that he's not allowed to go back over to Tom's house."

"I'll tell him, if you want," Javier said, pulling Laura in for a hug.

"Thanks," she said, squeezing him tight. "We can tell him together." After a few seconds, she said, "Oh, didn't you say there was a problem at work?" Javier's heart skipped a beat. He let go of Laura and ran towards the garage door.

"Thanks, honey," he called from the kitchen, "I'll be home as soon as possible."

"I love you," she called back, hearing the door slam shut. Laura sat down and sank into the chair, wondering what the emergency was. She had learned over the years not to ask since it was usually some mundane technical problem which she didn't understand. She hoped it wasn't anything too major.

Chapter 29

Javier burst through the front door of The School House, fearful of what he was going to find. He had expected to see a bar devoid of boys, filled with police officers arresting his men. What he found was business as usual. Six-thirty in the evening was typically a slow time of the day, and there were four or five customers – all faces that he recognized – and the boys were either playing games with them or with each other.

Everyone looked up in shock as Javier stood there. A number of boys waved and called out greetings to him. In the back of his mind, he noted that they usually tried to avoid his gaze when he walked through the bar. A couple of the customers also said hello as Javier relaxed and walked casually to the bar.

Juan handed him a bottle of water as soon as Javier sat down on a stool. Leaning forward, Javier said in a low voice, "You're about five seconds away from being fired. Why did you call me? What emergency?" Javier gestured to the bar. "Everything looks normal."

"It is now," Juan answered quickly. "But it wasn't before. Ask one of the boys." Juan scanned the room and pointed to where one of the customers was playing dominos with a boy. "Ask him!"

Javier glanced quickly at the boy. "Who, Tavi?"

Juan nodded his head fervently. "Talk to him. He's the one who saved everything."

Javier looked at Juan suspiciously before swiveling around on his barstool. "What's that guy drinking?" Javier said over his shoulder, as he watched Tavi talk to the customer.

"A...um...pina colada," Juan said nervously.

"Make him another one," Javier ordered. He looked at the two boys who were playing Connect Four at the bar. "You two, come with me." They obligingly hurried over. Javier grabbed the drink from Juan and walked over to where Tavi was.

"Excuse me, sir," Javier said politely, setting the drink in front of him. "Compliments of the house."

The man picked up the drink and took a sip of it through the straw. "Thank you," he said. "I appreciate it."

"May I borrow Tavi for a second?" Javier asked, putting his hand on Tavi's shoulder and digging his fingertips in. Tavi jumped up and the two boys squeezed onto the edge of the chair where he had been sitting. "These two will keep you company, if that's okay?"

"Sure," the man said magnanimously, waving his hand. "It's no big deal." He looked at Tavi with a smile. "I'm sure we'll get to know each other eventually."

Tavi smiled back and replied, "I hope so." Feeling the pressure of Javier's hand on his arm, he turned and quickly followed Javier up to his office.

Javier motioned for Tavi to pull a chair over from the wall as he sat at his desk. When Tavi was sitting in front of him, he said, "So, tell me about what happened today."

And Tavi told him almost everything that had happened.

After he had finished, Javier studied him appraisingly. "Good job, Tavi," he finally said. "Is there anything else you want to add?"

Tavi thought carefully for a moment before shaking his head. "Nope."

"I think you saved me a lot of trouble tonight," Javier said, smiling at Tavi. "How about you take the rest of the night off? Go explore, watch TELEVISION, sleep, do whatever you want, but you don't have to work tonight."

"Really?" Tavi asked excitedly.

"Really," Javier repeated.

Tavi turned to go, but paused after only taking one step. "Um…I was wondering…could Mac have the night off as well?" he asked hesitantly.

"What?!?" Javier said, smiling inside at Tavi's brashness.

"I mean...never mind," Tavi quickly said.

"It's fine. You earned it." Javier waved his hand. "Go." Tavi stood up and hurried to the stairs. As he reached the bottom, Javier called out, "Thanks again, Tavi." Tavi let the door close behind him without answering.

Javier called Vikram for the umpteenth time that night. On the third ring, Vikram said, "Hey, boss!"

"Where the hell have you been?" Javier demanded angrily.

"One of the boys is sick," Vikram said. "He almost died. I had to take him to a doctor."

"Fuck!" Javier muttered. "Where are you now?"

"Next to the triangle room. Why?"

"Just get your ass up here to my office now."

"Okay," Vikram said, wondering what Javier was doing at work. He hung up the phone, only to have it ring two seconds later.

"Where's Ben?" Javier asked.

"He's off today. He and his wife took a quick vacation somewhere. Remember? He asked you about it three weeks ago."

"Yeah," replied Javier grudgingly as he hung up the phone.

When Vikram reached Javier's office, he found Javier intently clicking the mouse on his computer. "What's going on?" Vikram asked.

Javier related the story that Tavi had told him. "And so," he concluded, "find out who this police officer is. We pay a large sum of money to make sure the police don't come here. Things like this shouldn't happen."

"Got it," Vikram said.

"And get the word to everyone on the streets that the usual bounty is in place for those two boys who didn't come back – Lucas and Jabar. Pass out photos to everyone, including the cops, and get them back here ASAP!"

"Got it," Vikram said again. Javier reached down to turn off his computer, and then stood up and stretched. "Where are you going now?" Vikram asked.

"Me?" Javier said. "I'm going home." He began walking towards the stairs and Vikram trailed behind him. "Make sure you get everything taken care of."

"I will," Vikram promised. "Have a good night."

They entered the bar, and Javier walked towards the front door as Vikram went to talk to Juan. "At least things can't get any worse," Javier muttered.

He walked out of the front door and nearly collided with someone who was rushing by on the street.

"Excuse me," the man said. He looked up and his eyes widened in surprise. "Javier!" Tom said.

Javier froze, his mind blank with shock. He watched Tom's eyes flick behind him and saw the realization dawn as Tom saw where Javier was coming from. He patted Javier on the shoulder reassuringly. "Don't worry. I won't tell anyone."

"It's…uh…it's not like that," Javier stammered. His work life and his personal life had never become entangled like this before.

Tom grinned and whispered, "Trust me. I understand." He walked a few steps and then pointed at Bangarang. "That one is my favorite. Maybe I'll see you in there sometime?" He smiled again, his pale blue eyes emotionless, and turned and hurried into his favorite little boy bar.

Javier closed his eyes. His heart was beating so fast and hard that he couldn't concentrate on anything. He reached up to wipe away the sweat from his brow and was surprised to find his fingers trembling. He took a deep breath and slowly exhaled as he struggled to regain control. He looked back to where Tom had vanished, every instinct crying out for him to rush after him and kill him so he couldn't talk to anyone. Javier took a half-step in that direction before hesitating with indecision. Arguing with himself, he turned around and headed for his car, his thoughts filled with fear for the first time in a long, long time.

Chapter 30

As soon as Tavi left the bar, he ran towards the alley where the bathroom for the circle room was located. Passing by it, he turned left and then made several more seemingly random turns. Stopping to catch his breath, he looked behind him to see if anyone had seen him. After a couple of minutes, the alleyway was still deserted and so he squatted down on the far side of the dumpster, reached behind it, and pulled out a loose brick. The brick was only about three-quarters as thick as a normal brick, having been patiently ground down by Tavi until he could hide his money in the hole behind it without having the brick stick out any farther than normal.

Tavi had anxiously tried to think of a safe place to hide his money. His shoe was okay for a couple of days at the beginning, but he knew that he couldn't use it for very long. He had seen others lose their savings because they hadn't been cautious enough. One boy had hidden his money in the pockets of his old pants which he never wore anymore. Another one had tried to hide his under the mattress of the bed he always slept on. Both of them had come home one morning to find that their money had vanished. Tavi doubted that another boy would steal their money, but he had learned over the last four months that people could do almost anything, and so all he could do was to try and be as careful as possible.

He pulled out enough small change to equal one talent, and then put the rest of the money back into the plastic bag. He pressed it into the hole and shoved the loose brick in on top of it. Even with giving the bar half of his tips, he had saved over eighty talents. He had no idea how much money he would need when he finally left, or what he could use it for, but he had become obsessed with saving money as it had become a symbol for the key to his escape.

He popped up quickly and looked towards the end of the alleyway from where he had come. He still didn't see anyone, and so he jumped out from behind the dumpster and ran back to the room, eager to tell Mac about their night off before Mac left for the bar.

He caught him just as he was leaving. "Mac!" he called out. The other boys turned around, curious as to why Tavi wasn't at work, but Tavi waved Mac over so that he could speak with him privately.

"What?" Mac said, hurrying over. "I have to get to work."

"No, you don't," Tavi said with a huge grin. "Javier has given us the night off."

"What?" Mac said in disbelief. "Why?"

"I'll tell you while we explore. Is there anywhere in the city you want to go see?"

Mac pursed his lips thoughtfully, and then turned and dashed back into the room. "Wait!" he said to Tavi. A few seconds later, he came out holding one of the tourist maps that Yuri had dropped off earlier in the summer. It showed the whole city and listed different places worth seeing. The boys had spent most of the summer studying them and talking to each other about the places they had been able to see, and the places that they wanted to visit.

"What's today?" Tavi asked Mac. "Friday?"

"Saturday," Mac corrected him.

Tavi pretended to study the map, knowing in his heart exactly where he wanted to go. He pointed to a description of the night markets at the bottom of the map. "How about we go here?" he asked. "We always work at night, and so I haven't had a chance to see them."

"Sure," Mac said. He glanced at the map and then looked around furtively. Without meeting Tavi's eyes, he said, "Um…let me go to the bathroom first."

"Okay."

Mac ran off in the direction of the bathroom, and Tavi went inside and sat on a sofa as he studied the map. It would be an easy commute, he thought, and then he wondered if Kurt and Kyle would be there. And if they were there, should he introduce them to Mac. He trusted Mac as much as he trusted anyone, but that didn't mean he completely trusted him. He was trying to decide what to do when Mac ran into house, slightly out of breath.

"Okay. I'm ready."

Tavi stood up, carefully folding the map back together. He put it into his pocket, and he and Mac headed off to the sky train station. On the way to the night markets, Tavi told Mac about what had happened earlier.

It was a typical day, and Tavi had gotten stuck with the early shift. There were only a couple of customers in there at that time, and so Tavi was playing a card game with a few of the other boys, gambling with matchsticks which they would later convert into money. The only bossman around was Juan, and he was so laidback that everyone had been pretty relaxed.

Until the two women entered the bar with the policeman.

There were always a couple of women who visited their bar each week. Usually they were with husbands or boyfriends, but sometimes women came in alone and would leave with one of the boys. From what Tavi had heard, it sounded a lot nicer than what happened to him each night, but he hadn't had the opportunity to experience it yet.

These women, though, were different. They were wearing long, thick dresses that came down to their ankles, they had on no makeup, and they were both wearing glasses and had frizzy, unbrushed hair. The only real difference between them was that one was short and fat, while the other was tall and thin.

They entered the bar with the policeman trailing behind them. The tall one stepped forward and said, "Boys! Come with us now. We are to here to free you. Hurry!" She reached down and grabbed the arm of one of the nine year old boys – Lucas – and pulled him to his feet.

The other woman – the short, fat one – pulled a bible out of her bag and went up to one of the customers. "Get thee away, Satan," she screamed at him. "How dare you touch these boys?!? I command you in the name of Jesus Christ to leave these innocent souls alone."

The man, one of their afternoon regulars, jumped to his feet and ran from the bar. The policeman made a halfhearted attempt to grab him, but the man shrugged him off and sprinted out the door. The other customer slinked out the side door before anyone could pay any attention to him.

The woman with the bible pointed at Juan, and said to the policeman, "Go arrest that man. He sells children for sex."

The policeman hesitated, obviously questioning himself as to why he was there. Frowning, he sauntered up to the bar and began speaking with Juan.

"Hurry, children!" the taller woman shouted. "Now is your chance. Let's go!" She rushed forward, still holding Lucas's hand, and began nudging the boys out of the bar, like a dog herding a flock of sheep. The short one joined her, and pretty soon they were all standing on the street in front of the bar.

Waiting for them outside was a small group of children, whom the women had found in the previous bar. Exhorting the children to follow them with promises of freedom, the women ran to the next bar, and had Tavi and the others wait outside.

Tavi had to admit that he was excited about the thought of finally being free. He had wondered if anyone in the city cared about what was going on, and was relieved to see that someone was finally saving them. He whispered eagerly with the other children as they waited for their saviors to come back.

After a few minutes, the two women came out of Bangarang with another ten children. All told, there were now around thirty children on the street in front of the bar, and pedestrians were walking by and giving them strange looks.

The women led the children away from the bars to a quieter area several streets away. The children were all happy and skipping and holding hands, as they imagined going home and escaping from the life they were currently living.

The two women led them to an old, beat-up car that was parked along the side of the street. Standing with their backs against it, the tall one said, "Children – we have freed you from your enslavement. You don't have to live in sin any longer." The children looked at each other happily, worshipping these women. "And so now," she announced, "you are free! You can go home to your families!"

The tone of the crowd of children abruptly changed from happiness to confusion to dead silence. The two women looked at each other, unsure of what was wrong. Tavi glanced around at the dismayed looks on the faces of the children around him and stepped forward. "Wait! So what do we do now?"

"Why, you go home. We rescued you from that place," the short woman said simply.

Tavi gave a short, bitter laugh. "And so that's it?" he asked. "You won't give us a place to live, or pay for us to go to school, or buy us clothes and food or anything like that?"

The women looked at each other again, realizing that this wasn't going how they had planned. The taller one cleared her throat and said, "We don't have much money. We can't take care of you. We could maybe find you an orphanage…"

"An orphanage?" Tavi said outraged. "I've met kids who live in those places. It's worse than what we do because they don't get paid." The crowd of children murmured their agreement.

The short woman looked like she was going to burst into tears. "I don't understand," she said. "You're sex slaves and we freed you. You're free," she repeated, as if Tavi didn't understand what that meant. "That means you can go home."

"Home?!?" Tavi shouted. He realized that he was being harsh with the women, but they had given him back the hope which he had thought was gone forever, and now it turned out that it was all a facade. "I don't know where my home is. I know that it's many buses away from here, and that it takes about twenty-four hours to get there, BUT I DON'T KNOW WHERE IT IS!"

The children's muttering grew louder.

"Well, I don't know what you want me to tell you," the taller woman said. "Here we came to save you and now you're acting ungrateful."

Tavi looked at the children who had come from The School House with him. "Do you know what they'll do if they find us here?" he asked the women quietly. "If we're lucky, they'll take us back and only break our arm. And if we run away again, then they'll kill us. So, where do you want me to go so that I can be safe?"

The women looked at each other and whispered quietly together. "We can each take one boy home and help take care of him," the shorter one finally announced.

"But…but...there are thirty children here!" Tavi said, frustratedly gesturing to the other children.

"What do you want us to do?" the taller woman asked.

Tavi stared at them, anger and remorse warring in his soul. He knew they were just trying to help, but that they didn't understand. He disappointedly shook his head and said, "Nothing. I'm going back. Hopefully they won't try to catch me before I do." He turned around and pushed his way through the crowd of children and walked towards the end of the street. When he glanced back, all of the other children were following him, except for Lucas and Jabar. The two women had gripped their wrists tightly, and as Tavi walked away, he prayed that they would be taken care of.

the

Chapter 31

Tavi finished his story as they were walking from the station to the night market. They walked in silence for a while, each lost in their own thoughts, until Mac asked with concern, "Do you think they'll get caught?"

"I don't know," Tavi answered, sniffing the air appreciatively as a cornucopia of smells swirled around him, making him lose focus for a second. "Um…I don't know. The women seem to care, but they don't seem too smart. And Javier has some cops working for him…" He trailed off when he saw the streets packed full of people who were meandering their way through the hundreds of stands that were selling clothes, and jewelry, and little carvings, and food. Tavi looked at Mac excitedly and they both ran towards the man selling ice cream.

"How much?" Tavi asked, as he and Mac stared hungrily at the tubs of different flavor.

"Ten cents," the man said, which was one tenth of a talent.

Tavi stuck his hand in his pocket and tickled the coins with his fingers. Suddenly, he remembered that he wasn't supposed to have any money. He looked at Mac guiltily and cleared his throat self-consciously. "Um…do you have any money?" he asked quietly.

Mac hesitated for a long second before he pulled a few coins out of his pocket. "I seem to have some tip money that I haven't turned in yet."

Relief flooded through Tavi. He pinched a couple of coins from his pocket and showed them to Mac. "Ah, what a lucky day," he said. "Me too." Tavi and Mac grinned at each other, both of them feeling less alone than they had only minutes before, and they turned to the man and started quizzing him about the different flavors of ice cream.

A couple of hours later, they were stuffed with foods that Tavi had never even heard of before. They had been wandering around constantly, examining all of the items for sale, and they hadn't even seen a tenth of the market yet. Spotting an empty space next to the corner of a building, Tavi and Mac walked over and sat down, resting against the wall.

"I'm so full!" Mac said, rubbing his belly with his hand. "I didn't know that things would be so cheap here."

"Yeah," Tavi said. "Too bad we can't come back here more often." A shadow seemed to flit over them and Tavi wanted to kick himself for reminding them what they had to go back to.

Mac took a sip of water from the bottle he had bought. He reached into his pocket and pulled something out. "Here," he said, opening his hand out to Tavi. There were two pills resting in the palm of his hand. "Do you want one?"

"Sure," Tavi said instinctively, reaching for one. "Wait...no!" he said after half a second, jerking his hand back as if it had been burned. "Why would you take one now?"

"I don't know," Mac said quietly, staring at the pills in his hand. "It just seems like we should."

Tavi looked at Mac worriedly. "Where did you get them?" he asked.

Mac shrugged, still looking at the pills. "Vikram. I always ask for two, just in case I need one for the morning. Usually I don't take it, but it's good to always have extras."

Tavi looked at the pills one last time, angry with himself for the desire he felt to take one and have all of his troubles disappear. He reached down and gently closed Mac's hand around the pills. "Come on, Mac," he pleaded. "We don't need those now. Just put them back – please?"

Mac looked at Tavi and then reluctantly put the pills back in his pocket. Tavi grabbed his bottle and took a swig. "How have you been doing with everything?" he asked quietly.

Mac closed his eyes and leaned his head against the wall. "I don't know," he said in voice almost too low to hear. "It's hard for me to sleep anymore and so Vikram has given me my own supply of the brown paste. I usually take some every night after the customer falls asleep."

Tavi felt a bolt of worry shoot through him. The same thing had happened to him a couple of times, but nothing like what Mac was talking about. "I didn't know it was that bad," Tavi said quietly.

Mac let out a shaky breath. "It's like I take the pill at night in the bar. The evening is like a dream. I take the brown paste and sleep like I'm dead. Wake up and try to escape from the hotel as quickly as I can. I come home and sometimes I shower for over an hour because I feel so dirty, but it feels like I'm dirty inside and I can't ever get clean." He wrapped his arms around his knees and started crying softly. "I don't know what to do, Tavi. Tonight was the first time I felt even a little happy in a long time, and now I just want to die again." He buried his face against his knees and sobbed as quietly as possible, which all of the boys learned to do really quickly.

Tavi put his arm over his friend's shoulders and pulled him close. He bit his lip, not knowing what to say. Without thinking, he blurted out, "I've been saving money to run away."

He was surprised when Mac looked up through his tears with a smile on his face. "I know. Down the alleyway past the old bathroom, behind the dumpster somewhere."

The shock on Tavi's face must have been obvious because Mac laughed with joy. "How did you know?" Tavi managed to stammer.

Mac frowned at the memory. "Fucking Brent," he said. "I saw you run off one time, and then I saw him creeping after you. I followed him for a bit before I ran straight at him with my hand up. The look on his face was so funny that I would have just laughed in his face if he hadn't run away so quickly."

Tavi smiled at the thought as Mac continued, "I looked to my right, and I saw you turning a corner, and so I followed you to make sure that Brent left you alone." He shrugged his shoulders and said nonchalantly, "I've done the same thing. I think I have almost eighty talents saved up."

"Me too!" Tavi said. "That must be enough money for us to…"

"To what?!?" Mac interrupted frustratedly. "It's like you told those women today – what are we supposed to do once we run away? My family is poor. They can't feed me, and I don't even know if I can look them in the eye after everything I've done. I'm supposed to be going to a good school in the big city!"

Tavi nodded his head in agreement. He had thought the same thing when the woman talked about him going home. He abruptly hopped up and reached down to help Mac up. "Fuck it," he said. "Let's just enjoy tonight. I wanted to try that pink stuff, and I heard people talking about games somewhere around here." He tugged Mac's arm and they merged back into the crowds. "Let's go have some fun."

As they searched for the booths that had the games, Tavi and Mac picked off pieces of the cotton candy they had bought and popped them in their mouths. Their hands and faces were so sticky that Tavi and Mac left the main thoroughfare to go find a public bathroom. Out of the corner of his eye, Tavi saw the two familiar figures he'd been keeping an eye out for all night, and he tapped Mac's arm and said, "Come on!" as he raced towards the alley they had disappeared into.

He was jumped as soon as he had taken two steps into the alleyway. Someone was on top of him holding him face down as another person rummaged through his pockets. Mac ran up and, without hesitating, kicked the boy who was searching Tavi's pockets in the face. He fell backwards, howling with pain. The boy who was sitting on top of Tavi glanced back in alarm just in time to see Mac tackle him, and as he struggled to fight back, Mac pinned him down and punched him twice in the face.

Covering his face with both arms to protect himself, the boy cried, "Stop! Stop! You win!"

Tavi pushed himself up and climbed to his feet, grabbing hold of Mac's hand as he prepared to punch again. "Wait," he said. Speaking to the boy on the ground, Tavi said, "Hello, Kyle." He looked across at the boy who had been kicked in the face. "And Kurt," Tavi continued with a smile. "You guys told me to come find you when I got the chance. Well, here we are."

Mac looked up at Tavi, and slowly got to his feet. "You know these guys?"

Kyle uncovered his face, squinting his eyes as he looked at Tavi, and said, "I remember you. Tavi, right?"

"Yep." Tavi reached down to help him up. "You guys don't seem to do so well at fighting. That's two for us and none for you so far."

"We do okay," Kyle said huffily, squatting down next to Kurt and checking his face. Seeing no blood, he stood up and said, "You're fine, Kurt. Get up and stop embarrassing us." Turning back to Tavi and Mac, he looked them up and down closely. "What are you guys doing here? Don't you have to work?"

"We got the night off," Tavi said simply.

"I've never heard of that happening before," Kurt said, struggling to his feet. "Did you run away?"

"No," Tavi insisted. "Things happened today, and our boss was happy so he said we didn't have to work tonight."

"Good for you," Kyle said, not pressing any further. "So what do you want to do?"

Tavi looked at Mac and shrugged. "I don't know. We've just been looking at the stalls. What do you normally do?"

Kyle thought for a second and said, "Usually we try to find a rich kid to jump and we take his money." Mac and Tavi sniggered at the thought of them beating someone up.

"But now, we were going to meet some other kids. You want to come along?"

"Sure," Tavi said, as Mac nodded his head. Without another word, Kurt and Kyle began walking down the alley with Tavi and Mac trailing behind. After a number of twists and turns which Tavi took careful note of, they turned down another darkened, non-descript street.

However, this road ended at a small park, and Tavi could see a number of people hanging out there. At the corner of the building across from the park, Kyle and Kurt entered a tiny store which had a small neon sign above the door. Tavi eyed it curiously as they passed under it, but couldn't figure out what the shape was supposed to be.

"Where are we going?" he whispered quietly to Kurt who was walking in front of him.

"The Candyman," Kurt said over his shoulder, as they walked into a well-lit convenience store. Tavi blinked his eyes at the sudden brightness and then yelped in surprise as a giant hand clamped down on his shoulder.

"Who's this, Kyle?" asked a voice next to Tavi's ear. He twisted around and found a short man with bright red hair and huge arms grinning at him. Tavi gulped involuntarily and stumbled backwards a step.

"Friends who may need you someday," Kyle explained. "The scared one is Tavi. His friend is…" he paused, realizing that the only way he had gotten to know Mac was when he was getting beat up.

"Mac," Mac said helpfully.

"Yes," Kyle said. "His name is Mac. Anyways, we have a couple of things to sell."

The Candyman's gaze swept over Mac and Tavi one more time before he brushed past them and went behind the counter. "Show me," he commanded.

Kurt and Kyle each dug into their bags. They pulled out a couple of books, a ring, a cell phone, and a gold necklace. The Candyman picked up each one and eyed them appraisingly. He opened up the cell phone, took out the battery, and checked the sim card which was nestled behind it. "What did I tell you?" he asked angrily, putting the battery in his pocket. "If you take a phone, then always remove the battery. Otherwise they can track you."

"You idiot," Kyle said to Kurt. "I thought you already did that." Kurt shrugged in response.

Tavi edged closer to the counter and reached out for one of the books. The Candyman slapped his hand away and gave him a dirty look. He whistled when he examined the ring and necklace and said, "You guys must've found a rich one tonight." He flipped through the books quickly before casually tossing them aside.

"One talent," he said.

"What?" Kyle asked in outrage. "This is the best stuff we've ever found. You can probably sell all of this for seventy talents."

The Candyman shook his head sadly. "Business has been slow lately. I can't be as nice as I have been."

"Come on, please," Kurt begged.

Sighing, the Candyman looked at them and said, "Fine. What do you think would be fair?"

Kyle immediately replied, "Five talents or ten percent of what you sell everything for."

"You mean the same thing we've always done."

"Come on," Kyle said. Gesturing towards Tavi and Mac, he said, "These guys are cool. Stop dicking around for their sake."

The Candyman frowned menacingly at Tavi and Mac, and Tavi's eyes widened in alarm. He reached a hand out to keep Kyle from talking.

But to his surprise, the Candyman burst out laughing and said, "Fine." He reached under the counter and slid five talents across to Kyle. "Five talents or ten percent of what I sell these meager items for – whichever one is the most." He turned his attention to Tavi. "You wanted to see the books?"

"Yes, please," Tavi said excitedly. The Candyman handed them to him, and Tavi flipped through both of them and then turned them over to read the back covers. "How much?" he asked, trying to hide his enthusiasm.

The Candyman studied Tavi's face, glanced at Kyle, and said with a grin, "Ten cents."

"Really?" Tavi asked hopefully, quickly digging into his pocket before he changed his mind.

"Yep." The Candyman held out his hand and Tavi paid him. Depositing the coin behind the counter, he fumbled around and pulled out a tiny coin, which he handed it to Kyle. "And here is your ten percent," he said with a grin.

Kyle took it as Kurt jeered at him. "Fucking Clarence," Kyle said with a grin.

"Clarence?" Mac said. "I thought your name was the Candyman."

The Candyman shook his head with a grin and turned his head towards Kurt, whose face had turned as red as the Candyman's hair. "Only this little troublemaker calls me the Candyman because he thinks my sign out front looks like a piece of candy. Everyone else calls me Clarence."

"I was wondering about that," Tavi said. "What is your sign a picture of?"

Clarence beckoned Tavi closer with his finger and whispered, "When I know you better, I'll tell you."

"Pssht!" Tavi said annoyed, stepping back.

"Did he tell you?" Kurt asked excitedly as Kyle listened with interest.

Tavi looked back at Clarence and grinned. "Yes, but I can't tell you until I know you better!"

"Aw…shut up!" Kurt said. "That's what Clarence always says too. Fucking Candyman," he whispered under his breath.

Clarence laughed and Kyle said, "Okay. We're gonna go meet the others. We'll be back later this week." He turned and headed for the exit.

Everyone said goodbye and turned to follow. Tavi hesitated for second and then turned back to Clarence. "Could you keep these safe for me for a while?" he asked hesitantly. "I don't really have a place to keep them."

Clarence's face softened and he gently took the books back from Tavi. "Sure, boy. Come by anytime if you want to read them."

Tavi beamed, the relief showing clearly on his face. "Thanks, Clarence," he said, running out the door. "It was nice meeting you!"

Clarence shook his head sadly as the boys' footsteps retreated in the distance. He looked up at the ceiling and murmured quietly, "Another one, Lord? How many of these boys are there in this wretched city?" He seemed to wait for a response, but upon hearing nothing, he slowly took the items off of the counter and locked them in a safe on the floor behind him.

Chapter 32

As Kurt and Kyle led the way into the park, they each pulled something out of their pockets and flashed a red light two times.

"What was that for?" Tavi asked, hurrying to keep up in the dark. He could feel Mac brushing against his right arm.

"To show them that we belong here and that we're not some rival gang," Kyle said, slipping the light back in his pocket.

"What?" Tavi stopped for a second in surprise and Mac bumped into him with a curse. "You guys don't all get along?"

"Are you kidding?" Kurt asked with derision. "There are a hundred different little gangs out there, and they'll all hurt you if they get the chance."

"Why?" Mac asked.

"Does everyone get along perfectly where you work?" Kyle asked.

"Well, no," Mac admitted.

"It's different, though," Tavi insisted. "You guys are struggling to stay alive. You should all be working together and make yourselves stronger."

"Heh," Kyle laughed, as they approached a group of kids hanging out on the playground equipment. "It's a nice idea, but it's never going to work. We steal from them and save our own butts by getting them in trouble. They do the same to us. That's what makes us stronger."

Tavi disagreed and wanted to argue more, but before he could say anything, flashlights from all directions blinded him and he shut his eyes and turned his head.

"Who's this?" said a girl's voice. "You didn't bring us two strays, did you?"

"I don't like them," a boy said. "Look at their clothes. Kyle, did you look in their pockets?"

"Calm down, you guys," Kyle said. "And turn those fucking lights off!" Two of the flashlights clicked off, while one of them wiggled around, shining its light on everyone. Kyle sighed. "Byron, what the fuck are you doing?"

The light clicked off and a voice said quickly, "Nothing."

The four boys who had just arrived blinked their eyes as they struggled to see in the dark. Tavi kept seeing white flashes everywhere and closed his eyes for a few seconds as he tried to get acclimated to the light. "So," said the first boy. "Who are these two? You were supposed to be visiting Clarence today."

"We did," Kurt said. "But we ran into these two on the way here, Pablo."

"And who are 'these two'?" the girl asked.

Tavi's vision came back to him, and he saw Kyle motion to him. "This is Tavi. The other one is Mac. We jumped them today thinking we could get something good."

"And then afterwards you decided to just bring them with you?" the girl asked, hopping off the slide and walking behind them.

"No, Chloe," Kyle said, carefully enunciating each word. "They beat our asses, just like Tavi did a few months ago. Remember? I told you guys about that."

"Who? That one guy who went psycho and put down both you and Kurt, and then stayed to talk about things?" Byron asked.

"Yeah," Kyle said embarrassedly.

"Psycho?" Tavi murmured.

"You did," Kurt insisted. "I've never seen anyone get as pissed off as you did."

"Ah," Tavi said, remembering what day it had been. "That was a terrible day."

"Anyways," Kyle said, "The girl who is circling behind us is Chloe. She keeps tracks of the other gangs. Byron's on the slide." Byron raised his hand in greeting. A nearby streetlight radiated enough light to show that he had a long ponytail. "He's our actor and figures out scams." Kyle pointed at the last boy, who was gently swaying in the swing. "That's Pablo. He steals like we do."

Tavi and Mac nodded to each of them. "Who's in charge?" Mac asked.

Everyone started laughing except for Tavi and Mac. "In charge? I don't want any of these boys in charge of me!" Chloe said disdainfully.

"Me neither," chimed in the others, laughing at the thought of it.

Tavi felt annoyed and wished they'd all stop laughing. "So, where do you guys sleep?"

If he had wanted to find the magic words to make everyone silent, then he had just found them. "What?" Pablo asked, jumping off the swing and walking towards them. He was dark-skinned and about six inches taller than Tavi. "Why the fuck do you want to know that?"

"Hey!" Kyle shouted, stepping in front of Tavi. "They don't know anything," he explained. "They're not on the streets yet."

At the same time, Kurt hissed at Tavi, "Don't ever ask that, man. Where you sleep is sacred because that's the time when you're most vulnerable. Don't be stupid!"

"What?" Chloe shouted right next to Mac's ear. He spun around in alarm. "You brought some boujies here?!?"

"No!" Kyle retorted. "They're working in a bar on Boys Street. They're just starting to figure things out."

"Man, if you brought spies," Byron moaned. He looked closely at Tavi and Mac. "Where do you guys work?"

Tavi cleared his throat nervously. "The…uh…School House."

The others grew still when they heard that. "Fuck, really?" Pablo asked. "Good luck. I don't know anyone in any of the gangs from there."

Chloe said quietly, "I met a boy from there when I first escaped a couple of years ago. He introduced me to Pastor Mike, but then when we were walking down the street, two cops grabbed him right there and I never saw him again."

"Do you know what his name was?" Tavi asked.

"Yuri," Chloe said, pausing when she heard Mac and Tavi gasp. "Why – do you know him?"

Tavi and Mac stayed with the children for the rest of the night. The others talked about the city, laughed about the scams that they had pulled, bragged about the fights they had been in, and argued about things they had stolen. When the night sky started getting lighter, they headed to the sky train station, hopping the gate so that they didn't have to pay. As they rode the train home, the children got off at different stops. Pablo got off near the night market and Chloe got off a couple of stops later. Kurt and Kyle got off one stop away from where Tavi had met them before, and he wondered if they had another place to sleep, or if they were just being overly cautious. When Tavi and Mac stood up to get off at their stop, Byron stood up as well and walked with them out of the station.

"Where are you going?" Tavi asked hesitantly.

Byron smiled good-naturedly. "I want to see where you guys live to make sure."

"Aren't you scared of getting caught by the bar you ran away from?" Mac asked.

"Nope," Byron said. In the daylight, Tavi noticed that he looked awfully young and innocent. "I didn't run away from a bar. All of the others did."

"Really?" Mac interrupted. "Even Chloe?"

A look of pain crossed Byron's face. "You guys think you have it bad, but Chloe started working when she was six years old. She would stand in a glass room with a number taped to her shirt, and men would sit there and point to the girl they wanted. She doesn't talk about it much but she went through a lot of shit." His face grew wary as he continued, "I probably shouldn't be telling you guys this, but she got away by stabbing the man she was with and then calmly walking out of the hotel. She was ten years old."

Tavi looked at Byron in surprise as they turned onto the street where the bar was. "Is she…safe to be around?"

Byron nodded his head. "Yep. She's amazing and really loyal. It just takes a while for her to trust people." He shrugged and added, "Especially since her bar is still looking for her two years later."

"Geez," Tavi said. He stopped in front of their house and opened up the door. A couple of boys were sitting on the sofa watching TELEVISION, apparently having just got home. "Well, here we are."

Byron popped his head in, looked around, and stepped back with a smile. "Okay. I was just checking."

"Why are you on the streets if you're not like us?" Mac asked, as Byron turned to walk away.

He kept walking as if he didn't hear them, and Tavi thought that he was going to leave without saying a word. However, he hesitated, and when he turned around, he said softly, "My parents were killed in a car accident last year and I have no other family. It was either this or the orphanage, and I chose to be free." He gazed at them meaningfully for a second, and then turned around, disappearing around the corner without saying another word.

A couple of weeks later, Yuri stopped by their rooms.

"Tavi!" he called to the back bedroom where Tavi was sleeping.

Tavi hurried out to the living room and his face lit up with joy when he saw what Yuri was carrying.

"Here," Yuri said, tossing his bag across the room to him. "Keep it somewhere safe." He turned around and walked out the door.

Tavi quickly glanced through the bag to make sure everything was still. He looked around for a safe place before tossing it into the dark corner of the room behind the television. He vaulted over the sofa and hurried out the door.

Yuri was disappearing around the corner of a building to his right. Tavi jogged after him, and found Yuri waiting for him when he reached the corner.

"Are you following me?" Yuri asked.

"No," said Tavi quickly. "I wanted to ask you a question." Yuri tilted his head and waited. "I met a friend of yours a couple of weeks ago."

Yuri wrinkled his brow. "Who?" he asked curiously.

"Chloe. She's this girl who…" Tavi trailed off when he saw the dark expression on Yuri's face.

"Stop right there," Yuri warned quietly.

"But she said that you…"

Yuri violently grabbed Tavi by his shirt collar and slammed him against the wall behind him. "I almost got killed because of that," Yuri hissed angrily. "The same will happen to you if you ever talk about that again." He banged Tavi against the wall one last time before he let go and stormed down the street.

Tavi watched him go, his heart beating rapidly in his chest. At the end of the street, Yuri kicked over a box in anger, picked up a stick, and smashed it against the corner of another building. Tavi could clearly hear his roar of anguish as Yuri bent over at the waist and put his hands on his knees. Not wanting Yuri to know that he had seen him crying, Tavi hurried back to his house.

When he ran through the door, he saw two of the other boys digging through his bag.

"Are you kidding me?" Tavi yelled, jumping over the nearest sofa and charging at them. "Leave my stuff alone."

"Hey, we found it," the larger boy, Junou, argued.

Without stopping, Tavi's fist smashed into Junou's jaw, and he collapsed to the floor in a daze.

The smaller boy quickly thrust the bag into Tavi's hand. "Here…I don't want this stuff anyways."

Tavi opened the bag and checked to make sure everything was there. He closed it up and looked at the two boys. "Don't touch my stuff," he threatened. They both nodded their heads in fright and Tavi stomped off to the bedroom, wondering if he could find a place to hide his bag or if he would have to fight everyone in the house.

He flopped down on a bed with the bag clasped to his chest. His eyes wandered over the ceiling and he noticed a vent near the ceiling on one of the walls. The covering was screwed to the wall and it seemed to be the right size. Tavi closed his eyes and fell back asleep, content with his new plan.

The next morning, Tavi left the hotel before his customer was even awake. He stopped at a convenience store to buy a screwdriver and then rushed back to the house. His bag was still under his bed where he had stuffed it before going to work the previous night. Working quickly, he unscrewed the cover of the vent, stuffed his bag in there, and carefully reattached the cover. He was fast asleep on his bed long before anyone else got home.

Chapter 33

"Is Billy home yet?" Javier asked Laura as he and Jasmine came in from the garage. He had picked her up immediately after school and spent the afternoon with her while she rode her pony – which she had ended up naming "Puppy".

"Mmm…not yet," Laura replied. She had been busy making dinner, but stopped to rinse her hands and give her husband and daughter a hug and a kiss.

Javier checked his watch. "It's a bit late, isn't it?"

"No, honey," Laura said. "He's in middle school now. He has things to do after school." She looked at her husband curiously. "Why are you so concerned all of a sudden?"

Javier flushed. "I'm not," he protested. "There's a winter baseball tournament coming up, and I was going to see if he and his friends wanted to play in it." He paused and said self-pityingly, "And then I thought we could play catch or something, but Billy's never here, so…"

Laura laughed and slapped him with a hand towel that was on the counter. "Stop being such a baby. He'll be home soon."

Javier pulled his wife in for a quick kiss, and then walked out onto the deck. Closing the sliding glass door behind him, he sat on the chair that was the farthest away from the house. His wife may not have noticed, but Billy had been acting strange lately – quite furtively, to be honest. Javier tried to think back and remember when it had begun.

After the incident with Tom and the beers, Billy had been cold to his parents for a few days. He had accepted his punishment for drinking with aplomb, but he seemed to be the most upset about not being allowed to go to Tom's house anymore. When Javier had pressed him on it, Billy had muttered something about not being his favorite anymore. That little comment had set off warning bells in Javier's head and he had suggested to Laura that they keep a closer eye on Billy over the next few weeks. He wished he could share with her what he now knew about Tom, but he didn't know how to explain it without letting her know about everything else.

After middle school started, Billy gradually mellowed, and he was back to his normal self. He seemed to enjoy his new school, he had a lot of friends, and he was doing well. For three months, everything was how it should have been, but then a couple of weeks ago, Billy started coming home from school later and later. His excuses sounded valid at first – projects, experiments, studying at the library – but Javier was starting to have his doubts.

Without thinking, Javier pulled out his phone and called Tom's house.

"Hello?" Tom answered.

"Tom, this is Javier."

"Oh hey, Javier," Tom said cheerfully. "I haven't talked to you since I bumped into you that one night."

"Listen, is Billy there?" Javier asked.

"Nope," Tom answered, and Javier could hear the smile on his face. "You said Billy wasn't allowed to see me anymore. I haven't seen him for a long time." In the background, Javier could hear laughter.

"Who's over there right now?" Javier demanded.

The laughter immediately cut off. "No one," Tom said quickly. "That was just the television."

"Tom, I swear to God, if you ever…" Javier began before Tom interrupted him.

"Have you been back to The School House lately?" he asked quietly. "I think I've seen you a few times."

Javier swallowed and clenched his jaw. "Tom, I'm not going to repeat myself. If you ever talk to Billy or any of his friends again…"

Tom cut him off and said, "Oops, the commercials are done. I gotta go, Javier. Hopefully, I'll see you around." And with a click, he hung up.

Javier hit the redial button in anger, but only got a busy signal. "Fucking shit!" he growled, staring at his phone. He pushed a button and searched through his phone book. Finding the number he wanted, he quickly dialed it.

After a couple of rings, a young man answered. "Bangarang!"

"This is Javier. Let me talk to Giovanni now!" Javier carefully studied his house. Laura was still in the kitchen making dinner, and he could see Jasmine on the sofa in the living room playing a video game.

"Javier, my friend," said a deep, gravelly voice after a few seconds. "What can I do for you?"

"Giovanni, I need some information about one of your customers."

"Okay," Giovanni said. "Let me get a pen." He paused for a second. "Alright, give me the details."

"His real name is Tom Jackson. He has a brown mustache and brown hair. He's about forty-five years old, slim build. He wears wire-rim glasses. Let's see…if he takes the kids back to his house, then he has a pool which he probably lets them use." He listened to Giovanni scribbling down the information. "If you could talk to your employees and the boys he takes home and find out what he does with them, what he likes, what he tells them, stuff like that."

"Sure, Javier," Giovanni replied. "I'll get back to you in a couple of hours. Can you tell me why you're so interested in this guy?"

Javier took a deep breath, relieved that he fnally had someone to share his worries with. "He coached my son's baseball team, and always had the boys over to his house. I think he's…" Javier hesitated, unable to find the words. "I think him and my son…" Javier took a deep breath and tried to focus.

"I understand," Giovanni said compassionately. "If any of these sick fucks got anywhere near my family, I would kill him. Let me know if you need some help dealing with this later."

"Thanks, Giovanni," Javier said. "I appreciate it."

"No problem. I'll call you soon. Ciao."

"Bye." Javier hung up the phone, feeling slightly better. He knew he should've done this four months ago, but he'd hoped that the problem would go away on its own. He cursed himself for getting soft, as he searched for another number in his phone and dialed.

He waved to Laura through the window as someone said, "Sergeant Frost."

"Hey, James. This is Javier. I need a favor."

"Sure, Mr. Lopez. Anything for you."

"I need any information you have about a Tom Jackson. His phone number is…wait a second." Javier looked at his phone and found Tom's number, which he quickly read off into the phone. "Let me know anything you've got. Supposedly his son died around ten years ago."

"Okay. Got it. Do you want me to call you back at this number?"

"Yep, that's fine," Javier said. Laura slid open the back door and walked over to him. "I have to go. Call me when you get the information." He hung up the phone without waiting for a response.

"Work stuff?" Laura asked, laying down and resting her head upon his chest.

"Yep," Javier said, absently caressing her back. "Just waiting for some specs on a piece of equipment so I can decide if we need it or not."

After a delicious dinner which was mainly dominated by Jasmine, Javier volunteered himself and Billy for dish duty. Billy, who had been sullen and withdrawn all night, sighed in exasperation and heaved himself out of his chair. He picked up some dishes from the table and carried them to the sink, as Laura gave Javier a sympathetic smile and took Jasmine to the living room.

They cleaned off the table in silence, not even making eye contact. When there were only a couple of glasses left on the table, Javier turned on the water and started filling up the sink with soap and water. Billy placed the last two glasses on the counter and impatiently waited for his father to hand him the dishes to be put in the dishwasher.

"How was your day?" Javier asked, handing Billy a handful of wet silverware.

"Okay," Billy replied.

"What'd you do after school? I was looking for you."

Billy looked at his dad cautiously as he grabbed a plate from him. "Why?"

Javier tried to repress his annoyance. "There's a baseball tournament in a few weeks. I wanted to know if you and your friends want to put a team together. We could start practicing soon," Javier said hopefully, feeling uneasy about letting his son see how much it meant to him.

Billy didn't answer at first. He just kept taking dishes silently from his father and putting them in the dishwasher. Finally, without looking at Javier, he said, "I think Coach Tom is going to coach us."

The wineglass that Javier was holding slipped out of his fingers and shattered in the sink. "What?" Javier said, using a tone of voice his son had never heard before. Laura ran into the kitchen to see what had broken, but her question got stuck in her throat when she saw how her son and husband were standing.

"You said I couldn't go to his house. You didn't say he couldn't coach me!" Billy snapped.

"Fine, I'm saying it now. You will have nothing to do with him!" Javier shouted. Laura rushed forward and put her hand on Javier's arm.

"What's going on?" she asked, flinching when she saw the look on her husband's face.

"No!" Billy retorted, turning around and walking off. "You can't say that. He's my coach and my friend. And I don't want YOU coaching me anyway!"

Javier turned to go after his son, but Laura pulled on his arm with all of her weight. "Javier, stop!" she commanded. "What is happening?"

He took a deep breath and glared at his wife. "He says Tom is coaching them for that baseball tournament."

"Oh," Laura said. She thought about it for a moment. "Well, I know you really wanted to do it, but I don't see anything wrong with it."

"Nothing wrong with it?!?" Javier roared, shaking off Laura's hand. "Tom's a...." He bit his tongue and looked away in anger.

"He's a what?" Laura asked. "I know he probably gave them beer, but I don't think he would do that again. Other than that, what's the big deal? He was a good coach and Billy looks up to him."

Javier shook his head and said quietly, "You don't understand."

Laura leaned against Javier's back and put her arms around him. "I do understand," she said. "I know it's hard for you, but Billy still loves you. Tom could never replace you."

Javier opened his mouth to respond, but then closed it, knowing it was useless to argue. He stared out of the window into the night, his mind working frantically.

Giovanni was the first one to call Javier back. When he saw who it was on the caller ID, he got up from the sofa where he and Laura were watching television and told her, "Sorry. I have to take this. It's that work stuff from earlier." She nodded her head distractedly, her attention focused on the television, and Javier stepped out onto the deck.

"Yeah, Giovanni. What have you got for me?"

"Let's see...He likes to have the boys call him "Coach," Giovanni began.

Javier shook his head in disgust. "Yeah, that's him. What do they say about him?"

"I guess he treats them well. He has the same three or four boys that he likes to use again and again. He likes to take photos of them and they often swim naked in his swimming pool."

"Anything else?"

"Nope. Just the usual. As I said, he's a bit gentler with them than other customers. From what the boys said, it almost sounds like he tries to seduce them. He doesn't do anything too kinky."

Javier's mind was racing as he imagined Billy and his friends spending time there. "You said he takes photos, right? Can you see if they know where he keeps them?"

"Just a second. Let me check." Javier heard the sound of the phone being set down, and then Giovanni yelled for someone. Javier walked around the deck, enjoying the cool night air, and waited for Giovanni to respond.

"Hey," Giovanni said.

"I'm here."

"He keeps them in an album underneath the sofa. He likes to show them to the boys. They say he pulls it out almost every time."

Javier gave an inaudible sigh. "Okay. Thanks, Giovanni."

"Hey! Remember what I told you. Just say the word and I'll help you take care of this guy."

"Yep. I appreciate it. Bye."

"Ciao."

Javier leaned back on one of the chaise lounges and stared at the night sky. Remembering things he had learned when he was young, he was able to pick out Orion and Ursa Major, and was looking for the Seven Sisters when his phone rang again, jarring him from his memories.

He saw that it was Sergeant Frost and slowly raised it to his ear, not sure how much more he wanted to hear that night.

"This is Javier," he answered.

"Hi, Mr. Lopez. This is Sergeant Frost."

"Thank you for calling me back so quickly," Javier said. "Did you find anything out?"

"Thomas Arnold Jackson, age forty-three, never married. Does that sound right?" Sergeant Frost asked.

"Sure. I guess so," Javier said. "Is there anything else?"

"He was locked up for about seven years because of statutory rape. There have also been several charges for indecent behavior with a minor, but the charges were all dropped before the cases could go to trial."

"What? Why? And how could he coach a boys' baseball team with those charges?" Javier demanded.

"I don't know. It just says charges got dropped. Is this one of your customers you're asking about?" Sergeant Frost asked.

"No." Javier replied shortly. "What about his son? Does it say anything about how he died?"

"Son?" Sergeant Frost repeated, sounding confused. "He never had a son."

"But he said…" Javier trailed off. "That lying fuck."

Sergeant Frost waited for a few seconds for Javier to continue. As the silence stretched uncomfortably, he cleared his throat and offered, "Is this something you might need my help with, sir?"

Javier shook his head, focusing back on the present. "Nope. You've been a huge help. Thank you, Sergeant."

"My pleasure, Mr. Lopez. Have a good night."

Javier hung up the phone and resisted the urge to throw it against the house in anger. As if sensing his emotional upheaval, Laura got up and slid open the back door. "Is everything okay?" she asked with concern.

"Yep," Javier said. "I just have to make one more phone call."

"Okay." Laura smiled at him as she slid the door shut. "Hurry up, though. They're about to show us who's getting voted off of the show."

Javier waited until the door closed tightly before he called Tom's number.

"Hello?" Tom answered cheerfully.

"Tom, this is Javier. I've been checking up on you. I want you to know…"

Tom interrupted, his voice cold and threatening. "No, I want you to know, you annoying fuck, that you had better stop calling me. You don't know who you're dealing with. I know you, Javier. You're one of those men who pretend you're happily married but you secretly crave the nice tight bum of a little boy. I know what you like, so stop being so high and mighty. You don't know what I can do," he warned.

Javier knew for certain that he was going to kill Tom. He just didn't know when or how. "Are you finished?" he asked.

Tom answered laughed and said, "Billy sure is a handsome boy, isn't he?"

Javier wanted to scream at Tom, threaten him, drive over to his house right then, but he knew that he had to stay in control of himself. He closed his eyes and said quietly, "Goodnight, Tom."

"Goodnight, Javier," Tom replied cheerfully.

Chapter 34

The next evening, Javier waited around the house for as long as he could so that he could try speaking to Billy again. However, Billy never showed up. He usually called if he was going to be late for dinner, but by six-thirty, they still hadn't heard from him.

"I'm sure he's just finishing up that project he's working on," Laura said unconcernedly, as she set the food on the table.

"Did he say which class it was for?" Javier asked.

"Nope," Laura replied. She sat down next to Javier and took his hand. "He's fine. Stop worrying so much." She turned her attention to Jasmine and asked, "Do you want one piece of chicken or two?"

"Two," Jasmine said, reaching across the table and trying to get the food herself.

Javier tried to focus on his wife and daughter during dinner, but his mind kept wandering as he pictured what Billy was doing at that moment. When dinner was finished, he checked his watch, and Laura said, "Didn't you say you had to go into work tonight and deal with a new shipment?"

"Yeah," Javier said regretfully. He kissed her on the cheek and headed for the garage. "I'll be home as soon as I can."

He went out of his way and drove past Tom's house on the way to work. The house was dark and Tom's car wasn't in the driveway. Silently cursing both Billy and Tom, Javier drove to work and parked in his usual parking space. He walked around to the front of the building and didn't notice the small form hunched over in the darkness by the alleyway.

Javier opened the door to The School House and strolled inside. Vikram was sitting at the bar with Yuri. Javier walked over and sat down on a stool next to them as Juan handed him a bottle of water.

A plaintive cry ripped through the bar. "Dad?"

Javier spun around, spilling his water on Yuri. Billy was standing in the doorway, staring at his dad, and then his eyes roamed around the bar, taking in everything.

"Billy?" Javier said in confusion, rising to his feet.

Without warning, Billy spun around and ran out through the front door. Javier glanced wildly at Vikram and then sprinted through the bar. He burst out of the front door, only to see Billy climbing into Tom's waiting car.

Javier jumped down the two stairs and tried to reach the car in time, but he knew it would be in vain. Before he got halfway there, Tom was pulling onto the busy main road. At the last second, he raised his arm out of the driver's side window and waved good-bye to Javier.

Javier screamed in fury and ran to his own car. It took less time than usual, but by the time Javier had pulled out of the alleyway and turned onto the main road, Tom's car was long gone.

Javier drove around aimlessly for the next couple of hours, constantly looking everywhere for Tom's car, but knowing in his heart that he wouldn't be able to find it. He didn't know what to do. He wanted to be able to confide in Laura and share with her about the danger that her son was in, but that would involve a lot of other explanations. He considered lying to her and telling her that Billy had called him and was spending the night at a friend's house, but he knew that the truth would come out eventually. Finally, he admitted to himself that it was time to tell Laura that the man she had married was a lie. He drove slowly to his house.

As he turned down his street, his phone rang. The caller ID said "*Billy*".

Javier sped past his house as he thrust the phone to his ear. "Billy!" he cried. "Where are you?"

Silence greeted him, and after a few seconds, he opened his mouth to speak again. But before he could say anything, he heard Billy whisper, "Dad?"

"Billy! Tell me where you are. I'm going to come get you."

Javier's stomach clenched in fear when he heard Billy start sobbing into the phone. "Please, Billy. Just tell me where you are."

"I'm at a bus stop across the street from the Wilshire Hotel," Billy said, again speaking so quietly that Javier could barely hear him.

"Okay," Javier said, stepping on the gas pedal. "I'll be there in eight minutes. Wait for me!" he commanded.

Billy hung up without saying a word.

Seven minutes later, Javier slammed to a stop in front of the bus stop. Cars screeched to a halt behind him, honking their horns. Javier didn't care. He jumped out of his car and ran around the front of it to the bus stop.

"Billy!" he called out, looking everywhere.

He sighed with relief when he saw Billy walk towards him from a nearby alleyway. He ran towards him and cried, "You're okay!" But when he caught sight of Billy's face, he froze.

Billy wasn't okay. His eyes were red from crying, and he had dark circles under both eyes. His hair was a mess, his shirt was torn, and he was swaying slightly as he staggered towards his father, slightly drunk.

Javier took a couple of cautious steps towards his son. "Oh, Billy," he said sadly, holding out his arms.

Billy pushed his hand away in disgust. "Don't touch me," he said viciously.

Javier recoiled at the sound of his son's voice, and let his arms fall to his side. He turned around and followed Billy back to the car.

After driving in silence for ten minutes, Javier turned off the busy road and headed for a nearby park. The small parking lot was empty at that time of the night, but the car's headlights flashed over some children hanging out on the playground equipment before he shut off the car.

"Billy," Javier said cautiously. "We have to talk."

"What are you going to tell Mom?" Billy asked.

"That depends on you," Javier said. "Do you want to tell me what happened?"

Billy stared straight ahead, tears trickling down his face. He clenched his fists and tensed up his whole body as he fought down the sobs that threatened to overwhelm him. "How could you, Dad?" he finally asked. "How could you do that kind of stuff?"

"Billy. This isn't about me," Javier began, hoping to deflect these kinds of questions until he could decide how to answer them.

"Answer me!" Billy screamed. "How can you touch those boys and kiss them and have sex with them? Is that what you want to do with me?!?"

"What?" Javier exclaimed, surprised and shocked. "No, Billy. You completely misunderstood everything." His mind raced as he tried to think of a suitable explanation for why he was there – he was meeting a friend, he was delivering something, his business deals with them, he...he....

"Then tell me, Dad," Billy cried. "How did Tom know you were going to be there at that bar tonight?"

A lucky guess, Javier thought automatically, but knowing that none of his excuses would answer that question. He sighed and did what he never thought he would have to do – he told the truth to someone in his family. "I own that bar," Javier said, surprised to find his body trembling from nervousness. "I have never ever touched those boys. I love your mother. I am not a sick pedophile like that."

Billy finally looked at his father, obviously wanting to trust him. "I don't believe you," he said doubtfully.

Fuck, he thought. "If you want, we can stop by after we leave here and you can go ask them."

"Fine," Billy said immediately, nodding his head.

"Now tell me what happened," Javier ordered.

"Dad," Billy protested.

"I'm serious, Billy. This is really important. Tell me everything."

Billy sighed and stared at his fingers in his lap as he pressed them together and made little shapes with them. He sighed again and then said, "It started in the summer. At first, it was just normal fun, but after a while, Tom only had four or five of us come over usually." He shook his head at the memory. "We were proud because we were special. We would just swim and have fun, but one day, Tom left some magazines lying around. You know…" Billy hesitated.

"What did they show?" Javier asked quietly.

"Just naked girls. And we looked at them and it was no big deal. But one time he asked us if we wanted to watch a video, and then he played a porno for us, and after that, there was always a movie playing every time we were there." He shrugged and said confusedly, "It was kind of strange. It just became so normal. And then once or twice, we would go skinny dipping in the pool at night, but it was just stupid fun. It was dark and no one could see anything," he said defensively.

"Okay," Javier said. "I understand."

"But at that last barbecue, there were only three of us there at the end, and Tom had given us a beer to celebrate. He said we were men now because we were going to middle school. I didn't really like it, but he kept making us drink. And then, the movie was on, and Tom said, 'Look at his penis. Are your guys' that big?' And we laughed, and then Tom pulled his pants down and showed us his."

Javier shoved the murderous rage that filled him to a small corner of his mind and focused on Billy. "Oh, Billy," he said compassionately, as Billy kept talking, eager to get it out now.

"And then he took down Paul's pants, and me and Matt took ours off, and then Tom pointed at the television and asked us if we had ever tried that. He then put his mouth on

Matt, and…and…" He shuddered as he relived the memory. Javier tried to put his hand on Billy's shoulder, but Billy flinched away. "Matt smiled and said it felt good, and Paul and I got jealous, but then Paul's mom showed up, and we quickly pulled our pants on and came home."

Thank God for Jane, Javier thought. "And did you go see Tom again?" he asked softly.

"No," Billy replied. "You guys said not to, and I was busy with school. But then a couple of weeks ago, Tom called some of the guys and told them about the baseball tournament, and we all agreed to be in it. We had a couple of practices, and Tom would drive some of us back to his house afterwards before dropping us off near our houses." Billy wiped his eyes, his voice becoming more and more monotonous. "Tom showed us his photo album and kept asking us to be in it. Photos of boys naked and stuff. Finally we agreed and…"

"Did he touch you?" Javier asked with concern.

"No." Javier almost cried with relief, until Billy said, "Not then."

"What?" Javier asked softly.

"Today after practice, Tom asked only me if I needed a ride. We went to eat pizza, and he started talking to me about how nice it is for men and boys to be together and how much better it is than with a woman. And he told me to remember how happy Matt was…" Billy paused for a second, before continuing, "Even though, I haven't really seen or talked to Matt for a long time. But Tom kept saying all of these things, and some of those videos and magazines also had men together, and his photos too."

"And then?" Javier pressed.

"I said he was wrong. I talked about you and mom, and he said that you were lying to us, and that you liked boys as well." Javier closed his eyes in pain. "And he told me where to wait and I saw you…" Emotion threatened to overwhelm Billy as tears streamed from his eyes. "I saw you go in there, and that meant that Tom was right. So I got back in the car with him, and we went to the Wilshire Hotel. He told them I was his son and they laughed and said how handsome I was. In the room, he poured me some wine, and we drank for a bit and watched porn on the television, and then he unzipped my pants and he...and he..." Billy swallowed hard and glanced at his father, shame covering his face. "He started sucking me and I just closed my eyes and it felt good, but...but...when it was finished, I felt...I feel so dirty and disgusting and I..." Billy shivered, unable to explain how he felt. He suddenly scrabbled at the door, threw it open, and leaned over and vomited on the ground outside.

Javier reached for a bottle of water from the backseat and handed it to him after he was finished. Billy rinsed out his mouth and spit the water out of the car window. "I'm not gay, am I, Dad?" he asked fearfully. "I really like this girl at school."

"No," Javier said. "You're not. A sick man just took advantage of you. You're not gay because of what happened tonight." He tentatively reached out and patted Billy on the shoulder. When Billy didn't move away, Javier felt his heart break with relief and gently squeezed his son's shoulder. "What happened next?" Javier asked, dreading to hear anymore.

Billy shrugged his shoulders again. "Tom went to the bathroom and I quickly pulled on my pants. He came out and saw me leaving and tried to grab me." Billy pointed to his shirt. "That's how this happened."

"And then you called me," Javier finished softly.

"What are you going to tell Mom?" Billy asked.

Javier had been wondering the same thing. "Do you want her to know?" he asked.

"No!" Billy said quickly. "I don't want anyone to know."

"Okay," Javier agreed. "But maybe it'll be good for you to talk to a professional. Someone who can help you through all of these things you're feeling."

Billy shrugged noncommittally.

"What do you want to do about Tom?" Javier asked him.

"I hate him," Billy said, shuddering again. "When I think of him and the way he smiled at me, I just feel so disgusted and…" He clenched his fists again and couldn't continue.

"I'll take care of it, Billy," Javier vowed. "He'll never bother you again."

Billy nodded his head. He looked over at Javier. "Dad," he said. "I can't go to school tomorrow."

"Okay," Javier said. "I'll tell your mom you're feeling sick, and you and I can stay home all day and play catch and relax."

"Thanks," Billy said quietly.

"Okay, you ready to go home?" Javier asked.

Billy looked at him suspiciously. "I thought you said we could stop by that bar so that you could show me that you're the owner."

Javier nodded his head in resignation as he started the car. "Okay."

The drive to The School House didn't take very long, and no words were spoken as Billy and Javier were both lost in their own thoughts. Pulling into his parking space, the two teenagers jumped to attention from where they were slouching against the wall. "Mr. Lopez," one of them said, both of them glancing with curiosity at Billy as he climbed out of the passenger door.

"I won't be long," Javier said. "You know what to do."

"Yes, sir," they both replied.

Javier led Billy into The School House, and held the door open behind him. As soon as he entered, Vikram ran over from the bar and said, "Javier! I thought you wanted to meet the new…" He trailed off when he saw Billy slink in behind Javier. "Who's this?" he asked.

"Vikram, this is my son, Billy." He stepped back and let Billy and Vikram look at each other. "Please answer all of his questions honestly, so that we can get out of here and go home."

"Okay," Vikram replied. "What do you want to know, Billy?"

Billy pointed at Javier. "Who's my dad?"

"Javier Lopez." Vikram glanced at Javier, who nodded his head and said, "Tell him everything he wants to know."

"Javier Lopez," Vikram said again. "He is the owner of this bar and he is my boss."

"Does he touch the boys who work here?"

The shock on Vikram's face was answer enough. "No! He would never do that."

Billy shoulders slumped with relief and he looked away from Vikram and studied the room. He saw the boys playing games and sitting on the laps of the customers. Javier tried to follow his gaze with his own eyes and winced at how it must look to someone who'd never seen it before.

He cursed quietly as remembered what he had forgotten to do. He pulled out his phone and dialed a number. "Giovanni," he said when the person answered.

"Javier," Giovanni replied in good humor. "You call me more often than my wife does."

"That man I asked you about earlier. Could you please call me the next time he stops by? I need to find him."

"Of course," Giovanni said, suddenly serious. "Did something happen?"

"My son," Javier said, not wanting to say too much in front of Vikram or Billy.

Giovanni growled, "Then I would be honored if you would let me help you."

"Thank you, Giovanni," Javier said sincerely. "I appreciate it." He hung up the phone and looked at Billy and Vikram.

"What was that about?" Vikram asked in confusion.

"Was that about Tom?" Billy asked at the same time.

Javier ignored Vikram and looked at Billy. "Yes."

"Can I come too when it happens?" Billy asked.

Javier studied his son's face, regretting everything that had happened that day. "We will see," he hedged.

"Please," Billy insisted.

Javier sighed and said, "Fine. If you still want to come later, then you can." He turned to Vikram and said, "We'll deal with the newbies tomorrow. I have to take Billy home now." He turned and walked with Billy out of The School House.

Billy was silent on the drive home, and Javier wondered what he was thinking about. As they pulled into the garage, Billy looked at Javier and said, "You know what, Dad? I think – because of you – that all of the boys who work in your bar feel the way I do right now. I think that makes you a hundred times worse than someone like Tom." Billy held his father's gaze for a heartbeat before opening his door and climbing out of the car.

Javier stared blankly into the space his son had just vacated. He gripped the steering wheel tightly, wanting to yell at Billy that it wasn't the same thing, and that what he did paid for everything they had, and...Javier felt his son's revulsion wash over him like a tailwind as his son exited the garage, and his hands fell to his lap as he began sobbing like a baby.

Chapter 35

The following day, Billy stayed in his room until late afternoon. Javier checked on him frequently to make sure that he was okay, but Billy appeared to be sleeping and so Javier just let him be. After an unenthusiastic round of catch in the evening, Javier was grilling hamburgers on the deck in the backyard while Billy watched him from a chaise lounge.

Breaking the silence, Billy blurted out, "Can I have your knife?"

Javier made a show of concentrating on the burgers, reluctant to answer. Finally, he said, "I'm not sure if you should have it yet."

"But you said you had one when you were my age," Billy reminded him.

"Yes," Javier said slowly, "but I grew up differently than you. It was a lot tougher and there were a lot of people I had to defend myself against."

Billy waited only a second before saying bitterly, "Did you ever have a man molest you?"

Javier closed his eyes in pain and set the spatula down. He reached into his pocket and pulled out the knife. He turned around, walked over to Billy, and handed it to him. "Don't tell your mother," he warned.

"There are a lot of things I can't tell Mom about," Billy said, repeatedly flicking the knife open and closed. He pulled it close to his face and studied the blade. "How do I make this sharper?" he asked.

"Billy, I'll show you later," Javier said sternly. "Put it away for now. Your mom and Jasmine are in the kitchen." He stared at Billy until he complied, and then went back to flipping the burgers.

After dinner, Javier left to go to work, promising Laura that he would be home as soon as possible, and promising Billy that he would let him know if he heard any news about Tom. He felt like all of the secrets were piling up and that they would soon come crashing down like an avalanche, but he had no idea what he could do to fix everything.

Vikram was waiting for him at the bar. When Javier grabbed his bottle of water from Juan, Vikram asked, "Can you look over the two new boys now?"

"Yeah, I have time," Javier said. "Bring them to my office." He glanced around the bar as he walked to the stairs, trying to see it through Billy's eyes, and he cringed at what Billy must think of him. He slowly trudged up the stairs to his office, lost in thought.

A few minutes later, Vikram hurried in with two boys, both around ten years old. He placed them carefully in front of Javier's desk and stood behind the first boy. Javier distractedly waved his hand which Vikram assumed meant he should start introducing the boys.

"This one is ten years old," Vikram said, placing his hands on the small black boy in front of him. "His name is Michael. He was one of the best students in his class, and his parents only wanted six hundred." He paused and waited for Javier to ask a question. When he didn't, Vikram tried to answer the questions Javier should've asked. "Um, he has good teeth and clear skin. His parents are both tall, so he should grow quickly. He seems good-natured and speaks well for his age."

Javier looked up from his desk and suddenly focused his attention on Michael.

Finally, Vikram thought with relief, waiting for a question.

Javier looked at the other boy and studied him carefully as well. Vikram cautiously stepped behind him and waited for Javier to say something.

"Okay. They can go," Javier said, with a wave of his hand.

"But…" Vikram started to protest, but years of working with Javier had taught him better. He swallowed and said, "Okay. Thanks."

Vikram put his hands on the boys' shoulders and pushed them towards the door. As Vikram exited the office, Javier said, "Vikram, stay for a second." Vikram poked the boys in their backs and told them to return to the room, and then he went to stand in front of Javier's desk.

"You started out like them, didn't you, Vikram?" Javier asked thoughtfully.

Vikram hesitated for a second, stunned by the question. "Uh…yeah. It was before I started working for you, but…yeah."

"Do you think it's wrong what we do?" Javier asked.

Vikram took a deep breath and said, "You want me to be honest?"

Javier nodded his head as he took a sip of water.

"It's what we do. There is no right or wrong. There's only the strong and everyone else."

"But if we stopped doing it and tried to change…" Javier said, struggling to find the words.

"Then someone else would take over and do what we do, and they would make the money, and maybe treat the boys even worse," Vikram said. "There's always someone else waiting to take over."

Javier leaned back in his chair and scratched his head in frustration. "After what happened to Billy yesterday, I realized that all of these village rats are probably the same as Billy with their own families that worry about them."

Vikram scoffed. "Their families sold their own kids for money."

"But we told them we were taking them to a school," Javier argued. Vikram shook his head in disagreement, but

Javier had a flash of inspiration. "Maybe we could change, and we could start a school for these boys. I know people on the city council who could help us become official."

"A school?" Vikram repeated in disbelief. "Javier, how would you make money then? What would you do about the boys in Bangarang and The Poker and all of the other places? You can't save everyone. If you want to be fair, then start giving the boys their tip money back and let them leave after they've worked off their debt, or maybe help them get work or go to school after they finish here, but what you're talking about right now is…" Vikram bit his tongue before he could say the word 'crazy'.

Instead of being angry, though, Javier was nodding his head. "Maybe we could do things a bit more humanely. There's no reason why we can't be kinder to them, I suppose." He chewed his lip thoughtfully. "And we could still open up a school for them, right?"

Vikram sighed and shook his head. "They would still be having sex with men every night," he pointed out.

"Fuck!" Javier said, pounding his fist on his desk in frustration. Suddenly, his cell phone rang. He reached into his pocket and saw that the caller ID was blocked. "Who is this?" he answered.

"Javier! It's Giovanni. Your friend just walked in."

Javier grinned so fiercely that Vikram felt a twinge of fear. "Thanks. I'll be over in a couple of minutes." He hung up the phone as he pushed back his chair to stand up. "The pervert who touched Billy is at Bangarang," Javier said to Vikram. He walked around and put his hand on Vikram's shoulder. "I trust you more than anyone, Vikram, and I need your help tonight. We'll finish talking about how to make things better later, okay?"

Vikram nodded his head, surprised by Javier's intimacy. "Sure…of course, Javier." Javier spun around and Vikram had to rush to keep up with him.

Javier slammed open the front doors to Bangarang and stalked into the bar, with Vikram trailing a few feet behind him. It was set up pretty similar to The School House, except

Giovanni had a few giant birdcages hanging from the ceiling scattered around the room. Locked inside of them were young boys wearing only white underwear as they reclined on white pillows and blankets and deigned who to talk to and who to ignore.

Tom was sitting at the bar with his hand on the leg of a boy around Billy's age. He seemed to sense Javier approaching, and turned casually to look at him. His face broke into a huge grin when he recognized Javier.

"Oh, man, Javier," Tom crowed. "I did not know that you were this stupid. How dare you follow me in here and think you can start something?"

Javier slowed to a walk and cautiously approached Tom as he studied the bartender behind the bar and then glanced at the stairs to his left.

"Do you realize that I'm a V.I.P. here?" Tom said louder. He stood up from his stool and stepped towards Javier. "You have made a huge mistake!" he warned Javier. Turning back to the bar, Tom spoke to the bartender and said, "Brenden! Throw this trash out of here. He's bothering me."

Brenden gazed at Javier for a split second, and then walked around the bar. He was huge, even bigger than Javier. From the side door, another man who was about the same size approached them. Tom glanced over his shoulder at Javier with a smile, waiting to see how he would respond.

Javier's lip quivered for an instant, as if he was fighting hard not to smile. He looked towards the stairs, and then without saying a word, he walked over and greeted the man coming down them with a hug and a kiss on each cheek. Tom's face grew pale and he nervously eyed Brenden and the other man who were standing behind him.

"Javier, my oldest friend," Giovanni boomed, and the whole bar stopped for a second to see who the boss was talking to.

"Giovanni," Javier said. "Thank you for the phone call." He turned around and he and Giovanni started walking slowly towards Tom.

Tom leaped out of his stool and took a step towards them, but Brenden quickly grabbed his arm and threw him back down.

"Mr. Delvecchio!" Tom called out anxiously.

Giovanni didn't say a word as they approached to within three feet of Tom.

"Mr. Delvecchio," Tom said again. "I'm so glad you're here. That man is harassing me in your bar."

Giovanni gazed at Tom with a look of disgust on his face. Without taking his eyes off of Tom, he said to Javier, "Is this true?"

"Of course not," Javier said calmly. "I haven't spoken to this man tonight."

Tom swallowed hard as they both continued to stare at him. He quickly glanced behind him, and gave a yelp of pain as Brenden tightened his grip on his arm.

"On the other hand, Giovanni," Javier said quietly, the pain and anger evident in his voice, "this man touched my son, took naked photos of him and his friends, and sucked his dick last night, and now Billy's pretty fucked up."

"Is this true?" Giovanni asked Tom with the same tone he had asked Javier a few seconds before. Fear bloomed on Tom's face and he jumped up, only to have Brenden slam him down again.

"You've made a huge mistake," Giovanni said softly. "Why would you touch one of our boys when we give you..." he motioned disdainfully at the bar... "these to play with?"

"I didn't know!" Tom protested.

Giovanni murmured rapidly and quietly to Brenden and the other man. "Take him out back. Tie his hands and feet behind him, tape his mouth, and put a hood on him. Throw him in the back of my car, and cover him with a couple of blankets. When you're finished, come back to work."

"Yes, sir!" Brenden said, quickly dragging a stunned Tom out the side door. He opened his mouth to yell, but was gone before he even had the chance.

Javier shook Giovanni's hand. "Thanks," he said. "Are you sure you want to finish it? We could do it no problem."

"I'm sure," Giovanni replied. "I enjoy things like this from time to time."

Javier kept his face blank, realizing that this was one difference between him and Giovanni. Personally, he didn't enjoy this kind of stuff. "Okay," Javier said. He paused to think for a second and then said, "My boy wants to be a part of this. How about Vikram and I go pick him up, and we'll meet you somewhere?"

Giovanni nodded. "Take the highway east out of the city. Get off at exit one forty-three. Then take your first right and then the first left. I'll be waiting down that dirt road."

Javier glanced at Vikram who nodded in understanding. "Okay," Javier replied. "We'll see you there." Javier quickly left with Vikram following him, anxious to get this over with, but still uneasy about bringing Billy along.

Chapter 36

Javier slowed down when he saw Giovanni's SUV parked on the side of the road in front of him. He pulled in behind it, only for Giovanni to turn his headlights on and start driving off slowly. He stuck his arm out of the window and waved for Javier to follow him. After a couple of minutes, he put on his right blinker and turned into a trail that Javier doubted he would've even noticed in the daytime. The trees seemed to press in closer and closer on each side as the incessant jarring of the trail got worse. Without warning, the rough trail ended and they entered a smooth clearing among the trees.

Javier left the headlights on as they climbed out of his car and walked towards Giovanni, who had already dragged Tom from his car and dropped him onto the ground. Javier, Billy, and Vikram quietly stood in a circle around a hooded Tom, whose arms were tied behind his back with duct tape, as were his feet. Javier reached down and yanked off the pillow case. Tom thrashed his head back and forth, his mouth duct taped shut, and his eyes rolled wildly as he tried to focus on something to comfort him.

He didn't find it.

He first looked at Giovanni, Javier, and Vikram, and his throat made a small whimpering sound as he stared into their merciless faces. His attention swung to the person standing near his feet. The fear disappeared briefly from his eyes when he saw Billy's face, and he made a sound of recognition. Billy's expression didn't waver, however, and

Tom's eyes were drawn to his right hand, where Billy was constantly flicking open and closing a switchblade knife.

Giovanni was the first one to kick him as Tom's body heaved with panic, and the rest of the men – including Billy – immediately followed suit. After a minute of this, everyone stopped, breathing heavily. Tom lay on his side, tears streaming from his closed eyes, and he noisily tried to breathe through his nose as the occasional snot bubble formed.

"You have plans for that knife, boy?" Giovanni asked Billy, reaching into his pocket and bringing out his own knife.

Billy hadn't looked away from Tom. He stared at him with a mixture of revulsion and hatred written across his face. He licked his lips and whispered, "I want to take his pants off."

Vikram looked at the others and quickly kneeled on Tom's chest and stomach. He reached down and unbuttoned his pants as Giovanni and Billy started pulling them down. Javier watched his son intently, ignoring Tom's moans.

Giovanni stepped back once Tom's pants were past his knees, but Billy bent forward again and pulled down the front of his underpants until they were below the balls.

"Billy," Javier warned, as Billy started breathing faster and faster. "I don't know if you want to…"

Before he could finish, Billy quickly grabbed Tom's penis and sliced it off at the base. Tom's body spasmed in pain, almost dislodging Vikram, as blood gushed from the stump that was left.

"Billy!" Javier shouted, stepping forward. But before he could stop him, Billy had thrown away the penis and stabbed Tom in the scrotum and again in his lower abdomen. Blood came pouring out as Javier stepped over the body and grabbed the arm that was holding the knife. He reached under Billy's armpit with his other hand and lifted him up. "Let go of the knife," he whispered. "Let go of it, Billy."

Billy squeezed the knife with all his might for a second, before relaxing his hand and letting it fall to the ground next to Tom. Billy began sobbing into his dad's chest.

Javier stepped to the side, swinging Billy with him, and said over his shoulder, "Can you guys finish him?"

"Yep," Giovanni said. It was as if time had stopped for a second, but Tom's unceasing moans suddenly filled Javier's ears and he hoped Vikram and Giovanni would hurry up.

He saw Vikram stand up out of the corner of his eye, and then suddenly Giovanni leaped down and repeatedly stabbed Tom in the chest and stomach. His moans grew louder and higher-pitched as Giovanni grunted and laughed with each thrust.

"Vikram!" Javier hissed. "Do it!"

Vikram reached into his pocket and flicked out a knife. He quickly knelt behind Tom's head, reached down, and slashed his throat. A few seconds later, silence filled the clearing, and Javier could hear the chirping of insects in the forest around them. He turned around, still holding Billy tight against his chest and saw Giovanni for the first time. His face and shirt had been splattered with blood, and he looked like a demon from hell at the edge of the dim light from Javier's headlights.

"Giovanni," Javier said, keeping his voice steady. "You have some blood on your face."

Giovanni looked up at Javier, his eyes filled with an emotion that actually frightened Javier. Giovanni slowly licked his lips, and then stood up, took off his shirt, and wiped his face with it.

"What should we do with the body?" Vikram asked.

"Throw it in the woods over there," Giovanni said, still breathing heavily. "The animals will eat it before anyone finds it." He reached into the backseat of his car and pulled out a clean shirt. "Check his pockets first," he suggested. "We don't want to leave any ID on him."

Vikram nodded his head and rummaged through Tom's pockets. He pulled out a wallet and a ring of keys. Tossing them next to the knife Billy had dropped, he grabbed Tom by his shirt collar and dragged him backwards into the trees. When he returned a couple of minutes later, everyone was already in their cars, waiting for him. Giovanni waved him over, and he climbed into the front seat of his car so that Javier could drive Billy home. On the way back to The School House, Vikram shared with Giovanni the conversation he and Javier had had earlier that night.

Chapter 37

Tavi spent every moment he could with Kurt and Kyle and the rest of their friends. Every morning, he would rush from wherever he had spent the night and get to the park as soon as possible, but at least two of their gang were always there before him, calmly waiting on the swings or the slide or the seesaw, and they would hop up with a smile and let him follow them around. The majority of the time it was Kurt and Kyle, but occasionally one of them was replaced by Byron or Chloe, and on one occasion, it had only been him, Chloe, and Byron, which had been a nice change.

Tavi tried to get Mac to come meet them as much as possible, but after the first few times, Mac stopped showing up. No one else really seemed to mind, since Mac had been getting quieter and more morose as the weeks went by, but Tavi was beside himself with worry and didn't know how to help his friend.

Mac was perpetually drugged up, and the Mac that Tavi knew was slowly disappearing. He would take a pill in the evening and then some brown paste at night to help him sleep. He would wake up in the morning and take another pill, usually stay with the customer until noon, and then come home, take the brown paste, and sleep until it was time to go to work. He was becoming so thin and fragile-looking that even Vikram had stopped by their house one day to talk to him about it, but it hadn't made any difference.

One day, Tavi came back to the house in the late afternoon, filled with joy. Kyle had let him help jump a boujie boy for the first time, and he'd been allowed to keep one of the schoolbooks they had found in his bag. Kurt and Kyle had both laughed at him when he had asked if he could take it, and said that he could always have all of the schoolbooks if they could have everything else. Tavi had laughed along with them, but had still clung to the book and read it the whole way home.

As he walked down the alleyway to the house, Mac popped out from around the corner and whispered loudly, "Tavi!"

Tavi looked up in surprise, his attention still focused on his book. "Hey, Mac," he said with pleasure. "It's good to see that you're up and awake this early."

Mac gave a wan smile and motioned for Tavi to come with him. "I have something I need to show you," he said. He started walking away from the house, and Tavi wondered where they were going. Mac led him into the bathroom they used to use when they were stuck in the circle room.

"What are we doing in here?" Tavi asked.

Mac walked straight towards the far right urinal, used the wall to help him climb on top of it, and stood up straight, stretching his arms above him. He gently lifted the tile, and reached into the hole towards the closest corner. After feeling around for a second, he smiled and pulled his hand back down, holding a bag with a string tied around the top.

"What is it?" Tavi asked.

Mac shook it, and the jingle of silver told Tavi that it was Mac's money bag. Mac gave Tavi a warm smile and put it back from where he had taken it. He slid the ceiling tile back into place and hopped down to the floor.

"I just wanted you to see where I kept it," Mac said. He had a sad look in his eye and Tavi knew that something important wasn't being said.

"Why?" Tavi asked.

"So that you can have it in case anything happens to me," Mac said simply. He slipped past Tavi and walked out of the bathroom.

Tavi spun around and grabbed Mac by the shoulder. "What do you mean in case anything happens to you?!?"

Mac shrugged and said softly, "You know how you get that feeling when you're going to die soon and the world is just a dark place and there's nothing you can do to stop it?"

"No!" Tavi shouted. "I don't."

"Well, I do."

Tavi dropped his hand in defeat, not knowing what to say. "Mac," he began. "You just have to not take the brown stuff so much or the pills." He studied Mac's face and added, "And you should come with me to meet the others. They've been asking about you."

Mac smiled the same sad smile and Tavi wished he could smash it off his face. "Maybe you're right," Mac said. "I'll try." He patted Tavi affectionately on the shoulder and walked slowly back to their house while Tavi constantly peeked at him from the corner of his eye.

And Mac did try. He met up with Tavi and Kurt and Kyle at the park the next two days in a row, and then three days the following week. But after that, he stopped showing up, and they continued to roam the city without him.

Tavi would rush home each day to tell Mac about what he had missed, and to try to get him enthused about something again. Each day, Tavi would have to shake Mac to wake him up, and Mac would spend the next half hour or so in a fugue state, blinking at the world around him with bleary eyes.

Tavi was late getting back the last night he ever spent in that house. Kyle wanted Tavi to meet Pastor Mike that day at the church, but they had gotten distracted by a boujie walking alone, and by the time they had realized what time it was, Tavi was already behind schedule.

He ran straight to the bathroom and took a shower. After drying off and getting dressed, he checked the cheap watch a customer had once bought him and realized he had to be in the bar in ten minutes. Running back into their rooms, Tavi leaped towards the bed he usually slept in and slid the book he had stolen that day under the pillow. Only then did he notice that Mac was still in bed.

"Mac!" he shouted, shaking him vigorously. "Mac, wake up! It's time for work!" Mac's head flopped around loosely. When Tavi stopped shaking him, his face was tilted towards Tavi and he could see that Mac's eyes were half open.

He leaned down in alarm and pressed his cheek against Mac's nose, hoping to feel his breath. Instead, he smelled the overwhelming scent of the brown paste. Carefully lifting apart his lips, Tavi saw that Mac's entire mouth was coated in the stuff.

Tavi let go of Mac's lips and slapped him on the face. "MAC!" he screamed. When there was no response, Tavi looked around frantically, but he was all alone. Jumping up from the bed, he ran out of the room and into the bar, screaming hysterically, "Someone, please help!!! Mac's not moving! I think he's dead!!!! PLEASE!!!! SOMEONE HELP!!!!!!"

Chapter 38

After Tavi led Vikram and Yuri to Mac's body, they held him down and forced his mouth open so that they could rub the brown paste in his mouth. He attempted to spit it out, but fell asleep into a dreamless state against his will. He woke up slowly the next morning, his head pounding and his mouth coated with a vile, bitter substance. As the previous night's events permeated through his consciousness, he closed his eyes and rolled over to look at Mac's bed, praying that it was only a dream.

Mac's body was gone, but the perfectly made bed was enough of a surreal touch to convince Tavi that it was real. None of the boys ever made their beds. Tavi curled up into a ball and sobbed quietly into his pillow, as little moments with Mac played across his mind like scenes from a movie. However, he kept hearing one sentence repeated over and over in the background of every scene – *"You know how you get that feeling when you're going to die soon?"*

"He knew he was going to die," Tavi whispered. But then he remembered how much brown paste was in his mouth, and about all of the pills that Mac had been saving up, and Tavi knew – Mac had killed himself on purpose.

He rolled over onto his back, momentarily hating Mac for leaving him all alone. It wasn't that he didn't know the other boys, but he didn't trust them like he had trusted Mac. He lay on his back, his eyes randomly roaming over the ceiling until they came to rest upon the vent on the wall. He stared at it blankly for a long time.

When he finally blinked his eyes and came back to the present, nothing had ever been more obvious than what he now knew – he couldn't stay here any longer. If he didn't leave soon, then there was a chance that he could become hopeless like Mac, or confused like Sven and Francois, or even heartless like Yuri seemed to have become. And Tavi refused to become like those people. He wanted to be the same person he was a year ago, before Yuri and Vikram had come to his village, before Will and Mac and Chouji were dead, before he'd had sex with hundreds of men.

Tavi felt his eyes growing teary again as he mourned everything that had happened over the last year. Wiping them away angrily, he made a vow to himself that he would never let anyone control his life like that again.

He rolled off of the bed and dug deep between the mattress and the box springs. After a few seconds of floundering around, he felt the screw driver and pulled it out. He jumped up on the nearest bed to unscrew the cover to the vent. After it swung down, hanging by the bottom right screw, Tavi grabbed his bag and sat back down on his bed. He reached under the pillow and stuffed the book that he had stolen the previous day into his bag. Looking around for a place to hide it, Tavi sighed and put it back in the vent, this time only screwing in the top left screw a couple of turns. If need be, he could unscrew it with his fingers and have his bag within a couple of seconds.

Tavi checked his watch, wondering if he should run away now or wait until the next morning. Seeing that it was already half past noon, Tavi decided that one more night would be worth the extra three hours he would have to escape before anyone noticed that he was missing. He jumped down from the bed, stuck the screwdriver into his pocket, and ran to where Mac had kept his money. If he hurried, then he should be able to make it in plenty of time before the boys from the circle room used it.

Once inside the bathroom, Tavi shut the door and slid a trashcan in front of it to alert him if anyone tried entering. He tried to emulate the way Mac had climbed to the top of the urinal, but he kept slipping and his respect for Mac grew a little bit. He finally managed to balance on top of the urinal, lifted the ceiling tile, and felt around until he found Mac's bag of money. Without counting it, he hopped down quickly, shoved it into waistband of his pants, and ran out of the bathroom.

As soon as he exited, someone grabbed him and threw him against the wall. He gasped at the impact and found himself face to face with Yuri.

"What are you doing in there, Tavi?" Yuri asked curiously. His eyes wandered from Tavi's face down to his pants, and they narrowed slightly at the bulge protruding from Tavi's groin.

"I...uh…" Tavi thought as quickly as he could. "I had a terrible dream that Mac died and I'm trying to find him. Have you seen him?" Tavi asked hopefully.

Yuri's expression softened and he took a step back. "Mac really is dead," Yuri told him. "He took about fifty pills last night and a fistful of paste."

"What?" Tavi cried in disbelief. "I thought it was just a dream." He pictured Mac's smiling face, and tears actually started welling up.

"I'm sorry," Yuri said, turning to walk away. "Go back to the rooms."

Tavi did as he was told and ran as fast as he could. He sat there breathing heavily for thirty minutes until he was sure that Yuri hadn't followed him. He left the rooms again, casually looking to his left as he turned right. Without hurrying, he walked to the dumpster where he had hidden his money. Each time he turned a corner, he glanced behind him to see if anyone was following him. There was never anyone there.

Confident that he was alone, Tavi squatted behind the dumpster and pulled out the brick. He reached in to grab his money, but all he felt was more brick. He forced his body between the wall and the dumpster so that he could look. His eyes told him what he already knew – someone had taken his money.

He spent the rest of the day in a daze, unable to comprehend what had happened. There had been close to one hundred talents in there and now it was all gone. He didn't take off the pants with Mac's money stuffed in them for the rest of the evening. When he went to work, Tavi smiled and flirted as well as he ever had before, and by nine o'clock, one of the men was already paying Juan his bar fine. As they stepped outside to go to the man's hotel, Tavi said quickly, as if suddenly remembering, "Oh…I forgot my bag. Can I go get it real fast?"

"Sure," the man, sliding his hand down Tavi's back and patting him on his butt. "Hurry back!"

Tavi ran to the rooms, knowing they would be empty. He leaped over the sofa and ran across the beds with his shoes on. Reaching up, he quickly unscrewed the top left screw, letting the vent cover swing down. Tavi pulled out the bag, opened it up, and threw Mac's money inside. He swung it over his shoulder and ran back outside. When he got back to the man, he had been gone less than two minutes.

"That was fast," the man said, smiling at Tavi.

Tavi smiled back. "I missed you," he said, as he reached for the man's hand so they would walk down the street holding hands together.

The pill Tavi took that night left him feeling jittery when it wore off, and he was only able to catch a few minutes of sleep off and on throughout the night. When his watch said eight o'clock, and the room was dimly lit from the sunlight shining around the edges of the curtains, Tavi slowly rolled out of bed, doing his best not to wake the man up.

He whispered a curse when he banged his knee into the corner of the bed, but he finally found his pants on the floor and bent down to pick them up. While he was leaning over, he saw his t-shirt under the bed, and grabbed that as well. When he stood up, the man was sitting two feet away from Tavi on the bed, with a look of displeasure upon his face.

"Where do you think you're going?" he asked.

"Nowhere," Tavi exclaimed. He set his clothes on the foot of the bed, and crawled back towards his pillow.

"Wait!" said the man, reaching over and grabbing something from his bedside table. "Stay like that. I like you in that position!"

Tavi groaned inside of his head. This was the last thing he wanted. Suddenly, he felt the now familiar sensation of a finger pushing lubricant into his anus. He gritted his teeth and cried out in pain as the man gripped his hips and started thrusting. Tavi tried to think about something else, and started naming all of the sky train stations in order in his mind. From somewhere in the back of his mind, he noticed the man speeding up and prayed that it would be over soon.

He abruptly felt air rush into his stinging anus which seemed to be as wide as a canyon. The man ripped off his condom, hopped forward, grabbed Tavi's head, and shoved his penis into his mouth. Tavi tasted the disgusting blend of the man's penis and the rubber from the condom. The man refused to let go of Tavi's head and moved it back and forth repeatedly until he thrust too far and Tavi gagged.

The man did it again, as he started moaning and crying out. Suddenly, Tavi felt the warm, bitter semen shooting against the back of his mouth. "Swallow it," the man groaned, holding Tavi's still. "Swallow it all, you little bastard." He put his other hand on Tavi's throat and gently started massaging it up and down.

Tavi had no choice and gulped as quickly as he could, hoping the man would pull back so that he could breathe. When the man felt Tavi swallow, he pulled himself out of Tavi's mouth and fell back onto the bed, breathing heavily. "Wasn't that good?" the man asked proudly.

Tavi couldn't lie anymore. He could feel and taste the semen in his mouth and on the back of his throat, and the texture and flavor of the man were everywhere inside of his mouth. Curling his lip up in disgust, Tavi ran into the bathroom, shut the door, and repeatedly gargled and brushed his teeth for ten minutes. He then climbed into the shower and let the hot water wash over him for what seemed like an eternity. When his skin was finally numb from the water beating upon it, Tavi scrubbed himself with soap and a wash cloth until he finally felt clean on the outside. After he dried off, he stood in front of the mirror naked, and saw what looked like a normal, innocent fourteen year old boy. He reached for the nearest thing he could find, which was the complimentary shampoo bottle, and threw it at his reflection in the mirror.

He stomped out of the bathroom, only to find the man lying on his side, facing the bathroom, with a smile upon his face. "Finally!" the man said. "I thought you had died in there."

Mac is dead, you asshole! Tavi thought, squeezing his eyes shut for moment.

He glared at the man, beyond angry for making him think of Mac. Tavi scooped up his underwear and put them on. He then walked to the foot of the bed and quickly pulled on his pants. "Wait!" the man said, sitting up. "What do you think you're doing? You can't leave yet."

"Yes I can," said Tavi, pulling on his shirt. "You don't own me."

The man stood up angrily and approached Tavi, his penis flopping before him. Tavi stuck his hand into his pocket, and when the man was a couple of feet away, Tavi pulled out the screwdriver and stuck it in the man's belly button. The man froze and gasped in surprise.

"If you say anything else, I promise I'll stab you," Tavi said. He pressed the screwdriver a bit deeper into the man's belly, and a trickle of blood ran down his stomach. "You have two seconds to turn around and lock yourself in the bathroom. Ready? One…" Before Tavi could say 'two', the man stumbled backwards, spun around, and locked himself in the bathroom. Tavi wiped the tip of the screwdriver on the bed as he glanced around the room. He saw his bag next to his shoes by the door, and he hurried over to get them.

He didn't notice the man's pants, though, and he tripped over them just enough for him to lose his balance for a second. Cursing out loud, he stepped over them before being struck with an inspiration. Throwing guilty glances at the bathroom door, Tavi searched through his pockets until he found the man's wallet. Pulling it open, he quickly grabbed the cash that he could see, and then stuffed the wallet back into the man's pants. Without bothering to count the money, Tavi shoved it into his back pocket, slipped on his shoes, picked up his bag, and ran out the door.

Within ten minutes, Tavi was on the sky train and heading towards the park. At that time on a Saturday morning, the sky train was mostly empty, and the only other person in the car with him was an old lady. Tavi pulled the money that he had stolen from the man out of his back pocket.

One hundred and fifty talents and all paper money! He counted it three times to make sure that he wasn't adding an extra hundred somewhere. That was more money than he had lost from his stolen savings.

He then pulled Mac's money bag out of his bag and carefully opened it up. Lying on top was the plastic bag full of his lost money. Inside of it was a note. Tavi pulled it out of Mac's bag, glanced back in to make sure Mac's money was still there, and then took the note out of the plastic bag.

Tavi,

I'm sorry I took your money. Hopefully I'll have the chance to tell you about this before you notice it missing, but I have a feeling that things may be ending soon, and so I'm writing you this letter.

Today I found Brent digging around the dumpster where you hid your money. He had been climbing inside of the dumpster – that idiot – and hadn't had the time (or the brains) to check the wall. I threw a piece of brick at him and hit him in the face, so the next time you see him, ask him where he got that cut on his forehead.

Anyways, I figure your money will be safer with mine. I promise you that nothing is missing. I didn't even bother to count your measly 102 talents.

Tavi, I don't know how much longer I can go on. My waking hours are living nightmares, and when I sleep at night, I just relive everything the drugs are supposed to block out. I can't do anything anymore without feeling men's bellies pressing against my back, or men licking me and kissing me, or sticking things up my ass. I hate myself, Tavi. My family is counting on me to get an education and a good job so that I can take care of them, but I've become a drug addicted whore. I can't even look at myself in the mirror anymore with shuddering at everything I've done.

Each morning when I wake up, I look at the pills that I've saved, and I wonder what would happen if I took all of them at once. Would it take away the pain forever? Would I finally be able to rest and not feel dirty and ashamed anymore? Would I be able to me again?

I know now that I'm going to do it. I'm sorry, Tavi, for leaving you. You're the best friend I've ever had, and you're the one who has helped me last for as long as I have. Please use my money and escape as soon as you can – before it is too late for you as well. You have a gift, Tavi. Your willingness to help those around you gives them hope, and you should use that gift and help others like us.

I'm sorry I'm not strong enough to help you.

Your friend,

Mac

Tavi carefully folded up the letter and put it inside of Mac's money bag. He then placed the money bag inside of his sack and rested his head against it as a pillow. He stared thoughtfully out of the window at the early morning sun reflecting off the tiny waves on the river and wondered what he was going to do.

Chapter 39

Tavi had the entire playground to himself, and he spent the next hour familiarizing himself with the rest of the park that he had never explored, looking for a safe place to hide and sleep. He found several thick bushes which he thought he could maybe squeeze under, but he didn't relish the thought of trying to live there. In the distance, he noticed one of the bridges that crossed over the river, and he wondered if anyone slept under there.

Disappointed with what he considered a wasted morning, he made his way back to the playground and was happy when he saw the top of someone's head on the other side of the slide. He hurried around with a smile on his face, only to stop short when Pablo turned and fixed his gaze upon him.

Out of the five children who hung out at the park, Pablo was the only one he didn't feel comfortable around. He had only seen him a couple of times since the night they had first met, and each time, Kurt or Kyle would hustle Tavi away and invite him on one of their excursions.

"What are you doing here?" Pablo asked.

Tavi was unsure whether he should admit everything to Pablo, or if he should just walk away and wait for the others to arrive. Realizing that he would have to trust Pablo eventually if he wanted to be a part of their group, Tavi answered, "I ran away this morning. I'm done. I'm never going back."

Pablo frowned. "Whatever. You still didn't answer my question – what are YOU doing HERE?"

Tavi's mind quickly ran over the events of the last day – Mac's death, Yuri, the man in the hotel – and he felt his anger at the unjustness of it all start simmering inside of him. "I was hoping to find a place to hide and then be a part of your group," Tavi said evenly.

Pablo threw his head back and laughed. Distracted by a branch snapping behind him, Tavi spun around and saw Kurt and Kyle approaching. "What's so funny?" Kyle asked, as they came and stood next to Tavi.

Pablo's laughter melted into chuckles. "This guy just ran away from The School House, and thinks we're going to help him." He shook his head at them and grinned. "He doesn't realize what kind of danger that would put us all in."

Kurt and Kyle both turn toward Tavi and patted him hard on the back. "Great! It's about time!" Kurt said happily, as Kyle nodded his head.

"Wait," Kyle said slowly, looking back at Pablo, "why wouldn't we help Tavi?"

"Because I think he's too much of a risk," Pablo said simply.

"It's not your decision," Kyle said.

"It's partly my decision. We'll wait for…oh, here they are," Pablo said, as Byron and Chloe showed up.

"What's up?" Byron said, settling himself on a swing as Chloe quietly scrutinized the four boys.

"Tavi ran away and wants to…" Kurt began before Pablo interrupted him.

"I'll tell him. Tavi claims he ran away and that he wants to join us. First, I don't know if he really ran away; he could be a spy. And second, he ran away from The School House, and if they catch us with Tavi, they might make all of us go back." Chloe slid her eyes towards Pablo and gave a little frown.

"Well, I think we should take a vote. I say Tavi can stay," Kyle said.

"Me too," Kurt and Byron said simultaneously. Chloe continued to stare at Pablo.

Pablo ran his hand through his hair in frustration. "And that's it?" he cried. "After two years, you guys just stop listening to me." He jumped off of the slide, his face turning red with anger. "I think he's going to be too weak. I say he has to prove that he can fight well enough."

"That's stupid," Byron said. "We've never done that before."

"And he's already beaten up both me and Kyle," Kurt exclaimed.

Pablo snorted. "Chloe can beat you two up." He stepped towards Tavi and shoved him in the chest. Tavi stumbled backwards in surprise and fell to the ground. He looked up at Kurt and Kyle in alarm, but they just shrugged their shoulders in resignation.

Tavi felt the anger inside of his chest boiling, and he slipped his bag off of his shoulder and onto the ground and hopped to his feet. Pablo charged at him without warning and tackled him to the ground. Tavi tried to throw him off, but Pablo outweighed him by over forty pounds. Pablo punched Tavi a couple of times in the ribs, and then tried pinning Tavi's legs with his own. Tavi swung a couple of ineffective punches, but Pablo was faster than anyone he had ever fought, and he grabbed Tavi's hand and slammed his arm to the ground.

Tavi felt Pablo shifting his position, and he struggled in vain to get free. The anger that had been building all day was being tempered with his disappointment at how this morning was turning out. He was afraid of what would happen if he lost to Pablo and that fear was making him weaker.

Pablo inched up enough so that his face was near Tavi's head. Whispering so quietly that no one else could hear, Pablo said, "I'm going to sell you back to Javier and collect the bounty."

"NOOO!" Tavi screamed and his whole body bucked, startling Pablo and throwing him off balance. Tavi's rage exploded and he freed a hand and punched Pablo under his chin. As Pablo fell back, Tavi grabbed the back of Pablo's head and smashed his forehead into his face. Pablo cried in pain, and rolled to his side. Tavi brought his legs up and kicked Pablo in the head, knocking him flat to the ground. Screaming inarticulately, Tavi sprung forward and began punching Pablo as hard as he could in the face, on his head, and in his neck and throat. Pablo curled into a tight ball to protect himself, crying out for help. Tavi jumped up and raised his right foot over Pablo's head to stomp down on it.

"Stop, Tavi!" Kyle said, tackling him to the ground. Kurt jumped on him as well as Tavi struggled to get free. "You won. Stop!"

"He said he's going to sell me back to Javier!" Tavi screamed. "He knows Javier!" He struggled for a few more seconds before he lay there panting, his eyes begging to be let up.

"Wait!" Kyle commanded. He slowly got up and told Tavi, "Stay here, okay?" Tavi felt too weak to argue, and with Kurt still sitting on his chest, there was no reason to.

"You see, I was right," Kurt whispered proudly to Tavi, as Kyle, Byron, and Chloe approached Pablo, "Psycho!"

"So, first of all," Byron said, "I think we can all agree that Tavi can fight well enough, yes?" He helped Pablo get to his feet, and Pablo limped over to sit down on the slide. He touched his nose with his hand. When he saw the fresh blood, he pinched it tight with his fingers and closed his eyes.

"Yes," Pablo answered quietly. Kurt decided that Tavi wasn't an immediate threat anymore, and so he climbed off of him and helped him up. They joined the half-circle around Pablo.

"Just tell them the truth," Chloe said, surprising everyone. "If you can't trust the people here after all of this time, then maybe it's you who doesn't belong."

Pablo opened his eyes and stared at the ground. He gently let go of his nose, and looked at his friends' faces crowded around him. Sighing deeply, he said, "You guys know Chloe's story, right? She was with Yuri, he got caught, she ran, me and her met up, then later we met with Byron, and finally you two came along." Kurt, Kyle, and Byron nodded their heads.

"Well, the truth is slightly different. When we started out, it was me and Yuri. We ran away at the same time from The School House." Tavi inhaled sharply when he heard this, but Pablo ignored him and continued. "It was my second time running away, but I couldn't take it anymore. You know what they do if they catch you a second time, right?" he said, finally looking at Tavi.

Tavi nodded his head. "Death," he said.

Pablo nodded his head and continued, "But we were doing well. We'd found places to hide out, and we were free for about three months. One day, we found Chloe being attacked by two boys and so we jumped in and saved her." He gave her a half-smile. "She was so small and fragile that Yuri insisted she come with us. After a couple of days, we took her to meet Pastor Mike so that if she was ever on her own, she would know where to get some food. Anyways, after we left there, we were walking down the street, when a police car slammed to a halt right next to us. Two cops jumped out and grabbed me since I was the closest to the curb. I tried fighting back, but they were too big and too strong. They started dragging me to their car, and I knew they were taking me back." He shook his head at the memory.

Chloe picked up where he left off. "Yuri could've escaped. We were in front of an alley and we had both run into it as soon as we heard the car doors open and Pablo yell. But then Yuri looked back and saw them dragging Pablo, he gave me a push down the alleyway and told me to go hide. He ran at the men and jumped with both feet at the knee of the nearest cop. The cop fell down screaming, and they both let go of Pablo. In like two seconds, the one who was still standing grabbed Yuri, slammed him really hard against their car, pulled his hands behind his back, and put handcuffs on him. He opened the door to the backseat and threw him in the car. Pablo was in the alleyway with me by then and we knew there was nothing we could do, so we ran."

Pablo finished softly, "And so I don't tell anyone I'm from The School House. If anyone whispers it to the wrong person, then I'm dead."

"Wait – so Yuri saved you?" Tavi asked in confusion.

Pablo nodded his head. "Yeah."

Tavi tried to reconcile the Yuri that he knew with the Yuri from Pablo's story. He thought about the glimpses he had seen when Yuri seemed happy and wondered which was the real Yuri now. "I think he's changed a bit since then," Tavi said.

Pablo answered, "Yeah, but you should've seen what they did to him. First rule you should learn is that roofs are really good for spying and creeping. Learn how to get up to them easily because a lot of the buildings are so close together that you can travel quite far sometimes only using the roofs."

"You've never told us that," Kyle complained.

Pablo shook his head and said, "I can't even explain it. That one secret made me not want to tell you guys anything, just in case." He looked around the circle and said, "I'm sorry."

Kurt, Kyle, and Byron nodded their heads in understanding while Chloe just snorted. "I knew about that," she said. "You guys showed me the first day I met you."

Pablo smiled and then turned to Tavi. "So I went back one morning a week or so after Yuri was caught. It was the hardest thing I've ever done, but I had to see him. I hid on one of the nearby roofs and kept watch over the bathroom we always used. I guess he was in the locked rooms then because he came by at about five o'clock. I whispered down to him, and when he looked up at me, I almost started crying. Both of his arms were broken, and his entire face was swollen and bruised. I've never seen anyone who was beat even half that bad." The others watched him in silence as Pablo swallowed hard, lost in his memories. "He just shook his head at me and whispered for me to never come back. And when he disappeared into the bathroom, I ran away and I haven't seen him since."

"I wonder why I never heard about you," Tavi said. "All anyone says is that no one ever gets away from The School House."

"I don't know," Pablo said. "I still wake up about a thousand times every night whenever I hear a noise. I still have nightmares about getting caught. But that's why I didn't want you here – they're all going to be looking for you now."

Tavi gulped and looked around the circle at what he hoped were his new friends.

"I need help. Can you guys please help me find a place to hide?"

No one would look him in the eye. After an interminable silence, Kyle looked up and said softly, "No, we can't."

Chapter 40

Javier unintentionally glanced at Billy when he saw *SalesManager2* on his caller id. Billy had been hovering around Javier for the last two days since their meeting with Tom, and Javier was hoping that everything that had happened could be safely put behind them forever.

"Yeah, Vikram," Javier answered as he stood up from his chair. "Hold on for a second."

Laura looked up from where she was reading on the sofa with Jasmine. "Will you have to work tonight?" she asked, with only a faint wrinkle between her eyebrows to indicate that she was worried.

"Definitely not," Javier reassured her. He stepped towards the sofa and gave her a quick kiss on the forehead. "I think I might be stepping back for a while and taking less of a hands on approach." He shared a look with Billy, who had also stood up, and said, "We're probably going to be shifting our clientele demographics, which would mean no more nights for me."

"Yay, Daddy!" Jasmine said, without looking up from her book. Javier smiled and stroked her head before heading for the deck in the backyard.

"What's up?" Javier asked Vikram as he tried to slide the glass door shut behind him. He looked back in surprise when Billy stopped the door from closing and stepped onto the deck with Javier.

"I need to talk to you," Billy whispered, his eyes glittering oddly in the moonlight.

"We have a small problem, boss," Vikram said into Javier's ear.

For the second time that week, Javier felt overwhelmed with how little control he actually had over his life. "Wait two minutes," Javier said to Billy. He pointed to a chair on the deck. "Sit there. This shouldn't take long."

As Billy trudged over to the chair, Javier walked to the railing and said irritably into the phone, "What is it, Vikram?"

"One of the boys is gone. I have Yuri out looking for him now and I was just getting ready to have his photo taken to the cops and our people on the streets."

Javier sighed and stared into his backyard, listening to the breeze as it gently stirred the leaves in the darkness beyond the light. Normally, he would have started shouting, threatening Vikram and anyone else who could be blamed, and promising a painful reminder to the boy who had dared to defy him. He turned around and looked at Billy, who was intently watching him from the chair.

When Javier didn't reply, Vikram nervously continued, "Um...Juan just told me about it now. He said that Tavi didn't come in to work last night, but he thought he might be sick. And...um...as soon as I found out, I went to the boys' room, and they said that Tavi hadn't been seen for two days."

Two days ago, Javier thought. That was the night I let my son help murder a man. Unable to look at Billy any longer, Javier sat on a chaise lounge and stared into the night sky.

Vikram was still talking. "Anyway, I just wanted to let you know. I will take care of everything and we should find him as soon as..."

"Let him go," Javier interrupted quietly.

Vikram was so quiet that Javier wondered if they had been disconnected. "I'm sorry...what?" Vikram asked after a few seconds.

"Let him go," Javier repeated. "He got away and hopefully he will have a better life. I only wish that we could've given him some money before he left."

"Javier!" Vikram protested. "You can't...I mean, you can't just let him go! If the other boys see that nothing will happen, then they'll all be gone within a week!"

Javier smiled in the dark at Vikram's short-sightedness. "It's okay, Vikram. I want to try and help these boys like we agreed a few days ago. Maybe get them into a school and sponsor them. And then we could try and help other boys from other bars."

Another long pause. This time, though, when Vikram spoke, he enunciated each word carefully, as if he were speaking to a child. "We did not agree on that. I thought we agreed that it wasn't possible."

Javier felt his anger stirring and shook his head in the dark. "Vikram!" he warned quietly. "I am still your boss and I am still the owner of The School House. You can either do what I say or find a new job. You WILL let Tavi go!"

Javier heard Vikram let out a deep sigh. "Yes, sir," he finally said softly. "I understand."

"Good," Javier replied. "I'll see you at work tomorrow." He disconnected the call and dropped the phone onto the table next to him. He closed his eyes and wondered if he would be able to make the changes he wanted to.

"Dad?" Billy said hesitantly.

Javier's eyes flicked open and he gazed at Billy. "Hey Billy. What's up?"

Billy swallowed and licked his lips nervously. Oh no...It's something bad, Javier thought, as Billy whispered, "I can't find your knife."

Javier froze as his mind frantically tried to consider the ramifications of what Billy was telling him. "You mean the one I gave you?"

Billy nodded his head, his eyes never leaving Javier's face.

"When did you last see it?" Javier asked quietly, sitting up on the chair and leaning closer to Billy, his forearms resting on his knees.

Just then, Laura slid open the glass door and both Javier and Billy flinched in surprise. Laura laughed lightly and asked, "Are you guys okay out here? Do you need anything to drink?"

Billy flicked his gaze from Javier to his mother, but he didn't say a word.

Javier smiled at Laura and said, "No thanks. We're just having a guy talk out here. We'll be in soon." He glanced at Billy who nodded his head in agreement.

"Okay." Laura smiled as she slid the door shut.

"When did you last see it?" Javier asked again as the door closed shut.

Billy ran his hands through his hair in a nervous gesture that Javier had never seen before. He shook his head as if confused and said, "I've been thinking about it all day. It has to be that night we…with Tom."

"Fuck," Javier whispered. The fear that had been growing in his belly suddenly exploded. "We have to go back there tomorrow morning and find that knife." He jumped up from his chair, walked to the railing, and stared into the neighbor's yard. He felt Billy hesitantly stand next to him, and he quickly reached out and pulled him close. Wrapping both arms around his son, he squeezed him tight and promised, "Don't worry about it, Billy. I swear it'll be okay."

End of Book 1

Preview of 'Boys for Sale – Redemption'

"Do you remember that movie you told us about?" Jack asked, picking up several rocks and tossing them aside after inspecting each one.

"Which one?" Tavi threw another rock into the water.

"The one about the lions and the wildebeests."

A long pause. "Yeah."

"And what happened when the lions jumped on the baby wildebeest and tried to kill it?"

Tavi threw another rock hard into the river. This one only skipped twice before sinking. "The wildebeests came back."

At the edge of the shore, underneath an inch of water, Jack saw it. The perfect skipper. He leaned over carefully to avoid getting his shoes wet and grabbed it. Running his fingers over the edge, he knew it would make it. "And do you remember what you promised us?"

Tavi finally stopped looking for rocks and looked at Jack. "No. What?"

"You said you would lead an army into the bars and we would free every single kid there."

Tavi stared at Jack and the corner of his mouth twitched up. "And?"

"It's time. Before too many more kids leave, we all go at the same time, we go in with our pipes, and we free every single kid we can find."

"And then?"

Jack bent low and threw the rock as hard as he could at an angle across the river. Even before it left his hand, he could feel the perfectness of the rock as it rolled along his finger and flew spinning across the surface of the river. He smiled with pride as it skipped twelve...fourteen...seventeen times before landing on the far shore. "And then we run for our lives. But if we stay here, they're just going to pick us off anyway. If we're going to get caught, let's go out with a bang."

About Me:

Between studying for my Master's degree in Education and teaching really smart students in Seoul, South Korea, I've discovered that when I do have a little bit of time off, my happy place is a small, mostly deserted island in Thailand (Ko Jum), and I find that living in a bungalow for a few weeks right on the beach is the perfect place for me to focus without any distractions. Also, since the only thing there is a small restaurant, a beach, and a dirt road leading to a village which is five miles away, there's not much to do besides swim, read, and write.

My first attempt at writing and finishing a book became T.A.G., The Assassination Game, a 600 page novel. It was based on something I wished was real, but I was tired of reading books with protagonists who were all good, and antagonists who were clearly bad. Personally, I liked the story, but I think my dad gave me the most honest feedback when he said, "I didn't really find any of the four main characters to be likable." Apparently I went too far to the extreme, but hopefully after a bit of editing, it'll appear on Amazon someday.

After that I wrote a book based on the idea 'what if imaginary friends weren't so imaginary?' However, that was all hand-written in two notepads, and it's still unfinished. Usually, when my vacation ends, I stop writing since there are too many other distractions in life - unfortunately. Hopefully, that one, too, will be finished someday.

Boys For Sale, and it's follow-up novel which is brilliantly named Boys For Sale 2, were inspired by a speech given by David Batstone in Seoul in January of 2011. I was shocked by how many children are bought and sold as sex slaves and the things that happen to them...and I was moved by how much some people give in order to save these children. One of his anecdotes led me to the character of Tavi, and as I imagined what he had to go through to get to where I met him in my mind, the story just seemed to write itself...

One Last Thing...

When you turn the page, you should be given the opportunity to rate this book and share your thoughts on Facebook and Twitter. If you believe the book is worth sharing, would you take a few seconds to let your friends and family know about it? And if you have a few minutes and a few words to say, it'd be great if you could leave a review on my Amazon page. If it turns out to make a difference in someone's life, they'll be forever grateful to you. As will I.

All the best...and thank you for reading my novel.

Marc Finks

10/11/2012

Printed in Great Britain
by Amazon